TAWNY TAYLOR

ELLORA'S CAVE
ROMANTICA PUBLISHING

W9-CQB-147

What the critics are saying...

ॐ

MARK OF THE BEAST

"This story is an erotic suspense full of chases and mild violence." ~ *Cupid's Library Reviews*

"Mark of the Beast is an intense, action-packed, sexy read!...a great start to her Animal Urges series..."~ *Joyfully Reviewed*

"Mark of the Beast started out with a bang and continued to excite until the end. The story is full of action and steamy passion." ~ *Coffee Time Romance*

"Just when I'm sure all mixtures of shifters have been designed a new one comes along and leaves me astonished. Tawny Taylor has come up with a winner that has a possibility of becoming a fascinating series full of suspense, chicanery and animalistic passion." ~ *Fallen Angels Review*

"The first in what looks to be a promising series by Tawny Taylor, MARK OF THE BEAST starts off with a bang." ~ *Romance Reviews Today*

TOUCH OF THE BEAST

"Tawny Taylor continues her Animal Urges series with a story chock full of action, adventure and lots of blistering sex." ~ *ECataromance*

"Touch Of The Beast is the second book in the Animal Urges series. Katie and Raul's story is full of fascinating and extremely graphic eroticism. I loved the HOT sex scenes between the two. Throughout the story, sex is almost a character within itself." ~ *Just Erotic Romances Review*

"Tawny Taylor is great at creating wonderful characters and interesting plots that will keep you turning the pages...Love scenes are incredibly heated and will leave readers panting for more. TOUCH OF THE BEAST is the second book in the ANIMAL URGES series and I can't wait to see what the next book will bring." ~ *Romance Junkies*

"Animalistic attraction has nothing on this couple –and I mean that literally. From dodging bullets, to tracking a pack of killers, Katie and Raul lead the reader on a merry chase...If you want a heated romance, a bit of suspense and a dab of the paranormal, *Touch of the Beast* is the book to read." ~ *Romance Divas*

An Ellora's Cave Romantica Publication

www.ellorascave.com

Animal Urges

ISBN 9781419956300
ALL RIGHTS RESERVED.
Mark of the Beast Copyright © 2006 Tawny Taylor
Touch of the Beast Copyright © 2006 Tawny Taylor
Edited by Sue-Ellen Gower
Cover art by Syneca

Trade paperback Publication May 2007

With the exception of quotes used in reviews, this book may not be reproduced or used in whole or in part by any means existing without written permission from the publisher, Ellora's Cave Publishing, Inc.® 1056 Home Avenue, Akron OH 44310-3502.

This book is a work of fiction and any resemblance to persons, living or dead, or places, events or locales is purely coincidental. The characters are productions of the authors' imagination and used fictitiously.

Content Advisory:

S – ENSUOUS
E – ROTIC
X – TREME

Ellora's Cave Publishing offers three levels of Romantica™ reading entertainment: S (S-ensuous), E (E-rotic), and X (X-treme).

The following material contains graphic sexual content meant for mature readers. This story has been rated E-rotic.

S-*ensuous* love scenes are explicit and leave nothing to the imagination.

E-*rotic* love scenes are explicit, leave nothing to the imagination, and are high in volume per the overall word count. E-rated titles might contain material that some readers find objectionable — in other words, almost anything goes, sexually. E-rated titles are the most graphic titles we carry in terms of both sexual language and descriptiveness in these works of literature.

X-*treme* titles differ from E-rated titles only in plot premise and storyline execution. Stories designated with the letter X tend to contain difficult or controversial subject matter not for the faint of heart.

Also by Tawny Taylor

⊗

About the Author

༃

Nothing exciting happens in Tawny Taylor's life, unless you count giving the cat a flea dip—a cat can make some fascinating sounds when immersed chin-deep in insecticide—or chasing after a houseful of upchucking kids during flu season. She doesn't travel the world or employ a staff of personal servants. She's not even built like a runway model. She's just your run-of-the-mill, pleasantly plump Detroit suburban mom and wife.

That's why she writes, for the sheer joy of it. She doesn't need to escape, mind you. Despite being run-of-the-mill, her life is wonderful. She just likes to add some...zip.

Her heroines might resemble herself, or her next door neighbor (sorry Sue) but they are sure to be memorable (she hopes!). And her heroes—inspired by movie stars, her favorite television actors or her husband—are fully capable of delivering one hot happily-ever-after after another. Combined, the characters and plots she weaves bring countless hours of enjoyment to Tawny...and she hopes to readers too!

In the end, that's all the matters to Tawny, bringing a little bit of zip to someone else's life.

Tawny welcomes comments from readers. You can find her website and email address on her author bio page at www.ellorascave.com.

Tell Us What You Think

We appreciate hearing reader opinions about our books. You can email us at Comments@EllorasCave.com.

ANIMAL URGES

 හ

Mark of the Beast

~13~

Touch of the Beast

~117~

MARK OF THE BEAST

లు

Trademarks Acknowledgement

ఴ

The author acknowledges the trademarked status and trademark owners of the following wordmarks mentioned in this work of fiction:

Citgos: Cities Service Oil Company

Krispy Kreme: HDN Development Corporation

Lean Cuisine: Societe des Produits Nestle S.A.

Manolo: Blahnik, Manolo

Pilates: LeRiche, Mary Pilates

The Incredible Hulk: Cadence Industries Corporation d.b.a. Marvel Comics Group

White Chocolate Dreams: International Coffee & Tea, LLC DBA The Coffee Bean and Tea Leaf LTD LIAB CO

Chapter One

ಬ

"I'm an idiot." Abby Clumm threw down her useless cell phone, wrapped the quilt tighter around her shoulders then hefted the shotgun up to take aim at the front door. "What was I thinking, coming out here alone?" Something strong and big and scary was doing its best to shred the wooden barricade into toothpicks.

She had no interest in becoming that animal's entrée. Quite the opposite. She preferred being at the top of the food chain.

Darn it, but there was nowhere to go, nowhere to hide. Outside, miles and miles of wilderness stretched as far as the eye could see. The nearest neighbor was probably at least a half mile away. She didn't stand a chance of escaping an animal attack out there. And inside the rural cabin she'd rented with her best friend, her chances weren't much better. A garden shed had more square footage than this place.

All one room, with what could barely qualify as a kitchen, a tiny living area and a cot for a bed, there were no potential barriers to hold back whatever beast was outside, trying to find a way in. Unless the ugly circa 1970s couch would do it. She doubted the brown, gold and rust plaid would shock the animal to death.

No. Once that door gave way, she was dead meat. It wasn't like she actually knew how to shoot the gun she was holding. She didn't even know if the stupid thing was loaded.

Argh! This wasn't supposed to be happening. Her best friend, Katie, was the one who knew about this survivor-type stuff. Hunting, camping, shooting. Abby was a city girl through and through. She could hunt down a deal on Manolos but she could not hunt an animal, even if it was standing five feet from her with a target plastered to its chest.

Which was why Katie was supposed to have arrived at their rented cabin, about ten miles outside of Anchorage, before Abby. Of all the times for air traffic controllers to stage a strike. She bet those stubborn controllers, who doubtless made more money in a month than she did in a year, didn't know her blood was on their hands if something happened tonight. She thought about scribbling down a note demanding legal recompense for her nonexistent descendants, but when the frenzied digging at the door stopped, she got all hopeful and thought just maybe the bear or whatever had left.

Of course, she wasn't about to open a shutter to check. She might be an idiot for getting herself into this situation in the first place, but she wasn't *that* stupid. Everyone who watched thriller movies knew if she opened a shutter the deranged, rabid animal would be standing there, waiting, slobber dripping from its teeth, its huge paw raised and ready to slam through the triple-pane glass. Three quarter-of-an-inch pieces of glass wouldn't hold up against an animal that could shake a solid door like this one had.

Her hands trembling, her heart beating a frenzied rhythm against her breastbone like a bongo drummer on crack, she sat on the back of the couch and lowered the gun. Darn thing weighed a ton.

"Please, please, let it be gone."

Shaking, she waited, her senses on high alert. Silence hung heavy, like an angry black storm cloud.

"I want to go home. I want a Crispy Kreme and a White Chocolate Dream Latte. And a mall." She set the gun on the floor, making sure the dangerous end—the one the bullets came from—was pointed away from her. "This wilderness stuff is for the birds, literally." She chuckled nervously at the cheesy pun and switched on the radio. She needed human contact, even if it was one-sided. Being alone in a scary, foreign place sucked.

She briefly considered heading back into town and dishing out the dough to stay the night in a hotel. Only one problem with that plan. The animal that had nearly ripped the door from its hinges might still be outside. Better wait until tomorrow. Granted, one night in comparative luxury didn't solve her problem. She couldn't go home until the strike ended. And she didn't have the money to stay in a hotel for more than a couple of days. What if the strike lasted a week? A month?

"God, this sucks!" She paced, chastising herself for letting Katie talk her into this so-called "Great Adventure". She'd been in Alaska all of seven hours, twenty-three minutes and she'd had enough adventure to last a lifetime.

Minutes, measured in the steady if slightly annoying ticktock of the wall clock, and the stream of 1980s tunes, slowly marched by. With each one that passed, her comfort level rose a tiny bit. Forty-two minutes later, she felt pretty confident she wouldn't end the night by becoming bear appetizer. It looked like the abominable snowman or whatever had given up. Yay!

She went back to the book she'd been reading, which she'd tossed on the couch when the attack had started. She settled herself in a cozy leather chair and kicked up her feet on the pine coffee table. She was just getting to a good part—a sex scene, of course—when someone knocked on the front door.

Katie? "Thank God!" She would've liked the option of checking through a peephole before opening the door, but since security didn't seem to be an issue in the boonies of Alaska—at least security against human beings—and peepholes didn't come standard on the cabin's heavy wooden doors, she slid the bolt aside and inched the door open instead.

That was so not her friend. But it—or rather *he*—was clearly a gift from Katie. He had to be. Another of Katie's naked-man kind of gifts.

Bless her, Katie'd sent a stripper out of guilt to keep Abby-the-City-Girl from getting bored and lonely.

"Uh...may I help you?" She grinned, blinked a few times and opened the door wider. If that was the abominable snowman, then this frigid, isolated place had just taken on some charm. "Did Katie hire you? I love that girl! For my birthday, she sent a stripper dressed as a cop. He was something...was he ever. But didn't anyone tell you you're supposed to wear a costume and then take it off *after* you come inside? That's half the fun. Oh, and where's your tunes? And your car?" She tried to peer around him. His frame was wide. The kind of wide she could appreciate.

"Wh-who's Katie?" Hugging himself for warmth, the guy standing outside stuttered between chattering teeth, "C-can I come in for a minute?"

Ah, so he was going to deny he'd been hired by Katie. That's the way Katie had played it last time she'd hired a stripper too. No problem. She knew there could be no other reason for a man to be standing nude on her front porch at eight o'clock in the evening. Especially since she doubted there were any nude beaches in the area, and even if there were it was damn cold for swimming. His erect nipples testified to that fact.

She wasn't too ashamed to say she'd noticed the cold had not negatively affected certain other erect...parts. That in itself was a wonder of nature worth the long flight from Detroit to see. Forget the mountains and glaciers and northern lights.

Back in Detroit, she would've never thought of letting a strange, naked man into her house, even if he was built like a god, had an erection that defied nature, and possessed the crooked smile of a devil. But after Katie's vague promise about making up for her tardy arrival, not to mention the rabid animal that had tried to rip down her door, and her sorry survival skills, having an extremely manly man for company didn't sound like such a bad idea.

So he didn't quite have the whole stripping thing down yet? That was nothing to hold against him, especially considering how he was built. As long as he didn't hear voices, have a parole officer or consider animal torture a hobby, all was well.

She was going with that. Beggars couldn't be choosers. "Sure. For a minute," she said, playing along with their game. "You look like you're freezing."

"Th-thanks. I am." He stepped inside and wiped his feet on the doormat. Bless his mother. Outside of teaching her son it wasn't exactly kosher to go a-visitin' wearing nothing but a smile and a coat of goose bumps, she'd taught him some manners.

"Um, since you're sort of denying having been hired by my best friend to assuage my anger, I'm curious. What's your story? Did someone steal your clothes?" It was a shame to cover the rippling muscles, bumps...and bulges...that comprised the anatomy of her visitor, but she had to feel sorry for the guy. Although his skin was the warm mocha of a suntanned beach bum's, his face was pale and he was shivering. Nothing looked funnier than a naked guy quaking with a hard-on. His dick was doing this funny little bobbing thing, which made it all the more tempting to stare. She pulled the quilt off her shoulders and handed it to him. "Here." He could do his routine after he'd warmed up a bit. A pathetic, shivering naked guy wasn't quite as appealing as a studly, hot naked guy.

"I'm not sure what my story is, to tell you the truth...thanks again." He accepted the blanket with a smile that inspired a few thanks on her part and wrapped it around his glorious body. Despite the fire she'd somehow managed to build without the aid of a push-button ignition switch, he stood by the door looking scrumptious if a bit pathetic. The look in his eyes reminded her of Zoë, the mutt that had parked her pathetic furry behind on Abby's front porch one frigid January night and given her a dose of the saddest puppy eyes ever. That had been almost five years ago. Zoë was now officially the world's most spoiled dog. Abby was not the kind of girl who could resist sad puppy eyes.

Speaking of puppy eyes...clearly this guy had nearly frozen off his more delicate bits by running around Alaska's vast countryside nude. *Must be his first time stripping. Poor baby, he needs someone to show him the ropes.* Either he was masochistic, undressing out in the cold instead of waiting until he was inside, or he had a brain the size of a gnat's.

Such a shame. The good-looking ones were always so stupid. Clearly this little truth didn't just apply to Michigan's less-than-brilliant crop of available bachelors.

"Why don't you go by the fire? You'll warm up faster," she suggested, motioning toward what had to be pure temptation to a guy who'd wandered who knew how far in near-freezing temperatures.

"Yes. That would be nice. I was just...didn't want to scare you. I can imagine what you're thinking." He brushed past her as he walked.

Crazy thoughts of getting cozy with him under that blanket—all in the name of sharing body heat, of course—passed through her mind. "Oh, you never know what I'm thinking," she said brightly. He looked harmless, in a devastatingly sexy sort of way. Despite the low IQ, Katie'd picked a winner. Abby decided right then and there that Katie deserved something extra special for her next birthday. Maybe twins. Going along with the ruse, she asked, "What happened?"

He shrugged. "I was sleeping. Then something woke me up—a dream. At least I think it was a dream. And I felt weird..."

"Hmmm. That's almost believable." Almost but not really. She was still going with the stripper story. It made the most sense. "Sounds like you were sleepwalking." Abby knew all about sleepwalking. She'd done it since she was a kid. It was a little disorienting at times, especially if she woke up in the middle of a dream. "Been there. Though I can't say I've walked out of the house naked before. Thank God. I can just imagine the field day Mrs. Knotsmidt would have with that.

She already thinks I'm an oddball." She nodded her head. "Better sleep in some sweatpants or something from now on. Just in case. It's a wonder you didn't freeze to death."

He glanced down at his quilt-covered form and then grinned guiltily. "Good suggestion."

Oh, what that grin did to her! Knocked her brain clear out of her head. It landed somewhere around her toe region. "Not that I'm complaining, mind you," she added before her grey matter had found its way back to its former position. She wasn't normally so forward, even with a naked stripper.

"Thanks," he said, sounding downright cheery.

"At least you didn't run into the bear or Sasquatch or whatever that was trying to rip down my door a bit ago. A naked guy I can handle, no problem. A wild animal with claws and teeth...no."

He studied her for a moment, his lopsided smile still firmly in place. She really liked it. Really, really liked it. The cop stripper had possessed a come-and-get-me smile like that too. Made a girl all soft and warm.

He combed long, tapered fingers through his hair. Her mouth went dry. Biceps. Oh, mama.

He did it again. He was clearly torturing her. "You're not from around here." It was a statement, not a question.

"Gee, whatever gave you that idea? Is it the accent? Or the fact that my friend called from an out-of-state area code and told you that?" she teased.

"No, actually it's the luggage." He pointed at the stack of suitcases still piled high on the cot. "Don't exactly look like the type who'd come out to a place like this by yourself though." His gaze dropped to her feet.

"That's because I'm not, as my kitten-heeled boots do testify. My girlfriend, Katie—the one who hired you—was supposed to come along. But some dumb strike delayed her flight. So, here I am, all alone. In the woods. With inappropriate footwear..." She sounded pathetic, which was exactly what she'd been shooting for. Maybe he'd be inspired to do an extra dance or two to ease her suffering.

Visibly perplexed, he looked at her for a long beat. Then his expression turned wicked. A good wicked. "Can't have that. I'll stay with you until your friend arrives. I think I owe you for saving me from freezing my," he cleared his throat, "vitals...off."

Whoo hoo! He wasn't just a stripper but a bodyguard and boy toy all wrapped in one scrumptious package. Okay, so she'd never worked so hard to get a stripper to perform his act before, but they were now on the right track. She was about to spend the night huddled up snug in a cabin with a guy who made her toasty with just a smile.

She hoped she had enough singles to tuck into his...hmmmm...no garter? Where did one place a tip if the tippee was naked? She'd figure it out. She had all night.

Then again, she felt it was necessary for propriety's sake to put up a small show of resistance to him staying the night. Not too strong. She'd hate to have him change his mind. "Oh, I don't know...that's so nice of you but I'd hate to impose. What about your other...er, clients?" This trip was starting to actually show some promise. Considering what she'd spent getting there, she owed it to herself to have some fun. In any form that presented itself, but especially any form that involved taking a closer look at the abominable snowman there.

Sex—at least the kind that didn't involve solitary satisfaction with the aid of a battery-operated appliance—was a distant memory. Her last relationship had ended almost ten months ago and lately she hadn't been in the mood to find herself a candidate for a fling.

Yes sirree, a vacation affair was not out of the question. If the candidate in question passed muster. It appeared that Mr. Abominable here had just announced his candidacy.

"I won't take no for an answer," he said with delightful decidedness. How she loved a man who could take control...when she wanted him to. So far, so good. "Not that I don't think you can take care of yourself, but it's not good for you to be alone. I have tomorrow off work. I can take you down to Portage Glacier if you want."

Her previously happy, pitter-pattery heart turned cold. Had she misread his intentions? "Glacier? As in hunk of ice?" Pooh. She'd had such high hopes for some...warmer activities.

His smile broadened. "Did you have something else in mind?" An evil glimmer sparked in his eyes.

Oh no, she hadn't misunderstood. They were definitely on the same page. Bless Katie, she was getting triplets for her birthday. "Uh..." Her heart set about pitter-pattering again and within seconds her face felt like it had been sitting inches from the roaring blaze in the fireplace. It had been such a long time since she'd come on to a guy. And never had a man who looked as great as this one given her the time of day, let alone a fuck-me look.

Alaska was cool!

She'd heard rumors of a shortage of women here. Maybe Katie hadn't been such an idiot for suggesting Alaska for their vacation after all. "Maybe," she said, "though it would be nice knowing your name...um, before we do anything..."

He stood up, conveniently leaving the quilt on the floor in front of the fireplace's hearth, and sauntered toward her. He moved with the strength and fluidity of an animal stalking prey. His body was absolutely perfect. Like romance-cover-model perfect. Smooth-skinned and suntanned. Muscular.

Big...hands.

By the time he was standing in front of her, she'd worked up a sweat just watching him. The air in the room had become thin and she was lightheaded.

He set one hand on each arm of her chair and leaned down until his nose almost touched hers. "Tarik Evert. Nice to meet you. And you are?"

She promptly forgot her name. She forgot a lot of other things too. They were all unimportant at the moment anyway.

"Tarik," she repeated somehow, even though she was sure her lungs had stopped functioning some time ago.

"Yes, that's my name but—"

"Nice to meet you too." Something huge wedged itself in her throat. She swallowed. Hard. Several times. She let her gaze slide south. It followed a bumpy route over some chiseled pecs and a washboard stomach.

My, my, my, did they come nicely packaged in Alaska.

"A couple questions first," she heard herself say. She was surprised she'd actually been able to speak.

"Sure." He backed away, reached down, snatched up the quilt and wrapped it around his shoulders.

That was such a bad thing. She couldn't see a bit of skin, except for above his neck and below his shins. Granted, the lack of exposed suntanned heaven did allow her to gather her thoughts a bit. "Are you married?" she asked, glancing at his left hand. That was always her first question when she met a man. Unlike a few of her friends, she did not do married guys.

"No. Not married. Never have been married. And probably never will be."

Big check. Never will be? She'd heard that before. "Infected with any diseases?"

"Nope. And I have proof if you need it…uh, at home."

"No, that won't be necessary." *Check.* "Committed any felonies? Or ever been profiled on *America's Most Wanted*?"

"Heck, no. I'm a law-abiding professional."

Check. "Professional?" Was he saying he was a male prostitute?

"Professional as in genetic researcher. I've worked for Omega Corporation since graduating from U.A.F. with a Doctorate in Microbiology. I'd give you one of my cards but I left them at home."

Of all the implausible stories. A scientist? Mr. Run-Around-the-Neighborhood-Naked? She giggled. "Imagine that. You left your cards *at home*. So you have a degree in microbiology? And you do research in genetics? How fascinating." If only he were telling the truth. She adored men with brains. Although this guy would be overqualified for the position of vacation flame if he had truly been a genetic researcher. But who was she to complain if he wasn't a genius? Absolutely scrumptious and safe. Willing...and clearly able. What more could a girl want for a short-time fling?

You pass!

"So, did I pass?" he asked.

"With flying colors."

He grinned and resumed his position over top of her. The blanket slid down his body, eventually landing in a heap at his feet. She wasn't sad to see it there. "I've always done well on tests," he practically purred.

She gave a little whimper as he slowly lowered his head to kiss her. "I'm not surprised," she whispered against his mouth.

The kiss started out soft and slow and deliberate. He brushed his lips against hers, teasing, tormenting. She arched her back and lifted her arms to wrap them around his neck. Anxious to feel his body pressed against hers, she pulled, sighing into their joined mouths when her wish came true and he lowered himself until he'd pinned her into the chair. She parted her legs, welcoming his hips between them. His cock prodded at the front seam of her jeans.

Their bodies smooshed together like that, it was no surprise the kiss deepened in a hurry. His tongue forced its way inside her mouth and wrestled hers into submission. It stroked and tasted and took until she couldn't breathe. Then it took some more.

Too many clothes. She had on too many clothes. Her blood was sizzling, carrying liquid heat through her body, up to her scalp and down to her toes. She released his neck and ran her hands over his shoulders. She dug her fingernails into his smooth skin and tipped her hips to grind her burning pussy against his cock.

He growled. Literally. The sound made her even hotter. She reclaimed her tongue from his mouth and made a feeble attempt at using it for speech. All she managed to do was whimper again.

As if he'd read her mind, he sat back and ran his hands down the center of her body. He stopped at the hem of her knit top.

Tense and trembling, she watched his face as he slowly lifted the cotton knit to reveal her stomach, bra. She put up a silent cheer of glee at the raw hunger pulling his features into tense lines. The muscles in his jaw visibly clenched, making him look both dangerous and sexy.

That was the world's perfect combination.

As he unfastened the front clip of her bra, she reached up to his brown-black hair. It was silky smooth, slightly curly. It suited him perfectly. She combed her fingers down the length then fisted her hands and pulled gently.

He had her bra straps pushed off her shoulders, and the cups had fallen to the sides, exposing her breasts. He traced a circle around one of her nipples and out of reflex, she arched her back. Aching need coursed through her body, hot and urgent, like a wildfire burning out of control. He tipped his head to look up at her face as he covered her nipple with his mouth.

Their gazes locked. He suckled her breast hungrily, the sensation sending pulse after pulse of heat down her spine to her belly.

She closed her eyes and lost herself in the sensations he stirred within her.

"You are so beautiful. So perfect. I couldn't stay away. I couldn't…" He moved to the other breast. He flicked his tongue over her nipple until it was a tight, ubersensitive peak. Then he pulled it into his mouth. Warm. Wet.

She shuddered, arched her back more and yanked harder on his hair. "Oh, God," she murmured, over and over and over. It wasn't like she'd never had a guy fondle her breasts before, but his expert technique, combined with the low rumble of his voice as he uttered those sexy words…she was in heaven.

She still had her pants on, and she was not happy about that. She released his hair and followed the lines of two perfect arms with her fingertips. When she found his hands, she grabbed them and pulled, placing them on the waistband of her jeans.

She knew he'd take the hint.

"My sweet kitten," he murmured, kneeling on the floor at her feet. His fingers moved deftly as he unfastened her pants. Then he pulled until they slid down over her hips. Eager to help, she lifted her bottom off the chair. He pushed on the garment, following behind the retreating cotton and trailing little tickly kisses down her legs to her ankles. He lifted one stockinged foot and slid one pant leg off then repeated with the other. As he stood, he let his hands glide up her legs. They stopped on either side of her hips. His thumbs traced the lace running along the low-riding waistband of her black satin panties.

"Mmmm. Sexy. I like," he said. "A lot."

She was so very glad she'd decided to wear some decent-looking underwear on her trip. Not a single pair of ugly undies would be found in her luggage. She hadn't planned on spending her first night in Alaska with a sexy stranger. But if she was honest with herself, she might admit she'd hoped it would happen. She made no apologies for her preferences. Unattached sex made sense. A lot less complications that way, as long as a girl was smart about things.

His fingers ran along the narrow band circling one of her legs. Instinctively, she parted her legs to let it explore further down. Only then, as the cool air hit the material, did she realize how wet her panties had become. Her pussy burned to be filled. Her breath caught in her throat when a fingernail grazed the thin, soggy material covering her labia.

He smiled. "I love your scent. It's so sweet and hot. I can't get enough." He licked his lips. "I want to taste you." Not waiting for her to find a way to drag some air into her lungs to respond, he hooked a finger in the crotch of her panties and jerked. The wet material ripped away. She didn't care that they'd cost a small fortune or that they were her favorite pair because they made her butt look smaller. At the moment she was only too happy to have them out of the way.

He set his hands on her knees and audibly inhaled. "Dammit, you smell good." He roughly pushed her knees apart and lowered his head to cover her pussy with his mouth.

The heat from his intimate touch ignited little blazes all over her body. Her chest. Her cheeks. Deep inside. She dropped her head back, gritted her teeth and gripped the armrests of the chair. Releasing her knees, he lifted his hands to her pussy, parted her folds to expose her clit, which was tingly and sensitive already. Then he dragged his tongue over it in a slow, lazy swipe that made her cry out in agony.

Her vagina clenched closed around painful emptiness.

Just because he wanted to make her suffer—or so she gathered—he then proceeded to run his tongue round and round her clit. With each circle, the tension inside her body coiled tighter, pulling her insides into knots. Then, glory of all glories, he slid a thumb inside her vagina. It wasn't nearly enough to satisfy her urgent need to be filled, but it eased the agony a bit. He timed the inward thrusts of his finger with the swirls of his tongue. The two together nearly brought her to climax.

Then, just as her body prepared for the first spasm, he stopped.

Frustrated beyond words, she opened her eyes.

He was kneeling on all fours. His skin rippled, like something was crawling beneath it. Then it darkened to almost black. Not deep brown, but the pure black of a panther's coat. He lifted his head back and let loose with a growl that sounded so foreign and animal-like she scrambled backward, tucking her legs under her bottom to get them out of his reach. Shaking, she wrapped her arms around herself.

What the hell?

There, as she watched, frozen by terror, a coat of pure white fur sprang from his skin, covering his body. His limbs changed into four thick legs. His torso lengthened and thickened, his head elongated. A mouthful of sharp teeth sprang from his gums.

A…polar bear?

A moment later, she leaped backward and lunged for the gun lying forgotten on the floor. The bear smacked the weapon with its huge paw, sending it flying across the room. It struck the front of the stove with a metallic bang then fell to the carpeted floor. The bear's gaze never left her as she scrambled backward until her spine was pressed against the far wall of the cabin.

What the hell? How had a man turned into a bear?

And then realization struck as she glanced down at the bear's paws.

That had been the beast that had nearly ripped the door down. She'd inadvertently let it inside.

When it licked its black lips, raised up on its hind legs and took one, two, three steps toward her, she just knew she was a goner. The bear was so huge its head nearly hit the eight-foot ceiling as it ambled toward her.

"I'm gonna die. I'm gonna die. I'm gonna die. Oh God!"

She'd never called herself a Christian but she decided right then and there it was time to pray.

Chapter Two

ဆာ

The pain. Unbearable. Excruciating. His muscles burned. His bones felt like they'd been shattered and glued back together. He was dizzy and confused. Still, one thing drove him. The excruciating hunger for the woman cowering before him. He didn't want to fuck her, he *needed* to fuck her. The compulsion threatened to take him over, completely. Just as it had earlier when he'd been lying in his bed at home and had caught a whiff of her scent.

That had been the first time he'd felt like this, the first time he'd changed into whatever beast he was now. It had surprised and confused him, both times.

Trying frantically to hold on to his humanity, which seemed to be fading quickly, he looked down. Thick white fur covered his arms and hands. His fingernails had lengthened into long black claws. What was happening to him? This was impossible.

He looked at his woman. Her eyes. She was terrified. He could smell her fear. The scent was bitter, like burned coffee. It called to the beast, to the predator he had become. He wanted to chase her. He wanted to take her.

Abby knew it was futile, that nobody would hear her, but she screamed again. Mid-shriek, though, she realized that her reaction to the animal seemed to be making things a whole lot worse. The louder she screamed, the fiercer the animal's stance, the more it bared its teeth and the louder it growled.

Somehow, she shut up, smacking her hand over her mouth to make sure she didn't scream again. Tears streamed down her cheeks. Her hand, which was still firmly holding back another shriek by some miracle, shook so bad she struggled to keep it in place. But with her silence, the animal's terrifying growling stopped.

In serious need of oxygen, she choked on a sob of relief and released her mouth to drag in a much-needed deep breath. Her eyes never left the huge animal standing on its hind legs in front of her. It sniffed the air, kind of shuffled back and forth.

It looked...confused.

To think a man lingered inside there somewhere. A man who seemed so normal and levelheaded. Right now did the human being — or more specifically the conscience only humans possessed — rule the animal or did raw, untamed instinct? How could she know? She believed she would be safe if it was the former.

And dead if it was the latter.

Her reactions mattered somehow. Why, she had no clue. Hadn't she read that animals could sense a person's fear? Was that it? Keeping her eyes on the animal, she consciously tried to slow her breathing, calm her nerves. It was close to impossible with an animal that big and potentially dangerous standing a few feet from her, but she knew she had no choice. More than any other time, she was grateful for the yoga she'd practiced for years. It seemed to be helping both of them. As she calmed, the bear tipped its head, regarding her like a puppy. Yes, it seemed to be true. Somehow the bear sensed her terror.

She closed her eyes and concentrated, willing her heart rate to slow. The fear to leave her.

Inside the animal lay hidden the heart and soul of a man. A man she didn't know, granted, but a man she'd sensed was not a cold-blooded killer. She rejected the fear. It would do her no good. A tentative peace took its place. Blinking open her eyes, she checked to see what the bear was doing.

It was on all fours now, its head lowered, its gaze traveling over her. Had she discovered the key to taming the beast? Could it be so simple? "It's okay, Tarik. It's okay," she murmured in the most soothing voice she could muster.

His mind fought a battle with the blind instinct trying to take over. Caught in the middle of an inner war, Tarik backed away from the woman. His body, this strange new body, wanted to claim her. But what little remained of the man he had once been wouldn't allow it. He sat back on his rump, raised his head and sniffed the air again. The bitter scent of her fear had faded.

Then she did what he hadn't expected. Her gaze focused on his face, she slowly stood, lifted her hand and stepped forward, whispering comforting words as she walked. Like magic, her gentle touch released him from the beast's grip. His roar of agony as the change reshaped his muscles and bones turned to a fading scream.

The room fell silent.

She visibly swallowed. Her eyes were wide as saucers. "Y-you changed. You're back."

He wanted to comfort her, to tell her it was okay. He wanted to protect her too. What would have happened if he'd lost the battle with the beast? What would he have done to her? "I don't know what's happening to me."

"I'll tell you what's happening. You turned into a polar bear. Holy effing shit."

"That's impossible. People can't change into animals. I know that for a fact. I study genetics for a living. There isn't a genetic disorder known that causes animals to change into other species. It just doesn't happen."

She raised trembling hands to her mouth. "I'd say it's impossible too, except I saw it with my own two eyes."

"This makes no sense."

"I don't understand it either. But it seemed that when I stopped being afraid, you changed back."

"Yeah." He thought back to the impulses and sensations that had coursed through him when he had been a bear. "I could smell your fear. It made me want to chase you...it was like an instinct. A compulsion. I could barely stop myself."

"But you did." Trembling, she wrapped her arms around herself.

He scooped up the quilt and, circling her, wrapped it around her shaking form. He caught the scent of her hair as he walked. His cock stiffened.

Dammit, his libido was in overdrive tonight, even more than normal. Because he had to, because being even a few inches away from her physically hurt, he moved closer, until his chest brushed against her back and her bottom rubbed his legs. He inhaled deeply, pulling the sweet aroma of her skin and hair into his nostrils. The need to take her swelled to painful intensity.

His brain told him he should leave before anything else happened. His body refused to budge. He'd been so close to taking her. She'd been willing.

Would she be willing again? Did he have the right to even try? He had to. God help him, he couldn't stop himself.

"You're so beautiful and you smell so good." He gathered her long hair into his hands and raised it to his nose. Lavender. He gently laid the tresses over one shoulder and nuzzled the sweet spot where her neck met her collarbone.

She stood stone still. Her trembling had stopped. Whether it was because of the warm quilt or something else he had no clue. Even though he was a man again, and not a bear, clear thought eluded him. Bizarre, burning impulses charged through his body. So urgent.

He wanted her. More than he'd ever wanted a woman before. This woman. Now. But he would not take her if she was scared.

"I don't want to hurt you. You believe me, don't you?" He sensed no fear, only mounting desire, so he gently pushed the quilt down to expose her shoulder and upper back. That was such a sexy spot on a woman—between her shoulder blades. He kissed her there and a coat of goose bumps sprang up all over her upper body. "It can get so damn lonely. Living alone. Having no one to talk to in the middle of the night. No one to share my hopes and troubles with. Have you been lonely too? You know what I'm talking about, don't you?"

His balls felt heavy. His blood like acid. The flavor of her skin lingered on his tongue. More. He wanted to taste every inch of her. He pulled the quilt lower, until he'd exposed her entire torso. The fine blond hairs at the small of her back stood on end.

He ran his tongue down her spine then dropped on his knees. This was the position to be in. Oh yes. The delicious curve of her rear end sat at just above eye level. He had to see it, had to touch her, to feel her slick passage again.

He knew the answer but he asked anyway, "Are you scared?"

"No," came her breathy response.

"I can't stop."

She didn't respond and he tried to back away. But before he'd stood up, she whispered, "Wh-who's asking you to?"

He reached down, under the quilt. Ran his hand up her smooth calf, the back of her knee. The blanket gathered on his forearm as he went higher. The back of her thigh felt smooth and warm. Her buttocks soft and tempting. He grabbed the blanket in his other hand and jerked. It fell to the floor. The woman didn't move.

"Your name. I want to know your name," he whispered.

"Abby."

"Abby," he repeated, teasing her labia with his fingertip. Her sweet honey, warm and fragrant, coated the tip of his finger. He knew what she tasted like, how hot and tight her

33

pussy was. He wanted to fuck her. Hard and fast. "Is that short for Abigail?" He pushed gently on her back until she bent over. He parted her ass cheeks and teased her anus with his moistened index finger. She shivered. "Are you cold, kitten?"

"No. Not cold." She moaned when he slid his thumb into her canal. Her inner walls gripped him as he slowly pulled it out and then pushed it back in. "Ohhhh." Her arms quaked. Her legs too. "This is crazy but I don't want you to stop."

"This way." He pulled his thumb from her and stood, leading her to the leather chair by the fireplace. He shoved the pine coffee table out of the way and motioned for her to sit, facing him. Then, kneeling again at her feet, he gently urged her knees apart.

A narrow stripe of dark blond curly hair covered her sex. Her inner folds were swollen, a deep red. They glistened with her juices. The scent of her arousal hung thick and spicy-sweet in the air. He licked his lips then bent down. He knew how delicious she tasted, how her flavor had beckoned the change. He had to be careful. He danced his tongue over her clit and slid two fingers deep inside. This time he didn't let his mouth go lower. Drinking her essence would surely call the beast again.

Her head thrown back, her spine arched, her breasts high in the air, she groaned and quivered. She pulled his hair, adding the pleasant tingle of his scalp to the already heady mix of sensations.

He stopped just before she climaxed.

"Oh God. Now," she pleaded. "Fuck me now."

He scooted closer, until his hips were flush with the chair's seat and then pulled on her bent knees until her bottom sat at the very edge of the cushion. Holding her knees for leverage, he positioned himself.

"Wait! Condom." She pointed at her luggage. "I'm on the pill, but a girl can never be too safe."

He nodded, went for the bag she pointed to and unzipped it. An unopened box of rubbers lay on top of her clothes. He quickly unwrapped one and rolled it on, dashed back to her and after muttering an apology thrust deep into her pussy. Her shriek of pleasure melded with his growl of satisfaction. His cock swelled inside her tight canal, filling every inch.

So hot and tight. Perfect. He withdrew himself then thrust again, settling into a slow but steady rhythm that would bring him to orgasm. He couldn't release her legs to stroke her clit. "Touch yourself," he said, knowing it was the only way she'd reach climax. Despite his deep thrusts, she needed more. "Touch yourself and come for me."

Her eyes closed, she lowered a shaking hand to her pussy and began stroking the tiny red nub. Slick heat coated his dick, sending white-hot pleasure rocketing through his body.

Soon. He would have release very soon.

"Faster," he demanded. He met the pace of her strokes in a desperate race toward climax. He needed it so bad it hurt. He needed her to find release even more. It burned him inside.

"That's it. More. More." He tipped his hips and released her legs, changing the angle of penetration. The head of his dick, wet and hot with her juices, rubbed the ridged walls of her pussy. He knocked her hand away, licked his forefinger and stroked her clit. He couldn't wait any longer. God help him, he couldn't hold back. "Come for me, kitten. I can't wait."

Her back arched, her toes curled. Her breathing turned to short panting bursts. And then he felt it, the wash of juices and pulsing spasms of her climax. She sighed then cried out, "Harder, please harder."

He obliged her, hammering in and out until the cum burst from his balls, pumped down the length of his cock and shot into her pussy. It just continued and continued. The heat. The pleasure. He didn't stop thrusting until he was spent and she was limp beneath him. Limp and smiling.

"Wow," she whispered. "So, uh, you're not an erotic dancer, are you?"

"Nope." He pulled out of her and, realizing the rubber had torn and he'd left her a wet mess, he went to the kitchen in search of a hand towel. He picked the gun up from the floor, checked to see if it was loaded — it wasn't — and set it on the table before returning with the towel.

She smiled a bleary-eyed thank you to him and pressed the scrap of worn cotton between her legs. She was shaking again — still. He grabbed the quilt, motioned for her to stand up, then sat and pulled her on top of him and wrapped them both in the blanket.

Warm and satisfied at last. And he'd made it through the lovemaking without turning back into the bear. He was a bear? A bear. How could that be?

He didn't want to think now. Didn't want to face the flurry of unanswered questions whipping around in the back of his mind. Later. There was plenty of time for questions later. For now he wanted to relax. To enjoy this woman, what she'd given him. As long as he could keep the beast under control, she'd be safe — from him.

* * * * *

Abby pretended to sleep. She slowed her breathing and relaxed her muscles. Eventually the trembling stopped as Tarik's warmth seeped into her muscles.

She'd just had sex with a man who turned into an animal. That was plain crazy. What the hell had gotten into her? It seemed since she'd boarded that plane back at Detroit Metro Airport she'd made one stupid decision after another.

First, she'd decided not to stay in a hotel. Sure, she didn't have a lot of cash, and the hotel bills would've tapped her out in a hurry. But it sure beat being lunch to a bear.

Second, she'd been stupid enough to believe Katie when she'd told her there were no polar bears this far south in

Alaska. Even if Katie had been right, and the man-bear-whatever holding her was a freak of nature in more ways than one, there were still grizzly bears and other animals that could do some serious bodily harm if she met them in the woods. She was stupid to have come out to the cabin by herself.

Third, she'd slept with a guy who she had just watched morph into an animal. That had to be the stupidest decision of all.

Now that she could think clearly, she could see how absolutely idiotic that one had been. She didn't know this guy. Although not knowing a man hadn't stopped her from having more than her share of one-night stands, none of the guys she'd slept with had had issues like this one. Granted, none of them had charged her rockets like this one either.

There was something about him. Especially after she'd watched him turn into the bear. A strength and dark sensuality, tempered with a touch of vulnerability. He was genuinely one of a kind, which made him that much more dangerous.

She needed to get out of there, away from him. Not just because she didn't belong in the woods any more than a penguin belonged in the jungles of Africa. And not just because he turned into an animal that weighed anywhere from five to ten times what she did and probably wouldn't mind swallowing her whole.

She needed to get out of there because of what he might do to her heart. Tarik was not a stripper like she'd thought. He was a genetic researcher who'd done some kind of experiment on himself, from the looks of it. Brilliant, fascinating, sexy…

Man oh man, she was in trouble. She knew herself well enough to know that if he was half as smart as he claimed, she could fall for this guy. She tended to do that if she let down her guard—fall for guys hard and fast. Especially sexy, intelligent, semi-vulnerable guys. Two weeks was nothing to some people. But to her, fourteen days and nights was ample time to set herself up for some serious heartbreak.

The itinerary for her vacation to Alaska did not include heartbreak. Vacation fling with someone she could never fall in love with, yes. Falling for a guy who wasn't just sexy but thoughtful and smart, hell no!

She really didn't need those kinds of complications in her life right now. Damn her weakness for people, animals, things that needed rescuing. That susceptibility had gotten her into this situation in the first place. If he hadn't given her those sad puppy dog eyes—and yes, her erroneous assumption that he'd been a gift from Katie—she wouldn't have been tempted to let him stick around.

She was her own worst enemy sometimes.

At the risk of making another stupid decision, she determined she needed to leave the cabin, find someplace safer to stay until she could fly back home or until Katie could join her. Either way, she wasn't going to see Tarik again.

Lucky for her, like most men after having mind-blowing sex, Tarik slept deep and hard. At the first light of daybreak, she scooped up her suitcases and headed out to the truck she'd rented. She threw them on the backseat and checked her cell to see if she had a signal. Nada. She'd have to wait to call Katie.

It was difficult, but she didn't go back inside for one last look at Tarik the man-bear. She didn't leave a note. She didn't wake him to explain. He was truly the most mysterious, interesting, gorgeous man she'd ever laid eyes on. To stand there and stare at him, remembering how it had felt to have him touch her, make love to her…she couldn't do it.

As she maneuvered the truck around the wide circle driveway, she whispered guiltily, "'Bye, Tarik. I hope you figure out what's happening to you."

Chapter Three

She was gone. Gone! His woman. The one he'd had only once and wanted again, already.

He searched the cabin. Her luggage was missing. He looked outside. Her rented truck was gone. A set of fresh tire tracks wound down the drive and out to the road.

A horde of emotions flared through him, ten times more intense than he wanted them to be. Fear for her safety, frustration, confusion, anger. They churned inside his gut like storm clouds. Wrapped in the blanket, no shoes on his feet, he ran down the rural dirt road, thankful for the lack of traffic. Her truck's tracks hadn't been covered.

She was alone out here. Alone and defenseless. What if she got lost? Or her truck broke down? What if a tire went flat? She needed him. She was obviously out of her element. He broke into a full run, raced past his own house without a thought, following the winding road that meandered through the pine forests. If she was headed back to Anchorage, she was going the wrong way. Did she realize that? His fears swelled with every moment that went by. Rage soon followed.

He wasn't just running now, he was charging. Into battle. Battle with the beast.

He lost.

Right after he'd stepped on something hard, a rock maybe, he felt the first twinges of the change again. "No!" he shouted. The dense forest around him swallowed up his voice. He fell to the ground as his bones shifted and his muscles stretched. This time the beast didn't have to fight so hard to take over the man. His fury and fear fed it until his thoughts were gone and only instinct drove him. He ran through the trees, battering anything in his way. He came upon a building of some kind and smelling her inside, kicked and clawed his way through the door.

No Abby.

He ran back outside and sniffed the air then turned toward the road. He heard the pop of a rifle, the whir of a bullet. He dashed for the trees. He ran until he couldn't run any longer and then he stopped. Finally, exhausted, the beast released him. Luckily he wasn't far from home. Weak and wobbly legged, he shifted back to a man.

The quarter of a mile back to his home felt like twenty.

He fell into a restless sleep, filled with nightmares. He awoke the next morning, wondering if they'd been dreams or memories. He'd never lived like this—on the edge. He barely clung to the normalcy he'd come to take for granted. Go to bed. Wake up. Go to work. That was how it was supposed to be. Instead, impulses kept running through his head. Strange, wild urges. Hungers. Needs. He tried to ignore them but they were so strong.

He dressed and drove the five miles to work, looking for a white rented Yukon as he drove. The beast inside didn't want to accept that Abby was lost to him, that she'd only been his for one night.

Or so he assumed it was the beast.

On second thought, it could've been the man that didn't want to accept the loss of Abby. At this point he wasn't sure of much of anything. He pulled into his parking spot, outside of Omega, cut off the engine and fisted his keys.

He'd been tempted to call off but decided he needed this—his normal day-to-day life—to keep him grounded. Something powerful pulled him. Something he didn't understand. He felt that holding onto the life he'd known before was his only hope of holding onto himself, his very soul.

He went into the building, smiled at Denise the elderly receptionist-slash-office manager-slash-gofer. For the first time since he'd started working at Omega, some eight years ago, she didn't smile back.

Had something happened to her too?

He opened his mouth to ask if she was okay when two huge guys he'd never seen before stepped out of the security office, which was located to the right of her desk.

They gave him a look. Not a friendly one. No, more like the kind of glare they'd give a guy who'd been caught embezzling a million dollars from the company.

What the hell was going on?

He felt like he'd stepped into a bizarre new world. Everything appeared to be the same but it was a façade. Something had changed. Something besides him. The people around him acted differently. Like strangers.

"What's up?" he asked.

The two guards rushed him, knocked him to the floor, and pinned his hands behind his back. He was so confused and shocked he didn't try to fight them off. Whatever mistake had been made would be cleared up. He'd done nothing wrong. He'd been a longtime, trusted employee. His boss, Alexander Torborg, was his mentor. His friend. Those men had no reason to be securing his hands behind his back.

They hauled him to his feet. He noticed, as the guards escorted him past Denise's desk, that she was watching the whole scene with a puzzled expression.

They led him to the elevator, took him down to the basement. He'd never been in the basement before. Had never had a reason to go down there.

"Want to tell me what's going on?" he asked, not expecting an answer.

Escorting him like a prisoner, the men didn't say a word.

The elevator doors opened, revealing a dimly lit narrow corridor, painted a dull gray. The ceiling was open, revealing heating ductwork, wire channels, the bones of the building. Their footsteps echoed on the scuffed tile floor. The guards stopped him next to a metal door.

What poor schmuck had been forced to take an office down here?

One of them unlocked the door while the other held onto the manacles securing his arms. Yes, they were like those old-time irons. Not handcuffs. Thick, hinged metal cuffs wrapped around his wrists. The edges ground into his bones when he twisted his wrists. Hurt like hell. Between the cuffs and the metal chain connecting them, the rig weighted a lot.

Had they expected him to be extra-strong? Did they know about his recent...troubles?

The room was empty. Painted the same color as the hallway outside and furnished with a cot, a dresser and a toilet, it looked like a prison cell.

One guard stood at the door while the other unlocked the shackles.

"Uh. Do I need to call a lawyer?" Tarik said just before they shut and locked the door. "Well, fuck!" He slumped onto the bed. "What a way to start the week."

Minutes later, the door rattled. He looked up to watch his boss walk into the room. The door slammed shut behind him.

Torborg's face was, as usual, completely devoid of emotion. His eyes were flat. His stance relaxed. "Tarik, I'm sorry I had to do this."

"So, mind telling me what's going on? Why am I locked up like a criminal? I've been working for Omega for years. I haven't done anything wrong. Haven't done anything to the company. And we've known each other a long time. You know I'm not the kind of guy who ends up handcuffed. Right? There has to be some kind of mistake."

Still standing by the door, Torborg nodded. "I'm afraid there hasn't been a mistake, although I understand you wouldn't do anything to hurt the company intentionally."

That was an interesting statement. Confusing but interesting. What exactly did Torborg think he'd done?

It made Tarik think. Had he stumbled upon something in his research? His most recent project hadn't brought him much attention from his superiors. In fact, he'd begun to question his work's value.

"Care to elaborate?" he said when Torborg didn't say more. He wasn't used to this kind of treatment. Up until today, he'd been a valued employee of Omega Corp. Torborg had been a family friend. He'd helped Tarik through a rough patch during his undergrad studies, had hired him right out of graduate school, and had treated him with a great deal of respect. Although his tone hadn't changed — as usual Torborg was the epitome of cool professionalism — Tarik sensed something had.

"I didn't see this coming. Thought we'd finally found the right combination, the right location on the genome. It worked on the rats."

"What are you talking about? What do rats have to do with me? With this?" Tarik motioned to the four solid-looking walls surrounding him. Confusion and frustration pulled his muscles into tight knots. Torborg was skirting an issue. A big fucking issue, like the proverbial elephant in the room. What kind of elephant was he dancing around? "I have a right to know why you've basically imprisoned me without a trial. You can't hold me here."

"I can and I will," Torborg shouted for the first time. Ever. Since they'd first met, Tarik had never seen Torborg, the CEO of Omega Corporation, lose his cool. He had always been the same. Flat, lifeless. Almost robotic. But brilliant. Intellectual. A man with vision.

This crack in his icy exterior said a whole lot more than any words he'd spoken so far.

Tarik shook his head. "This is bullshit and you know it. This is America. I have rights."

Torborg lifted his chin slightly. He visibly gathered his thoughts. "You'd have rights if you were human." He enunciated every word clearly, like he was speaking to a classroom full of first graders.

"Huh? Of course I'm human."

"No. Not technically."

This short and simple statement confused Tarik. Why should Torborg believe he was anything but a human being? He'd been born the son of a man and woman, like every other child. He had thoughts and feelings...understood consequences...made moral decisions...paid taxes...

...and changed into a bear from time to time.

Fuck! "What do you mean?" Tarik asked.

"It's part of our genetic engineering research. I can't tell you any more about the whys than that. You were created in Omega's lab, your genetic code altered before implantation into the woman you've known as your mother. Biologically, she was no more your mother than I am. We bought an ovum. From a donor. We replaced a small section of your DNA with that of a polar bear. The mark. On your hip." Torborg pointed at his hip, where the large black birthmark he'd always despised lay hidden under his clothes. "The Mark of the Beast. That's the only permanent sign of what you are."

His head started spinning.

"You don't exist, at least not according to the world out there. Your social security number is fake. All your identification. Even your school records. There's no record of a Tarik Evert ever having lived."

"What?" He sat stunned for several beats. Then, it all sunk in and he realized what Torborg had just told him.

This was wrong. Wrong! What had they done? To take an innocent human being and play with his DNA, to see what they might end up with? To lie to him all his life? To deny his very existence? Omega had crossed the line. This wasn't science. It was inhumane. Insanity.

Human genetics research had its opponents, mainly because of fears about experiments like this. Were there others who'd been created? Like him? "Why? Why!" Tarik demanded.

Torborg lifted his hands. "I've told you everything I can. I can't say more." His words were weighty. Someone or something was keeping him from being more specific. But Tarik didn't give a fuck. "You've shifted because of The Season, the urge to mate. I believe it should only happen once a year. It's already clear you cannot control it and we can't afford to have you…impregnating a woman."

It was all suddenly very clear. The urges he hadn't been able to deny. The loss of control. The sexual hunger. "You're afraid of what I might reproduce," Tarik said.

"As scientists, we have a responsibility to protect the purity of the human gene pool."

"Which is why you shouldn't have done this in the first place." He wasn't about to tell Torborg it might already be too late to protect the gene pool, since the rubber had failed.

"I have men searching for the woman, Abigail Clumm. She's in Anchorage. We're checking hotels. She must be brought in immediately and examined."

They knew? What would they do to her? A flash of heat shot through his body. He had an overwhelming compulsion to protect Abby, his woman, even though he understood Torborg's reasoning. "Leave her alone." Even to his own ears his voice had become an inhuman growl.

For the first time since he'd stepped foot in the room, Torborg showed fear. The bitter scent wafted to Tarik's nose. It stirred the instincts he'd struggled to control since changing back to a man earlier. He felt his muscles tighten. His heart race. His breathing quicken. The tingling in his bones started building. Soon it would change to pain as they stretched and broadened.

Seeming to realize what was about to happen, Torborg's eyes widened. He pounded on the door. Three loud bangs. "I don't want to kill you, Tarik. But if I must…to protect everything we've worked so hard to accomplish, I will." He backed himself into the wall next to the door and knocked again.

Tarik wanted to jump on him and tear the man to pieces for what he'd done. It was wrong to play with people's lives like this! To think his life's research might be twisted and abused. Used to manipulate men, women, children. Ruin lives. For what purpose? It couldn't be good.

The pungent scent of fear billowed off Torborg's skin now, like great plumes of wretched smoke. Tarik backed away from the man as far as the room would allow. Still, he knew what was about to happen. He couldn't stop it.

The pain swelled until it blinded him. Muscles stretching and pulling. Bones reshaping. Tarik screamed, but the sound that came from his mouth took the form of a loud, angry roar.

Torborg spun around and started pounding on the door. "Open this door, dammit!"

It nearly killed him, but Tarik forced himself to resist lunging forward and ripping Torborg's throat out. He knew he could kill the man. It would be so easy. In a sense, it would be so satisfying.

His mind was still working, somewhat. The drives of the beast muddied his thinking. The door flew open and he saw his chance.

Escape first. Find Abby. Protect Abby.

He literally trampled Torborg as he charged for the door. The man crumpled on the floor beneath his feet, mid-scream. Tarik barreled past the guards, who he suspected were taking aim at his back. His drive to find Abby pushed him forward. He ran to the elevator. Couldn't work it. His fingers had shortened. Found the door to a stairwell was propped open. He ripped the door off the wall and threw it at the guards shooting at him. That stopped them.

Minutes later, he charged out of the building and ran for his life, only one thought remaining in his mind.

Find Abby.

* * * * *

Some moron was banging on her hotel room door. Dammit, she hated hotels! She never could sleep in one. People were so rude, stomping down hallways, hauling screaming kids, knocking on the wrong doors. Argh!

Sleep. All she wanted was some sleep. It shouldn't be too much to ask.

Abby covered her head with the pillow and made an attempt at ignoring the idiot out there trying to kick in her door. It couldn't be Katie. She was still out in L.A. She'd checked. Several times. The strike hadn't ended yet.

"Go away, you've got the wrong room!" she shouted when he didn't let up. Had to be a guy. No woman would be so stupid. Yeah, yeah, that was a sexist comment. She was in no mood to be politically correct. The friggin' jerk didn't stop.

"Dammit!" She threw the pillow against the wall, ripped the covers off herself and stomped to the door. Leaving the security chain in place, she pulled open the door a couple of inches and giving the big, stupid lug standing in front of the door her meanest glare she said, "You've got the wrong room, asshole. Get. Lost."

"Abigail Clumm?" the man asked.

Not answering, she gave him a once-over.

Wasn't anyone she recognized. Didn't have on a uniform. She doubted he was a policeman. And even if he was, what would he want with her?

Still, despite her anger and resentment at having been dragged out of her bed, her curiosity got the better of her. "Who's asking?"

"My name's Joe. I work for Omega Corporation here in Anchorage."

His name did nothing for her but the company rang a bell. No, it rang a huge gong!

Omega. That had been the company Tarik said he worked for. Had something happened to Tarik? What did they want with her? And why were the hairs on her nape sticking up on end? "I'm sorry. I don't know anyone named Joe. And I know nothing about a company called Omega." She shut the door, locked it and sat on her bed, wringing her hands. Not exactly the most productive thing to do, but what choice did she have?

She hoped the guy would just leave. Leave her alone and go back to Omega. It was probably a silly thing to hope for, but oh well.

The knocking resumed.

Yeah, it had been silly all right. She considered calling the police but figured the guy probably hadn't done anything illegal so they wouldn't help her. She picked up the phone to call the front desk.

"Miss Clumm, this is an urgent matter," the pest shouted through the door. "I'm under orders not to leave without you."

"Peachy." She slammed the phone on its cradle and went back to the door. Making sure the chain was still in place, she cracked open the door again. "What's this all about? Why the hell would I go with you anywhere?" She didn't bother to keep the exasperation out of her voice. Let him know he'd pissed her off. She was on vacation. How dare he come here and ruin it for her.

"You were seen with one of our employees last night, Tarik Evert."

Seen? Seen how? How could anyone have seen her? She'd been in a cottage in the middle of the wilderness. People were spying on Tarik? Why?

Or had Tarik sent this guy to her for some reason?

The guy continued, "We believe you may have been exposed to a potentially dangerous material. We would like you to come to the hospital for a brief examination. To make sure you're okay."

Dangerous material? Huh? What kind of dangerous material? The only thing she'd been exposed to was Tarik himself. And a few bodily fluids.

Something was fishy about this story. Unless that turning-into-a-bear stuff was catchy.

But really. How likely was that?

She opened her mouth to thank Joe Whoever for his concern when the door crashed inward, knocking her on her butt on the floor. Joe charged inside, grabbed her—despite a really pathetic attempt on her part to stop him—and hauled her down the hallway and out through an emergency exit. With as much care as he'd show a rotten hunk of moldy meat, he tossed her into the back of a rusty white van, and paying no heed to her threats to have him and his company sued for kidnapping and battery, he slammed the door shut before she could stop him.

Well, didn't this just suck! Alaska sucked. Overgrown thugs who thought they had a right to snatch innocent women from hotel rooms sucked. She pulled her cell phone out of her pocket. No signal. Ugh! That sucked too! This was the absolute worst vacation she'd ever had.

The minute that door opened, there was going to be hell to pay. Someone was going to feel the pain...and it wasn't going to be her!

Chapter Four

൪

The big creep Joe was in for it. The minute he dared open that door, Abby vowed to let him have it. Fingernails, teeth, a knee in the groin. She'd let him know under no uncertain terms how little she appreciated being manhandled.

Just to give him a little taste of what was to come, and to possibly gain the attention of a passerby, she rolled onto her back and started kicking the door with all her might. She didn't expect it to come open. It was locked from the outside and she wasn't strong enough to kick through sheet metal. But it did make a satisfying noise. If there was anyone outside, they'd hear it.

When the van didn't start up, she took that as her cue and really started kicking hard. Bang, bang, bang, bang! It was a beautiful thing.

Until the door flew open and she was flat on her back, hardly in a position to fight off a pissed-off kidnapper.

Then, quite suddenly, the wisdom of creating a ruckus was lost to her.

He literally pounced on her like a friggin' cat doped up on catnip and pinned her down. Hands overhead. Legs to the steel floor. Upper body squashed to the point it was hard to breathe. She realized it was futile but the need for air inspired her to do as much squirming and fighting as she could.

Didn't help at all. If anything, it made him hold her tighter.

"You are absolutely the craziest woman I have ever had the displeasure of meeting!" he spat.

"Fuck you too."

Still holding her arms, he sat back, lifting his chest off hers. Evidently finding her not only crazy but hilarious, he dropped his head back and started laughing hysterically.

"Go ahead. Laugh. You won't be for long."

His expression sobered, sort of. His lips were quivering. "Oh yes, you and what army are going to whoop my ass?"

"I don't need an army to take you on, you egotistical piece of shit."

Yeah, she realized those were big words coming from a woman who barely stood over five feet and weighed in at less than one-twenty. But he'd pissed her off. And she had a tendency to run her mouth off when she was pissed.

Unfortunately, that particular habit rarely led to a good result. She could see this situation would be no different. He moved carefully, to keep her pinned down while reaching for a bit of rope lying next to the wheel well. Just great. He was going to tie her up.

"I shouldn't have to do this, you know. You should be willing to come quietly. It's for your own good, you deranged woman." He stretched to reach the rope, but lo, it was beyond his reach.

Ha! He'd have to move to get it.

She gave him a sneer. "Looks like you have a problem." She flinched when he lifted his arm to belt her.

God, he was a bigger psycho than she'd thought!

"Don't!" she screamed, turning her head. She closed her eyes and tensed up, expecting to feel the pain any second…

Okay. Any second now…

Oh, thank God, he didn't hit her.

She hazarded a glance his way. He was staring down at her with the reddest face she'd ever seen on a man. Looked like he was either suffering a serious case of constipation or had just swallowed some battery acid.

"You okay?" She jerked her hands, freeing them. Much to her surprise, he didn't put up much of a fight. The second he flopped over beside her, she saw why.

There was a red stain on his back. Blood was seeping from a torn gash in his jacket.

What the hell? She looked outside the back of the van.

A polar bear was lumbering around the side of the vehicle. *A polar bear?*

Tarik?

She shouldn't be so happy to see him again, especially in his bear form. No, it wasn't a good thing to be so giddy. She'd best be going around that way, away from him. Yes, far, far away.

"Oh hell!" She dashed after him but he moved a whole lot faster than she did. He was standing back, toward a crop of pines at the edge of the parking lot about twenty yards away. He was facing her, pacing back and forth, sniffing the air and snorting.

"Tarik?" she shouted. God, if that wasn't Tarik, she was in some deep shit.

The bear stopped pacing. It sat on its rump and tipped its head. Couldn't say she'd ever seen a polar bear at the zoo do that.

No, that was Tarik all right. He'd saved her. How had he known she was in danger? How had he known where to find her? Was that other guy, Joe, really going to take her to a doctor or had something far worse been planned for her?

What the fuck was going on?

So many questions. The only one who had answers was unable to speak at the moment. Even though he was resting, he looked uneasy, confused. She wasn't sure if she should approach him like before or not.

Fairly certain he wouldn't hurt her, she decided to give it a try. But he didn't let her get near. Whenever she took a step forward, he took two back.

"Tarik, I don't understand." This time when she walked toward him he didn't back away. "What's bothering you? What's happening?" She stopped a few feet from him. He was so huge. A beautiful creature. The only place she'd been so close to a polar bear had been at the zoo. And at least four inches of plexi-glass had stood between her and the animal's claws and teeth. Regardless, she wasn't afraid. Not at all.

"Won't you change back? Tell me what to do next? I'm so confused. What did that man want with me?"

He raised up on his hind legs, towering over her by nearly three feet. His hot breath huffed in her face.

The instinct to turn tail and run buzzed through her like a jolt of electricity but she remained still. Watching his face, she raised a hand and stroked the thick fur coating his stomach. "Tarik, please come back to me."

She could feel his skin rippling under her hand, even through the thick fur. A moment later, he was a man again. A naked, shivering man. A man with sad puppy eyes.

"You need to leave here," he whispered. "You need to leave now. They know your name."

"Who's *they*?"

"Omega." His expression was an odd mix of emotions, too many to read clearly.

"This, your problem, has something to do with your work? They know what? That you're changing into a bear?"

"Yes, they know. They did it to me." He lifted her palm to his mouth and kissed it. "I can't tell you more. I don't know any more. Besides it doesn't matter. All that matters is that you're safe. You need to go home, get away from here."

"That's not going to happen as long as the strike is still going on. The flights out of Anchorage have all been cancelled."

"Where's your truck?" He was starting to shiver harder. Although it was warm by Alaska's standards, somewhere in the upper 50s, it was still pretty chilly to be running around in one's birthday suit.

"You're cold. I can get something for you in my hotel room."

His fingers wrapped around her wrist as tight and unyielding as steel bands. He pulled her flush against him. She had more than a suspicion he hadn't done that to block the chilly northerly wind. "No. You shouldn't go back in there."

She tipped her head up to look him in the eye. It wasn't easy, but she managed to speak, "All of my stuff's in there, including the keys to my rental."

He grunted but released her. A bummer! "Fine. But I'll come with you."

"I don't think Joe's in any condition to get in our way. He looked pretty bad off. I think he's still alive, but barely."

Tarik's expression darkened. "Yeah." After a moment, he nodded. "Okay. Let's go. But you must be careful."

"I'll go in through the main entrance and let you into the building through the side door. My room is only a few feet from the door. Hopefully no one'll see you." Her face warmed. "Not that you don't look absolutely fabu—"

For the first time in too long, his lips curled into that naughty smile. "No need to explain." He gripped the back of her head with one hand, tangling his fingers in the hair at her nape. With a sharp yank, he dragged her against him. Then he slanted his mouth over hers and kissed her to bonelessness.

She literally drooped against him, relying on his other arm to support her as she kissed him back. Their tongues stroked and mated. Their breaths mixed. She moaned. He growled. She wished they were back at the cabin, in front of the fireplace, naked. At least he was naked. That was a mighty fine start.

He broke the kiss much too soon. "Let's go, before Omega sends someone else. I'm sure they know something's happened to Joe by now." He held her until she had her feet back under herself and her knees had regained their strength.

"Yeah." Her head kind of floaty and light, her feet skipping along the surface of the asphalt parking lot, she walked back into the hotel. It wasn't easy, considering she was still in space-mode from that amazing kiss, but she tried to pay attention to who was nearby as she went back to her room. The door was still slightly ajar, thankfully, since she hadn't had the chance to grab her keycard before being thrown over Joe's shoulders and hauled outside like a sack of trash.

It didn't look like anyone else had been in the room. Everything was where she'd left it. She dashed out to the corridor, and after listening for a moment to make sure no one would be coming down the hallway in the next few seconds, opened the door leading to the parking lot to let Tarik inside.

She pointed at room 113 and he nodded, preceding her. She handed him a blanket—giving the guy something to cover up his very scrumptious body was becoming a tradition. He smiled a thanks and wrapped it toga style around his form.

He said nothing while she ran around, throwing her clothes, shoes and cosmetics into her luggage. She left the keycard on the table next to the door when they left. Tarik, being one hundred percent gentleman, carried her heavy suitcases to the door.

When they stepped outside, they both halted mid-stride. The big white van was gone. Joe was gone too.

"How?" she asked.

"Where'd you park?"

"Around back."

Still carting her luggage, Tarik jogged to the end of the building and peered around the corner. Evidently he didn't see anything because he dashed around the corner and out of her line of sight. Fearful she was being watched or followed, she looked back over her shoulder. No one. Her nerves jumpy, she broke into a full run after Tarik. As she rounded the corner, she saw he had already put her suitcases in the backseat and was sitting behind the steering wheel. His uncovered arm jutted from the open driver's-side window. She handed him the keys then ran around the rear of the vehicle and climbed into the passenger seat.

While buckling her seat belt, she turned to him. "Do you think Joe's still alive?"

"Don't know. Don't want to know." He shifted the vehicle into reverse and punched the gas, backing out of the parking spot, then jammed it into first and popped the clutch, setting the truck lurching forward, wheels squealing.

Hands on the dashboard, arms locked, she looked over her shoulder several times. Would a big white van pull out of some hidden parking spot somewhere?

Didn't happen.

"Whose name is the cabin rented under?" Tarik asked as he pulled the truck out onto the two-lane road that headed north, out of Anchorage.

"Katie's. Why?"

"Good. We'll head back there. For now. Until I can figure out what our next move will be. It's not likely they'll find us, as long as we keep the truck hidden—"

"Uh. I'm no pro at this running from bad guys stuff, but I think that might be a bad move. They saw us. Together. *Reallllly* together, if you get my drift."

"Good point. Man, my mind is not working tonight. Think, think, think. We need somewhere safe. And some supplies. I think it might be worth it to swing by there and grab a few things. If we're careful."

A part of her put up a silent cheer at the thought of going back to the isolated cabin with Tarik. The other part, the one that was heartbreak-phobic didn't care for the idea. Yes, she supposed that part was the one she should be listening to.

But it was so darn difficult! There were so many things going on there — men trying to kidnap her, a severe case of *like* melting her brain...how was she ever going to make an intelligent decision with those kinds of pressures piling on her shoulders? Sloping and weak, they lacked the required weight-bearing capacity, normally buckled under stresses a whole lot lighter than this.

The *like* thing was particularly weighty. Despite Tarik's bizarre problem, or maybe because of it, she genuinely liked him. He was different from any man she'd ever met before. He was complicated. Intriguing. The kind of guy who had a lot going on under the surface. She had a feeling it would take her a long time to figure him out. A part of her wanted to take up that challenge, to discover all his secrets. His wants. His fears.

She spent the entire trip out to the cabin telling herself why that was such a bad idea. There was no way she'd ever consider living out in the boonies. If it took longer than ten minutes to reach the nearest mall, it was too rural.

Not to mention the cold!

Living in Michigan, she'd seen her share of snow. There were some years when the state didn't dig its way out of the dreaded white stuff until the end of March. Spring was cold and soggy at best. Fall was a mixed bag of hot, humid weather and frigid cold. Her energy levels dipped in the winter when daylight was brief.

She needed sunlight. Living in a place where three months of the year it was dark was out of the question. No way.

Which made the possibility of a long-term thing with Tarik all but impossible. He lived in Alaska. He worked in Alaska. And she assumed there was no way he'd leave Alaska.

Sooner or later he'd get this thing with Omega straightened out and he'd go back to whatever he was doing before he'd found out he was a part-time polar bear. Besides, it wasn't like he could roam around her subdivision in bear-mode without calling attention to himself. Wasn't every day there were polar bears trotting around suburbia. Some moron would probably shoot him or have him hauled to the zoo. And then she'd have to go there to visit him.

Not much of a life, no matter how she looked at it. Poor guy.

When she was a kid, she loved watching The Incredible Hulk. But she always felt sorry for Bill Bixby at the end. He usually made friends with someone but had to leave them behind and move on. Even at eight years old, she could see how terribly lonely his life must have been.

"No welcoming party. Better hurry, though. I have an idea." Tarik parked the truck behind the cabin, out of sight of what little traffic made it down the rutted, barely passable dirt road leading from the main road at least a half mile back. When he shut off the engine, he turned to look at her. "You've been quiet. Are you okay? You're not hurt, are you?"

"I'm fine. Just thinking. There's a lot to think about, you know."

He nodded. "Let's get inside. Then we can talk about some things." He shut the door after she climbed to the ground—those trucks were not made for short girls with legs the length of your average junior high-school student.

Before she had turned around, he was heading around the side of the cabin. He went for the gun first, checked to see that it was loaded then took a look in the refrigerator.

"What're you going to do with the gun? You're not going to shoot anyone? Are you? I mean, for some reason it's kind of okay for you to do that bear-whooping-ass thing, but shooting people…" She let the words trail off. This was for real! People were chasing her. And someone could end up shot. That someone could even be her, if they weren't careful.

"I'm taking it as a precaution." Still staring into the fridge, he grimaced. "I see we're going to need to stock up on a few things before we head out of town."

"What's wrong with what I bought? Can't we take this stuff?"

He frowned. "Soy milk? And what's this?" He pulled a prepackaged meal out of the tiny freezer. "Lean Cuisine? First, I won't touch soy milk. If it doesn't come out of a ranging animal, it's unnatural." He tossed the Creamy Basil Chicken dinner into the freezer and slammed the door. "And these meals wouldn't satisfy a guy half my size. The portions aren't big enough for children."

"Well they're big enough for me." That sounded wrong.

He grinned as he scooped up the gun and headed for the door. "Let's go."

Her face warmed. She followed him outside, grateful for the chill on her stinging cheeks. "You know what I mean."

"Sure I do."

If she could've, she would've put money on the fact that he brushed his side against hers on purpose as he opened her door. He sauntered around the vehicle, opened his door, set the gun on the floor behind his seat and climbed in.

"A buddy of mine is out of town for a few days," he explained while driving the truck back down the long, winding road. "We'll stay at his place for the night. Hopefully no one at Omega knows I have a key. He doesn't work with me, so no one should know who he is or that he's gone." He draped an arm over her shoulder. His fingertips traced little circles on the nape of her neck. "We'll be comfy-cozy."

She shivered. "I'm sure we will."

* * * * *

They drove about a half hour, down winding roads that cut through pine forests. A bumpy rutted driveway—didn't anyone in Alaska have a paved drive?—led to a cabin that was almost identical on the outside to the one she'd rented with Katie.

Tarik parked the truck behind the building and hauled Abby's luggage and the gun up to the front door. After unlocking the door — no small feat with his arms loaded — he pushed it open for her.

The cabin's inside looked almost exactly the same as well. Butt ugly furniture and all.

Did everyone in Alaska decorate their homes in Rustic Tacky?

Tarik set her suitcases next to the bed and headed to the fireplace. The view from behind as he bent over to pick up some firewood was interesting, considering what he was wearing. He tossed a couple of logs into the fireplace then wadded up some paper and lit a brilliant blaze with a long wooden matchstick.

Made it look so easy. It had taken her at least a half-dozen tries before her fire had grown beyond a measly flicker.

Show off.

"We'll have to be careful when we head down to the store, not call too much attention to ourselves," he said as he poked at the fire with a long metal hooky thingy.

Not call attention to themselves? That was going to be interesting, considering he was still wearing the toga he'd fashioned out of the hotel blanket. If that didn't get someone's attention, she didn't know what would.

"I don't want to go to Max's Place," he continued, standing directly in front of her for a moment before continuing back to the kitchen. He filled one of those old coffeepots with water and spooned some grounds into the little basket that sat at the top. Once he had the coffee started, he headed back in her direction. He sure was a busy bee. A sexy busy bee. "Max is a friend of mine. If any of Omega's guys ask him about me, they'd know I was still in the area." He sat down in a chair. "Come here." He punctuated his words with a come-hither eyebrow wag and pat on his thigh.

It took all of three steps to put her front and center before him. Like she expected, he grabbed her waist and pulled, until she was comfy-cozy on his lap. More than her cheeks warmed and it was hard to remember what they'd been talking about. A very curious unseen protuberance was poking her bottom through the blanket and her clothes. "Okay, maybe going to the store isn't such a good idea. How far away from here do you live?" She fanned her face. Was it getting stuffy in there or what?

He buried his nose in the crook between her neck and shoulder. "My place is back by your rental. Why?"

Battling a case of goose bumps, she tipped her head and scrunched up her shoulder. Why? Yes, that was a good question. What had they been talking about? Oh. Yeah. "You were going to get yourself some clothes, weren't you?" She leaned back a bit, taking her neck out of the line of fire and motioned up and down his body with an index finger. "I'd think a guy dressed like Julius Caesar might stand out in a place like this. The only thing you're missing is the olive branches or whatever those things were on his head."

He screwed his perfect mouth into a playful scowl. "Funny." One of his hands took a little tour of her body, starting at her waist and ending up under her shirt, cupping her breast through her bra.

Oh, what a naughty hand. Naughty in the nicest sense. Her head dropped back and her eyelids fell over her eyes. She felt her nipple hardening, thanks to his gentle caresses. "If you went there—uh, I mean at your house—you could grab yourself some canned food or whatever it is you eat." She had no idea how she'd managed to string together so many words, considering her head was spinning and her body was planning a party for the arrival of one hunky guest.

"I'm thinking there's another guy named "Joe" sitting at my place waiting for me to come home so he can escort me back to my prison cell in the basement of Omega's headquarters."

That last part sobered her up a smidge. They'd held him prisoner? What was going on? "They were going to lock you up? Why?"

"So I couldn't do this." He removed his hand from her breast, cupped her chin and kissed the daylights out of her. His tongue did all those naughty, yummy things his tongue had a tendency to do. It flirted with hers then got all serious, plunging in and out and getting bossy. In response, she kissed him back. Wasn't any way she could do anything but that.

For each thrust of his tongue, she gave him one in return. And while she was teaching his mouth a lesson or two, she let her hands go a-wanderin' over the bumpy terrain that made up his absolutely drool-worthy upper body. She yanked until the toga came untied and then set both hands free to wander at will.

Based on the low rumbling growl he gave when one of her fingertips grazed a nipple, she guessed he appreciated the thorough attention she was lavishing on his chest and stomach. That was, she assumed as much until he broke the kiss and pushed her fanny off his lap. She ended up wedged between the chair's arm and Tarik's hip but that was no problem, especially when he caught one of her hands in his and gently set it atop one very prominent part of his anatomy.

Being all too eager to drive him as crazy as he was driving her, she wrapped her fingers around his shaft and slowly pumped up and down.

His gasp was followed by a husky murmur, "Suck my cock."

Sounded like fun.

She sped up the pace a bit then slid off the chair and stood in front of it, straddling his outstretched legs. His cock stood front and center, looking big and tasty. She bent over, opened her mouth wide and took him in.

He tasted great, like outdoors and man and all things sexy and wild. She swirled her tongue round and round then traced a line down the underside to the curls coating his balls. She fondled them gently as she licked back up to the tip and took him as deeply as she could into her throat.

Under her forearm, she felt the muscles of his leg trembling. She felt the tug of his hand on her hair. The sting of his fingers digging into her shoulder. The sensations fueled the blaze burning inside her body.

Up and down, up and down he thrust his hips, fucking her mouth while holding her head still. Quite suddenly, he pushed her away.

Was something wrong?

She lifted her gaze to his face, saw the fierce hunger burning in his eyes. She didn't know why but she whimpered.

He was breathing heavily, his chest rising and falling with each gasping breath. The fine sheen coating his chest glistened in the flickering light of the fire and right then and there she decided she'd never, ever seen a sexier man. "Dammit woman," he said, sitting forward, "what you do to me." Looking like he might eat her up, he snatched up her hands in his and pulled, dragging her up against him again. Then he stood, taking her with him. Still holding her, he added, "It's my turn now."

What exactly did he have in mind?

Chapter Five

ಬಂ

He was losing control again. The beast was gaining strength, being fed by the delightful sensation of Abby's mouth on his cock. He had to stop it. Had to gather up his strength, hold off, even if there wasn't a cell in his body that wasn't screaming for a quick release.

He wanted to possess her. To spill his seed inside over and over and over again. Yet a tiny part of him knew he shouldn't, that to impregnate her could put her in more jeopardy than she was already in. Not to mention an innocent child. He'd taken her word for it the first time, that there could be no pregnancy but he didn't want to take that chance again.

He helped her to the floor, and once she was nude and lying comfortably on the thick rug before the fire, he pulled her knees apart. Her skin took on a golden glow from the fire. Her hair looked like flames fanned around her head. Her eyes were dark. They said more than he suspected she knew.

He moistened a fingertip with his mouth then parted her labia. Her clit sat nestled under her damp curls, glistening with her juices. She arched her back the instant he touched her there.

Dammit, she looked so lovely, her tits pushed high into the air, her nipples pink points, beckoning him. Her soft legs parted, her cream coating her pussy. He wanted to sink his cock into her tight heat and fuck her hard. Fuck her until she screamed his name, until she begged him to do it over and over again.

No. No. Not like that.

He'd take her slow. He'd build up the tension until neither of them could stand it anymore. They'd find bliss together.

Yes, that's how she deserved to have it.

He started by eating her. She smelled incredible and tasted even better. He flicked his tongue over her clit while gliding two fingers into her tight canal. In and out they went, in time with the rhythm of his tongue. She moaned and groaned, threw her head from side to side and tensed up her legs, parting them wider for him.

"Yes, my sweet. That's the way. Open to me. Open wide."

The sound of her ragged breathing was like a tonic. It sent waves of wanting crashing through his body. Building, building. He had to have her. He needed her. Now.

No. No!

He added two more fingers. She was tight around them. So hot and tight.

"Oh God," she shouted. Her body trembled beneath him. "No more. Please."

He didn't stop but he did slow down. His fingers dragged in and out of her at the pace of a turtle. Three tremors accompanied each push in and each pull out. His tongue continued to tease her clit but also slower. He used long swipes now instead of short flicks.

It was only when she screamed, "Fuck me now," that he stopped.

He gently rolled her onto her stomach then helped her onto her hands and knees. "Yeah. That's the way. I want to fuck you from behind. I'm going to fuck your pussy and then I'm going to fuck your ass."

"Oh God," she squeaked.

He reached around her hip and stroked her clit while entering her in an agonizingly slow thrust. He felt every ridge in her inner walls as he drove deeper. And every inch as he pulled out again. She tossed her head back. Her hair fell in a spray of flashing gold over her shoulders and back. Fucking gorgeous.

She rocked back and forth, meeting his thrusts as he settled into an easy pace. Her inner walls gripped him tightly. Her juices coated his cock in sweet, slick heat. His balls tightened. The fire of his need threatened to consume him completely.

He could sense she was getting closer, that she was on the verge of orgasm. It was the scent in the air. Musky and sweet. It drove him crazy.

Unable to wait any longer, he pulled out of her pussy and after dampening her anus with some of her juices, pressed slowly into her ass.

Abby tensed beneath him. "It hurts."

"This is the best way. Relax for me, kitten." He moistened his fingers adding more lubrication. Dammit, she was tight and hot. When she opened to him, taking him all the way in, he stopped to give her a chance to get comfortable. He fucked her pussy with his fingers and she started shaking. "Touch your clit."

"Yes. Oh God, yes." Her fingernails grazed his knuckles as she traced a circle over her clit.

He met the rhythm of her strokes with the thrusts of cock and fingers until she was screaming her release. He followed a single heartbeat later, pumping his seed into her ass until there was nothing left. It just about killed him but he withdrew from her and let her lie down. He pulled the blanket from the chair, gathered her to him and covered them both up.

She pressed a single kiss to his shoulder and he smiled.

This was so right. So perfect. He didn't want it to end, even though he knew it had to. And sooner was better than later. He cared too much for Abby to let it go on any longer.

* * * * *

Abby lay beside Tarik, soaking in the heat radiating from his body. His breathing had settled into the slow, steady pattern of sleep, his chest rising and falling with each breath. Lost in her thoughts, she watched him sleep. What to do? Things were obviously a whole lot more complicated than she could even imagine. His work was a big part of things. They'd tried to hold not only Tarik hostage but had also tried to kidnap her for some reason. Something to do with sex, if she'd understood Tarik's vague reference earlier. Or maybe it had something to do with kissing? She'd have to admit, her brain hadn't been running at top speed when he'd answered her question. What had he said? Something about not being able to 'do this'? She wondered what "this" he was referring to.

Good thing her brain was working okay now, not that it made coming to any kind of decision easier. There were so many unknown factors to consider.

She knew nothing about Omega, other than they didn't hesitate to operate outside of the law. How far they'd go, she had no idea. Had they truly intended on having a doctor look at her? Or had they had more nefarious intentions? Really, could she afford to assume anything but the worst?

Hell, no.

Whatever Omega had done to Tarik, they were going to some extreme measures to keep it secret. She had to assume that meant they might kill both of them if they had to.

She shivered.

This stuff was so out of the range of her normal life. Up to this point, the most unpleasant person she'd had to deal with was the bitch who'd stolen her boyfriend back in college. These guys were making Angel—her parents had obviously given their child the wrong name!—look like a creampuff.

And then there was Tarik himself. He wasn't just a handsome guy, a fuck buddy. He was a gentleman. He was a considerate and giving lover. And he was a human being who deserved to make his own decisions about his life. Somehow he needed to get away from Omega.

She knew she'd have to help him as best she could. It was that rescue mentality kicking in again. She couldn't help it. Sure, she wasn't some crazy ass-kicking chick who could take down five men single-handedly. But she had a brain that worked pretty well most of the time, a rental SUV that could handle the worst roads, and more than her share of determination. Sometimes being stubborn had its advantages. At least in this case, it might help keep one innocent man who'd committed no crime from being imprisoned — or worse.

Then, once she'd assured his safety, she'd head back home and try to forget Tarik had ever existed. It was for the best, not only for her own good, but also for his. She sensed he wanted a woman to love, someone who would be around for the long haul, even though he'd said he'd probably never marry. The long haul stuff was so not her. She was more a flavor-of-the-week kind of girl.

The only question remaining was how she'd help him? What was their next step?

She couldn't possibly take on a whole company, evil bosses and armed guards. She didn't know how to use a gun and violence wasn't her thing. She tended to run away from bullies rather than confront them. In this case, she figured running away was probably the best choice.

But run to where? They were literally in the middle of nowhere. There were no flights, thanks to the stupid air traffic controller's strike. She doubted there were any buses or trains that would get them far enough away to be safe. While she supposed Tarik could take to hiding out in some remote cabin, what kind of life would that be? How would he earn money?

Tarik needed a job, a place to live...a life.

Oy, she'd barely been able to provide that for herself!

"You look worried," his voice cut into her thoughts.

She'd been so consumed by her deliberating, she hadn't realized she'd been lying there staring at an awake man. How long had his eyes been open? "There's plenty to worry about, don't you think?"

"Not for you. I won't let you worry about anything. You're here on vacation. You can go home whenever you like. I'll take care of everything."

The last time a guy had said those words to her, she'd ended up having to pay a mechanic to put a new engine in her car. Her ex-boyfriend Jack had failed to put a belt on properly and her rods or whatever those vital engine parts were called ended up getting ruined.

"What're your plans?"

He shook his head. "I don't want you getting involved."

"Too late there, buster." She regretted those words the second they'd passed through her lips. Tarik looked like he'd killed a kitten or something. "Sorry," she said, reaching for him. "Sometimes I'm so flippant. I get sarcastic when I'm stressed out. I didn't mean to hurt your feelings."

He stood and opening a nearby armoire, pulled out a pair of pants. He held them up to his waist, obviously to check the fit. "What're you apologizing for?" He sat on the couch and shoved one foot into a pant leg then did the same with the other. "You're right. You are involved. And it's my fault. Which is why I'm handling this whole thing. I won't see you get sucked in any deeper." He yanked up his pants and fastened the fly.

Men had such fragile egos. Why was it necessary for them to take on the world by themselves?

She swallowed a sigh. "As much as I trust you could do this without my help, I still can't see turning my back and skipping off into the Alaskan sunset. I don't see you being the kind of guy to go all Rambo and charge into Omega with guns blazing."

"Frankly, that's exactly what I was thinking."

"Liar."

"Cool. My buddy left his cell phone. This could come in handy." He pocketed the phone he'd found on top of the armoire then sat next to her. His arms were crossed over his chest, a pose she found especially appealing because it made his biceps look huge. "I suppose you have a better plan?"

"Yes, as a matter of fact, I do. Though I haven't nailed down the finer details yet."

"Let's hear what you've got."

"Okay. It's really quite simple." She hesitated but he encouraged her to go on with a nod. "We run."

He stared at her for a minute but didn't speak. She had to give it to him, he didn't bust into raucous laughter. Nor did he flatly refuse to consider her suggestion. In fact, he seemed to be waiting for her to tell him more about The Brilliant Plan. Too bad there wasn't much more to tell.

"Like I said," she continued, figuring she'd be forced to talk her way through the problem. "I haven't settled all the details yet. But I'm thinking it makes more sense to just get away from all this instead of attacking a bunch of people with who knows what kind of weapons and power behind them."

He seemed to consider what she said carefully. "You have a point."

"You agree then? That we should leave?"

"I'm beginning to appreciate the fact that it might be a good plan, at least for now."

"I was trying to figure out where to go."

"I'm thinking heading for Canada would be best. I have a driver's license…though I'm not sure it's exactly legal."

"Oh boy."

"It's worth a try. If what my boss said is true and I don't exist here in the United States, maybe I can find a way to gain citizenship in Canada under an assumed name. Without any legal records here in Alaska, I should be untraceable."

"Good, then we'll head south. In my rental car, I guess. We'll need to fill the tank. I'm guessing the northwestern part of Canada is pretty much like this. Lots of nature. Not a lot of Citgos. Wish I had rented something smaller that gets better gas mileage. Back home, there are gas stations on practically every corner."

"We can head down to White Moose by way of Dawson City. It'll be a long drive, at least ten hours, but at least it should be relatively safe at this time of year. And we can break it up a bit, maybe have dinner in Eagle Ridge."

It wasn't easy but she resisted the urge to grimace. Long car rides were not something she enjoyed. In fact, she hated them. Granted, the scenery would probably be breathtaking. And she wasn't talking about the scenery outside.

But ten hours? Ugh.

Evidently, being a bear-man meant Tarik could read minds—or more likely, read her body language. As much as she tried to hide her lack of enthusiasm for the upcoming road trip, he knew she was not thrilled. He gripped her upper arms and stared long and hard in her eyes, like he was trying to hypnotize her. "You don't have to do this."

"I want to help you."

"We can find another way to get you home, a bus—"

"You think that's going to be better? It would probably take twice as long by bus. No, I'm fine. At least we'll be able to make pit stops and perhaps take an occasional break to admire the mountains or flowers or whatever. I wish those stupid air traffic controllers would get back to work. I'd fly home tomorrow. It was a blessedly short flight from Detroit. But then again, what if those thugs know where I live? Oh..." her words trailed off as she realized for the first time how unlikely it was that she'd be able to simply go home and resume her life like nothing had happened. This Omega wasn't some junior high bully picking on a convenient target. This was a company with a lot to lose and probably gobs of money and resources.

Probably long arms and lots of eyes, like the U.S. government. "We haven't thought this completely through yet, have we?"

"Not completely. No. It's possible they could find out where you live and work. I don't think you'll be safe until I settle things with Torborg. But I'm not ready to deal with him yet. I need some time to look into some things. And I know if I show up at Omega right now, there'll be an army there waiting for me. No, it's better if he comes looking for me and I confront him when I'm ready."

"But will he go looking for you? Or will he send Joe the Kidnapper?"

"I'm thinking he'll come himself and try to talk me into returning to Anchorage with him. If he doesn't, I'll just have to improvise, find a way to make him come to me. I've been working for the man for years. I've always considered him a mentor. A friend. I'll admit he's harder to read than ancient Greek, but I think he'd want to keep this as quiet as possible. Sending a bunch of assassins to fill me with lead won't accomplish what he's after. For one thing, he'd risk someone finding proof of what he's done."

"Your body?"

"My DNA."

"Oh."

He motioned toward the kitchen. "We'd better take all the supplies we can, in case we're forced to sleep in the truck. Blankets. Food. Cash. Clothes. Whatever we can find. We may be roughing it for a few days. I just hope my buddy does a better job stocking his pantry than some other person I know." He winked.

Abby really wished she could get over her rescue complex.

Chapter Six

ෝ

"They're gone. We tracked down the cabin the woman was renting and there's no sign she'll be returning. No luggage. No food. I've been to Tarik's place. He hasn't been there in a while." Security officer Raul Zant stood just inside Torborg's office, stiff as a Marine on the first day of basic training.

Torborg forced himself to set the phone he'd been holding in the cradle, rather than slam it. Things were not going the way he'd planned. Not by a long shot, and he was fucking tired of hearing bad news. Didn't anyone understand how important it was to get a handle on this situation? Had he failed to communicate that effectively? What the fuck would it take to make these morons understand? "Dammit, I need them in custody today. Now. Not later. Not tomorrow. Not next week. They must be stopped before something happens to complicate our situation further. I'm trusting you to find them and bring them back here without making a scene. You're Evert's friend. Hasn't he called? Talk some sense into him."

"No, he hasn't called. But I have good news."

"Good. I need some good news about now."

"We've located the rental company Miss Clumm rented the car from, and she hasn't returned it yet. We have license plate numbers and a make and model. We'll find her."

"Excellent. If they haven't already headed into Canada, they won't get across the border. I've had Evert's identification tagged."

"And they can't fly."

"Good." The red call indicator light blinked on his phone. Knowing who was likely calling, he stared at it. His gut wound into a tight knot.

"Sir, we'll have them here by tomorrow. I'd be willing to bet they're driving to the border. We'll catch them when they try to cross. I have agents heading to Eagle Ridge now."

"Excellent," he said, distracted by the light which was continuing to blink. Fuck, he'd have to take the call.

"It's too bad it came to this. I don't know what's going on here, but I've known Tarik for a long time. He's an okay guy…I don't believe he'd ever do anything illegal or immoral…"

Torborg heard the regret in the security guard's voice and knew he had to reassure the man he meant Tarik no harm. If he failed, he knew he risked losing the guard's loyalty. He needed everyone on his team right now, more than ever. "Let me make one thing clear. Tarik is like the son I never had, and I'm not intending on hurting him. But he's ill and needs treatment. We need to get him into the hospital immediately…before it's too late."

"Yes, sir. I'll do my best."

"I'm counting on it. Your friend's life depends upon it."

* * * * *

It was amazing how close a girl could get to a person when taking a road trip. In the time it took for them to drive to Eagle Ridge, Alaska, a tiny town that barely qualified as an intersection, she'd learned a whole lot about Tarik, both what he'd been raised to believe about himself and what he'd been told more recently. It probably wasn't P.C. for a girl to feel sorry for a guy, at least from the guy's point of view. Men tended to despise any form of pity. But really, how terrible.

Tarik had thought all along that he was your average brilliant genetic researcher, or at least a member of the species Homo sapiens. How awful to find out that everything he'd believed about himself was a lie, right down to the most basic of truths. He wasn't entirely human, nor was he an animal. He was some kind of genetic experiment.

Being the kind of girl she was, Abby found herself feeling more and more compelled to do what she could to help him deal with it all. He didn't talk a lot, at least not as much as she would've, had the roles been reversed. If she'd found out her parents weren't her parents and she'd been concocted by her coworkers years earlier in a petri dish, her DNA fused with an animal's, she would've been on a rant for hours. And she could pretty much guarantee that even out there in the boonies, there'd be plenty of people who would've heard her bitch about it. Anyone within several miles, she'd bet.

Tarik, in contrast, spoke softly, calmly. He talked science to her, about things she couldn't even begin to comprehend. It was kind of cute. He threw words like gene splicing and genome around like an NBA star would toss around a basketball. The way he spoke the words, with such quiet awe, it was like he verbally caressed them. It was clear he loved the work he did, and was very committed to the good that might come out of it someday.

She found herself wanting him to talk about her the same way, with equal respect and dare she say it…adoration. Love.

Whether she'd wanted to or not, during that car ride and meal in Eagle Ridge's only restaurant, while she listened and shared, she fell in love with Tarik, the man. Tarik the beast. Tarik the being. She realized it as she sat across from him, watching him devour a patty melt and basket of fries. He gave her the very last bite of the slice of chocolate pie they'd shared. Any man who did that was a keeper.

Her mood turned dark as they returned to the truck. Very soon they'd be going their separate ways. Tarik had it all planned out. They'd head into Canada. He knew of a town not far from the border where he could get internet access on his laptop. After doing a little research, he was going to contact his former boss and plead his case. They'd meet. Tarik would convince him to leave them alone, and then she'd either head south, toward the southern United States-Canada border, or to the nearest airport. Rumors were the air traffic controller's strike was just about over. In no time, she'd be back home and Tarik would remain in Canada and everything would be normal again.

Shit.

No, she wasn't exactly thrilled about that last part, but what other choice did she have? She had a job to go home to. Bills to pay. A best friend. A life.

Why did her life feel so empty when it had never felt that way before? She'd been content with the way things were going, all the way up until she'd stepped foot in this beautiful, wild place. Even when she'd first arrived in Alaska, she'd still been anxious to return home. It was sometime later, after she'd spent a night or two with Tarik that her attitude toward her former life had changed. She guessed it had been a gradual process, not sudden. There'd been no Big Moment when the violins had played and she'd suddenly seen her life with new clarity and all of life's mysteries had been solved.

Really, did it matter how it had happened? How she'd gone from being quite pleased with her life to downright depressed.

No. Because it made no difference in the long run. She still had to go home and go on with things because that was what everyone did, at least everyone who kept themselves out of the mental wards of hospitals.

Maybe, if she was still in a funk after a week or two, she'd follow Katie's advice and talk to that guy who ran the dating service downtown. Perhaps she'd finally had her fill of casual sex.

"You're very quiet again. Are you okay?" Tarik was sitting beside her, in the passenger seat. They'd both agreed it was probably best he didn't drive, just in case he decided to do the bear-morphing thing again. He hadn't changed into a bear in a while, since that time at the hotel, but she wasn't about to take her chances. Even though she was positive Tarik's mind still operated like a human being when he was in bear form, she didn't think he'd be able to drive. There were few things she feared more than being in a car accident, thanks to an unfortunate event that had happened when she was sixteen. A few weeks after getting her driver's license, the car she'd been driving was hit head-on by a driver who'd had a seizure. Years later, the sound of metal colliding against metal still echoed in her head.

"I'm fine. Just trying to plan my next move—our next move." She sounded tired, even to her own ears.

He took her hand in his and held it gently. His thumb brushed over the top of her hand, soft as feathers.

It was something, how tender Tarik could be sometimes. Quiet and warm and sensitive. And then at other times he was sexy and strong and wild. Such an odd—but wonderful!— combination. "I'm sorry you're caught up in this. I'd give anything to end it right now. It's like a nightmare I can't wake up from. I'm sorry for dragging you into this mess. Turn right at the next intersection."

"It's not your fault." She followed his direction and turned at the corner. "You had no idea what was going on. I feel bad for you. Learning everything you believed about yourself was a lie. Learning you have no family. No ties to anyone. That you basically don't exist to anyone or anything but Omega." *And me!*

"Yeah. Well. As soon as I can get onto the internet, I'm going to get the facts. And then I'll deal with Torborg. I still have friends in Omega. I'm hoping they'll help me. Or if I have to, I'll hack into the system. It's not like I haven't done it before. When I'm through digging up dirt on Torborg, he won't have a choice but to leave you alone."

She nodded and drove the remaining couple of miles to the customs station in Bear Creek, Yukon, listening to the radio. She half expected to hear the DJ break in with a news bulletin about a couple of dangerous felons making a run for Canada. A Bear Creek Police cruiser passed them about a half mile from the station, and she held her breath, expecting him to turn around and flip on the lights. He didn't. Still very nervous, she looked at Tarik just before pulling up to the little station squatting next to a school.

"If there's any delay getting through, we'll just turn back and find another way."

"Okay."

They rolled to a stop and Abby gave the man standing inside looking tired a friendly smile. "Good evening," she said as cheerily as she could.

He gave her a smile that said "I just want to go home". "Identification, please."

Abby handed him her Michigan driver's license then turned to Tarik. He lifted his hips, slid a hand into his back pocket and pulled out his Alaska driver's license and handed it to her. She didn't look at it before passing it to the border patrol officer. "There you are, sir. We're just heading into White Moose for some sightseeing. I'm vacationing in Alaska for the week."

"Uh-huh." The officer held one ID card in each hand. His gaze hopped back and forth from them to Abby's and Tarik's faces. Then he glanced down at the counter in front of him. "One moment." His eyebrows furrowed, he held up an index finger.

Abby gave Tarik a worried look but didn't say anything. He didn't speak either. His expression was blank.

"Miss, I need you to pull your car into the parking lot, please," the man in the booth said a moment later.

She swiveled her head and tried not to look like a shoplifter who'd just been caught with a watermelon up her skirt. "Sure. Okay."

This time, she gave Tarik a "what now?" look.

He whispered, "Back up."

"But what about my license?" she whispered. "I can't fly without it."

"Back up," he repeated.

And so, despite some serious reservations about leaving her sole piece of identification in the hands of the Canadian border patrol, she threw the car into reverse and hit the gas. As she turned to watch behind her, she caught the surprised expression on the man's face.

After she'd cleared the booth, Tarik grabbed the steering wheel and gave it a swift jerk, making the truck spin around. Before she realized it, they were driving forward again, although now they were headed back toward Eagle Ridge.

She sucked in a deep breath. "Now I have no idea how I'll get home. No way I can fly without my identification."

"We'll worry about that later. If you'd parked, we would've ended up in handcuffs. I've been back and forth across that border many times. No one's ever asked me to pull over. Torborg must've done something to keep me from crossing into Canada."

"What are we going to do now?"

"Check into a hotel and get a little sleep."

"Is it safe to do that?"

"Yes. I doubt he'll get the local authorities involved, since he's trying to keep this quiet. So, even if he knows we're in Eagle Ridge, it'll take a few hours to get someone over here. By the time they arrive, we'll be long gone."

"Then you have a plan?"

"Sure. But rest first. You're going to need it. I was hoping it wouldn't come to this. We've got to ditch this truck."

* * * * *

This time, as they carried their luggage and supplies into the dingy little motel room they were sharing, Abby told herself she'd have to be the one to get things rolling, so to speak. Her heart weighed more than a load of bricks. She was scared and confused and aching to be held. She ached to caress Tarik and comfort him. To make him feel special and adored and less like some kind of scientific disaster. She wanted him to feel like a man, a man who had someone who cared for him. Even if it was only for one more night.

She'd never been real good at being a seductress. Acting the part of seductee had always been more fun. She had to admit she had a bit of a submissive streak in her. In her book, nothing beat having a strong, sexually aggressive and skilled lover take complete control in the bedroom. Although Tarik hadn't exactly pulled out the handcuffs and whips, he'd proven he had the heart of a dominant. The whole animal thing actually made him seem even sexier. More dangerous. Wild. *Grrrrrooooowwwwllll.*

After Tarik had carted in the last of their gear and stowed the truck way in the back of the parking lot, he flopped onto the bed and gave her a crooked, tired smile.

Oh yes, things were heating up nicely.

Being in a mood to do something completely contrary to her nature, she turned on the charm, gave him her best come-hither look, and pushed her jacket off her shoulders. It landed on the floor behind her as she took a few hip-swinging steps his way. "Please tell me you aren't too tired."

"Too tired for what?" He blinked.

Yeah. Right. She wasn't buying the clueless act and he knew it. His smile was testimony to that fact. But would he continue to play dumb to see how far she'd take it?

Come and get me, Dangerous. I'm in the mood for some playtime.

A sparkle glimmered in his eyes. It appeared he either lacked the willpower to continue their game or simply didn't care to keep it going. Before she had drawn in a breath to give him a more direct invitation, he jumped up and practically tackled her. Her feet literally left the floor as he scooped her into his arms, turned and tossed her on the bed.

It became instantly clear the mattress had seen better days and the bed's frame hadn't been tested in some time. There were a couple of loud squeaks as she bounced, then a popping sound and then a loud thud. The mattress dropped about a foot and a half. Abby squealed in surprise and then fell into eye-watering, belly-clenching laughter. The tears flowed like champagne at a wedding. She couldn't stop them. And she just about peed her pants when Tarik got all studly and pounced on the bed with her, and a loud rattle and crunch followed. "We. Broke. The. Bed," she said between guffaws.

To her glee, he turned all jungle cat and lunged forward, knocking her on her back. Holding his upper body over hers on outstretched arms thicker than her thighs, he looked down at her like she was his next meal.

What an absolutely delightful place to be! *Hungry, are you?*

He licked his lips and lowered his head to give her a toe-curler of a kiss. It started out soft and sensual, mostly lips, a little bit of teeth. She loved a man who could take his time with a kiss. It suggested he'd take his time with other things too.

After teasing her mouth with his for a while, he set his tongue exploring. It delved into her mouth, caressed her own tongue, checked out the scene further inside then left to find new and unconquered territory — her ear. The entire left side of her body became covered with goose bumps and little bursts of heat shot through her bloodstream. She lifted her arms to reach for him, but he caught her wrists in his hands and pushed them up over her head until they were pressed against the mattress.

She was ready to melt now! Whimpering because she couldn't speak, she took one last, wandering look at the wonder that was Tarik and then let her eyelids fall closed, shutting her into the dark world of her desire. Sensations intensified as he ran his tongue down her neck. Touches felt stronger, more erotic. Sounds louder. She licked her lips, tasting the sweet flavor of his kiss and balled her hands into tight fists.

Did he have any idea how much she wanted him now?

"You're absolutely perfect. Do you know that?" he asked with a husky voice that made him sound like he'd just run a marathon. Before she could answer, he added, "I want you so much."

Take me! Take me! Hoping he'd get the message, she kicked off one of her boots then followed up with the other one.

The man proved once again how well he read her mind, body language, whatever. He unsnapped her jeans and yanked them off. When she started to move her hands to help him, he growled, "No. Don't move."

She was really loving this! "Okay," she said cheerily, returning her hands to their former position above her head.

"If I could, I'd tie you up. I can tell you've been waiting for this, for a man who'll take control in the bedroom."

Yes, yes!

"You want to surrender to your man, don't you?"

"Yes," she said on a sigh. *But only you. Only this man.*

"You will surrender to me."

She felt herself smiling as he roughly removed the rest of her clothing until she was flat on her back, arms up, hands clasped together above her head, breasts pushed high into the air.

Her legs were flat on the bed, pressed together. She knew they wouldn't stay that way long.

He ran a fingertip down her body, starting at the base of her throat. Down, between her breasts...the center of her stomach...into her bellybutton. It stopped just a bit north of her pussy. Her thighs clenched as expectation pulled her muscles into knots.

Her own breathing echoed in her head. Fast and shallow. In between panting breaths quiet little sighs and moans slipped between her lips. She wanted more. So much more.

He slid his hands between her knees and pushed outward, forcing them apart, wide, wider, wider. The cool air chilled her wet pussy, making her shiver. "Mmmm. I love the way you smell."

She loved the way he sounded. And looked. And felt. And smelled too.

His hair tickled the insides of her thighs as he lowered his head to taste her.

At the first touch of his tongue to her nether lips, she clenched her stomach and tipped her hips, silently begging him to deepen his touches. She needed him inside her. Her pussy was burning with the urge to be filled. How long would he make her wait?

He parted her labia with his fingers and flickered his tongue back and forth over her clit. The motion sent little jolts of pleasure buzzing up her spine. Bursts of white light exploded behind her closed eyelids and she sucked in a few clipped gasps.

More, more, more!

He pushed two fingers inside her while continuing to torment her clit with that agile tongue of his. Oh, she was going to die. Or had she already died…and gone to heaven?

To hell with thinking or wondering.

More, more!

Chapter Seven

ॐ

"I want to give you everything you've ever fantasized about. I want to *be* everything you've ever fantasized about."

A tremble wound up Abby's spine. Tarik didn't know it, but he had already lived up to that promise. And then some.

With every light flicker of his tongue and thrust of his fingers, he carried her closer and closer to climax. It was going to end fast this time, too fast. She moaned.

He stopped tormenting her clit and pussy, instead tickling the insides of her thighs with tender kisses. "What do you imagine? Tell me. What do you think about when you masturbate?" He ran his index finger along her slit but didn't push it inside. "I'm guessing you masturbate a lot. You're such a sensual woman."

Out of instinct, she rocked her hips back and forth. Her insides were burning up with a fever only he could cure. The problem was, she knew that even if he did bring her to climax, the fever would return. Again, and again, and again.

"Tell me," he repeated, reminding her that he was waiting for a response.

"A strong, dangerous man in control."

"Yes, kitten. Anything else?"

She felt him leave her, heard him unzipping her suitcases. "What are you doing?" She opened her eyes.

He was still dressed, standing over her stacked suitcases in the corner of the room. The top one was opened and he was holding a pair of socks in one hand, her scarf in the other. "Looking for stuff. Now close your eyes."

She giggled. "What kind of stuff?"

"You ask too many questions. I'm in control. That's all you need to know."

After rooting around in her suitcases for a while longer, he returned to the bed. The springs groaned under his weight and her nerve endings tingled as she pulled in a deep breath. The scent of Tarik and woods filled her nostrils. In her mind's eye, she imagined them together in the woods. She'd never done it outside. Never thought to. Not with all the bugs and snakes and critters. But with Tarik, she decided it might be fun. She would make love with him outside. Someday. And it would be wonderful.

While she imagined herself lying naked on a grassy clearing in a forest, he tied something around her wrists, securing them together. Then he kissed his way down her body until he reached her ankles.

"You are everything I've ever fantasized about. Did you know that, Abby?" he murmured as he pulled her ankles apart. Her heart was beating against her breastbone like a kangaroo trying to bust loose from a cage by the time he'd tied them. Her legs were wide apart. She was stretched out in preparation for some kind of delightful torture.

"If I had the chance, I'd make love to you like this every night. No, every morning, noon and night."

If. No, when. She wanted it to be *when*.

He trailed a slick path with his tongue up the inside of one of her legs. "I'd tie you up and tease you until you begged me for completion." He fucked her hard with his fingers until she was gasping and yanking on her restraints. He added a finger in her ass too, which acted to spike her temperature to at least a thousand degrees.

"More. Oh God. More!"

"Mmmm. You're an impatient little thing, aren't you?"

She heard the quavering of his voice. She wasn't the only one losing patience. "Yes." She pulled at the restraints holding her ankles. There wasn't a single cell in her body not screaming for release. She was burning up from head to toe. Aching and trembling and tense.

"Oh yes, wider. I want your legs wider. I want to see your pussy when you come. I want to smell that wonderful scent when I give you release." He untied her ankles and pushed them back, until her knees were bent and her legs were as wide as they could be. Then he tied them again. To what, she had no idea. She didn't give a damn.

"What about these tits? Do you like a little bit of pain when you fuck?" He simultaneously stroked her clit and pinched one of her nipples. The sharp pain and sweet pleasure blended together, threatening to send her over the edge. He stopped just before she sailed over the last hurdle to completion.

She nearly cried in frustration.

He kissed one corner of her mouth then the other. "Look at me."

She opened her eyes.

His were focused on hers. Wide and warm. They were dark but full of tenderness. "I came to you because I had to have you. I had to possess you. But I've stayed with you because I need you."

His confession brought tears to her eyes. She hadn't realized how much she'd longed to hear those words from him. And she hadn't realized how much she ached to tell him she loved him. But she wouldn't. No. She couldn't. It wouldn't be fair to either of them.

He settled over top of her and she shuddered as his dick prodded at her slit. He glided into her slowly, the leisurely pace of his thrusts making the most of every intimate stroke. He made love to her. Stroked her. Held her. Kissed her.

His cock drove in and out of her, taking, claiming, but his touches and whispered promises were sweet and sincere. What had started out as a hot fuck ended as lovemaking beyond her wildest dreams. Lovemaking she'd never forget, no matter how long she lived.

And when it was through, he untied her and held her until she drifted off to sleep. As she slipped into her dreams, she swore she heard him whisper, "I love you, kitten."

* * * * *

"Wake up, sweetheart." Tarik's deep, husky voice entered her dreams once again. In her mind's eye, she saw his face. He smiled. "Time to get up. We have a long walk ahead of us. We need to get going."

Slowly, her dreams faded and the sensations of the world around her penetrated the haze of sleep. She didn't want to move. Didn't want to open her eyes. She just wanted to go back to sleep and dream some more. There, in the world of her fantasies, none of the bad stuff existed. Only good. Tarik. He loved her.

"What time is it?" Her voice was gritty from lack of sleep. It felt like she'd drifted off only fifteen minutes ago.

"Just after three."

She groaned and dragged the pillow over her face. "Why do we need to leave so early?"

"We need to get moving if we want to clear the Canadian Customs before sunrise. I don't want to tangle with Torborg until I've had a chance to get online, but if we're going to get into town by a decent hour, we're going to have to catch a ride from someone to White Moose. It'll take us days to walk."

"We're going to hitchhike?"

"Sure. It'll be safe. Most of the time the only people driving these roads at night are vacationers in RV's and truckers. I figure either way, we'll be comfortable. Besides, those boots of yours aren't exactly the kind of footwear required for hiking. Your feet would be shreds if we walked. It's only a few hours down to White Moose by car. We can be down there by breakfast. I'll buy you steak and eggs at the White Moose Grill."

That set her mouth a-watering. Quite suddenly she realized she was starving. "Steak sounds good."

"Let's go." Since he was already dressed and ready to head out, he did a lot of pacing as she dressed, put on some makeup, ate a snack and gathered her things. She knew they'd have some walking to do, so there was no way they'd be able to take everything they'd managed to haul to the motel, but she was determined to take everything she could. She crammed as much into her rolling suitcase as would fit—the thing had to weigh eighty pounds!—wrapped a blanket around her shoulders and nodded. "Ready."

He gave her one of those no-way looks and pointed at the suitcase sitting on one end beside her. "You can't take that thing."

"Why not? It's heavy but it rolls. I need the stuff in there."

"Hot rollers?"

"Yes, hot rollers. We're heading into a city, right? What if we decide to go out for some drinks? My hair's frizzy if I don't curl it."

"You look fantastic without going to all that fuss. Besides, I doubt there'll be anyone there you'd want to impress. Take the small bag. Put a few clothes in it. Warm clothes. Some food. And let's go. We're not going to be walking along the road. If we're going to get past customs, we're going to have to cut through the woods. That thing'll slow us down. A lot."

The woods? They were going to be walking in the woods? In the dark? Was that safe? She'd spent more than enough time on this trip thinking she was going to be snack for a bear.

"Are you bringing the gun?" she asked.

"No, I wasn't planning on it. Why? I thought it made you too nervous."

"Well, yeah. It did. When I thought you might use it to shoot people. But I'm not about to hike in woods in the wilds of Canada without one. What if we run across a grizzly?"

"We'll leave it alone and it'll most likely leave us alone." He tossed the mostly empty carryon bag onto the bed and opened it.

"Most likely?" She pushed the larger suitcase onto its back and reluctantly opened it. She hated to leave all her belongings behind, but perhaps after it was all over, she could call the hotel and ask them to ship them home? That was an idea. She could live with that. She pulled out the warmest pieces she'd brought with her, along with some underwear, and packed them into the smaller bag.

"I'm just thinking the gun is a bad idea," Tarik said, as he set about pacing again. "I wouldn't want to get caught by border patrol armed on public lands. It isn't hunting season. I could be arrested. It's bad enough we're illegally crossing the border. Besides, I doubt I could shoot someone. No, it's better if we leave it behind. Honestly, I can't remember the last time I read about a grizzly attack in the paper."

Was he telling her the truth or telling her what he thought she wanted to hear? Being totally ignorant of animals while vacationing in Alaska was a bit of a complication. "Okayyyy." When she'd stuffed as much as she could into the small suitcase, she zipped it closed and nodded toward the door. "I'm ready. I guess." She didn't sound ready.

Standing like a sentry next to the door, he caught her shoulders in his hands and looked into her eyes. "Trust me. I'll keep you safe. No matter what."

She believed him. After giving him a nod and a weak smile she said, "Let's go." She followed him out into the dark night.

* * * * *

"Okay. You were right. I'm dying," Abby admitted after her suitcase became snagged once again on a fallen log. Northwest Canada's forests weren't as scrubby as Michigan's. The shrubs growing under the trees weren't as dense, but there were lots and lots of other obstacles to stumble over as one made their way in the dark. And her having never been the outdoorsy-type, she was that much less equipped to handle the strain. They'd been walking for what was probably less than an hour and already she felt like it had been days. She had a new respect for pioneer women who'd traveled on foot to parts unknown. They were clearly made of stronger stuff than she was.

Probably wore better shoes though too.

Tarik, being the gentleman that he was, offered once again to carry her bag. But she was stubborn and wouldn't accept his help. After all, she'd been the one to insist on taking the stupid thing in the first place. Why should she be a sissy and make him lug it around for her? She was no diva. She was a girl who took care of herself. Paid her share. Carried her own luggage.

Even if it was going to kill her.

"Wait. I just need to get a better grip." She stopped walking and pulled blindly at the stuck bag while cursing fallen trees and the lack of a full moon or flashlight. When it didn't break free, she added another round of colorful curses.

"Give me that," Tarik barked, sounding more amused than angry. He snatched the handle out of her hand and yanked it away from her before she could stop him.

"Hey! I was getting it."

"You're too damn stubborn for your own good."

"I've had a few people tell me that. Now give it back." Almost completely blind, she lunged in the general direction of his voice. She found nothing but air. "Where'd you go?"

"Here." His hand, big and warm and reassuring, closed around hers and he pulled her gently forward. "Take small steps. There are some tree roots here. I don't want you to fall."

"Thanks." It was a whole lot easier going without the added burden of the suitcase, on top of the challenge of walking in the dark in unfamiliar territory. "I promise I'll carry it once we get out of these woods. I can't see a thing."

"Really?" He sounded genuinely surprised. "You can't see anything?"

"Nothing. That surprises you?"

"I can see fine," he said, sounding bewildered. "I guess I never realized I was different from other people...outside of maybe being a little stronger than some of the other kids when I was a kid."

She wasn't about to tell him he was easy at least twice as strong as any man she'd ever dated. And she hadn't dated one hundred-pound weaklings either. Her last boyfriend had spent more than his share of time in the gym pumping the proverbial iron. He pumped more than that, she'd realized sometime later. Like the towel girl, the Pilates instructor and a few of the gym's regular customers. But that was beside the point.

No, it was clear by the tone of Tarik's voice that he yearned to feel normal, like he was no different from any other man on the planet. Like he'd always assumed he was.

And she was inspired, as she stumbled along behind him, gripping the waistband of his pants and using it to keep herself on her feet, to list all the ways he was exactly like any other male who'd trod upon the Earth.

"That whole seeing-in-the-dark thing is such a minor issue, when you look at the big picture," she said. "To me, you're like any other guy."

"Did you forget that I turn into a bear?"

"No. But it's not like you turn into a bear every hour, or even every day. It's been a while since I saw you in bear form. At least…what? What day is it? I've lost track."

"It's been less than forty-eight hours since I last changed."

"Doesn't matter. You're still one hundred percent guy to me. You pass gas when you sleep."

"Dogs do that."

"You scratch when you wake up. That's a guy thing."

"Apes probably do that too."

She jerked on his pants in a show of frustration. "Oh, for heaven's sake! You're looking for reasons to compare yourself to an animal. If you ask me, the average American male is at least fifty percent animal. If I understood your long and confusing explanation of genetics, you're less than one percent bear. In my opinion, that makes you genetically superior to your standard human male."

"Nice try," he said dryly. He was obviously not going to make this easy.

She stumbled over something on the ground and crashed into his back. While struggling to get her feet back under herself, she asked, "Can I ask, why is it so important? Why do you need to be like everyone else?"

He stopped walking. "Why? Because all my adult life I've been studying what makes mankind different from all the rest of creation, and trying to find ways to overcome our physical shortcomings. Disease, aging. Now I have to face the fact that I'm less than what I thought I was. A lot less."

"Or more."

"How can being part animal be more?"

"I can list people who were no doubt one hundred percent genetically human but who were no better than animals. Hitler. That serial killer, Son of Sam. Some politicians…need I go on? No person is the sum of their DNA. They're so much more than strings of protein, don't you think?

I mean, if you had a child who had a genetic mutation or whatever, would he or she be less than human to you?" Not knowing whether he could see her or not, but suspecting he could, she shrugged. "It's that half-empty, half-full thing, I guess. The way I see it—being a girl who couldn't care less about genetics—you're *more* than the average guy. You're stronger, smarter, loyal and brave, better in bed...and I'll probably never be content with another 'normal' man again."

Silence.

Uh-oh. What was he thinking? Did he think she was ready to drag him to the altar? She was so not going there. In fact, she was still operating under the assumption that they'd be going their separate ways once this whole Omega thing was straightened out, not that she was particularly thrilled about it.

"Could you just pretend I didn't say that last part?" she murmured.

He didn't respond, which meant he wasn't about to forget. Wouldn't you know it, her bear-man had to have the memory of an elephant? At least he started walking again.

A few minutes later, they broke through the dense forest. They were standing in a ditch. Up above was a road. Oh, what a beautiful sight!

"Does this mean we're ready to catch a ride?" she asked, trying not to get too hopeful. She reached for her suitcase, but Tarik refused to hand it over, regardless of the mean-eyes she gave him.

"I'm carrying it and that's the way it is," he said.

"See? Typical male stubbornness. You're definitely human in my book."

He grunted and started trudging up the incline toward the road, pulling her along as he walked. She was grateful for the help. Her legs were pretty much shot by then and she knew she wouldn't have made it up on her own.

He stopped when they reached the top, set the bag on the ground and gave her a long look. His back was to the moon, so it wasn't easy to make out his expression. And his eyes were hidden under a heavy shadow, but she could see his mouth. It looked yummy and kissable and scrumptious. She wanted to kiss him and make him forget all about that man-beast thing. Who cared if he sprouted fur from time to time? She didn't.

She licked her lips, preparing to act on that impulse when her all but forgotten cell phone rang. Stunned, since the minute she'd arrived in Alaska she'd been unable to get a signal, she scrambled to find it. Where had she put it? In one of her coat pockets? She patted herself, discovering the lump as it rang for the fourth time. Too late. Damn. But at least she could see who it had been. Maybe whoever it had been would leave a message.

She pulled it from her coat and flipped it open. The lit screen glared in the dark and she had to squint to read it.

Katie's cell number. Maybe she had some good news? Abby checked the signal indicator. Two bars. She might be able to make a call out. She hit the Send button and crossed her fingers.

Good news. Give me some good news.

Katie's cheerful, "Hey, stranger! Wh—" was like the song of angels.

"Oh. My. God! Katie! Where are you? I have so much to tell you but I don't know if we'll get cut off." Abby smiled at Tarik and mouthed, "My friend, Katie."

"Where are you?" Katie asked.

"I'm not sure. Somewhere in Canada." Abby looked up and down the stretch of road but saw no signs. "We're next to a road—"

"Canada? What're you doing in Canada in the middle of the night? Why aren't you at the cabin?"

"Long story. Where are you?"

"At the cabin, which, by the way, is empty. Where's your stuff? And I'm not happy with you. You didn't come and get me at the airport. I had to rent a car."

"You're here? In Alaska? And you have a car? And your phone works? There is a God!" She hopped up and down and grabbed Tarik's arm. "She's here! She can come and get us."

Tarik nodded.

"Listen," Abby said to Katie, not wanting to risk losing the connection—when she got home she was switching cell phone companies to the one Katie used! "I'm going to give the phone to somebody else, and I want you to take down some directions. Okay? And make sure you bring all your stuff. And your driver's license. You're not going back. Got it?"

"What's going on?"

"Just get a pencil and listen. I'll tell you when you get here."

For the first time in who knew how many days, Abby felt like things were going to be okay. She handed Tarik the phone and he gave Katie detailed directions on how to find them. Then after making Katie promise to call when she arrived in Bear Creek, they skidded back down the sloping ditch to wait for her.

She was more than grateful for Tarik's offer to hold her as they sat on a fallen log to rest for a bit. She was cozy and safe and warm in his arms. There, with a bazillion brilliant stars overhead, he kissed her. It wasn't a demanding, taking kind of kiss. It was a sweet, romantic, gentle but oh-so-sensual kiss. A kiss she knew she'd never forget.

"Let's go. We'll head back to the hotel and wait for your friend there."

"I can't believe I just hiked a million miles for nothing."

"We could stay here. We wouldn't have to risk crossing back over the border. But I figured a hotel room would be a lot more comfortable, since it'll take close to ten hours for your friend to drive down." He kissed her nose and then pulled her to her feet. "If I have to, I'll carry you."

"Like hell you will. I can walk on my own two feet, thank you." She softened her response with a smile. "This girl is no wimp."

"Yet another reason to love you."

Her heart did a happy little polka in her chest. Tarik did love her. She hadn't been dreaming the first time she'd heard it.

Chapter Eight

ഇ

"We've located the truck, sir," Zant said from Torborg's open doorway. "As we suspected, they've headed into Canada. We found it behind a motel in Bear Creek." The man hesitated for a moment, like he'd wanted to say more. But he remained silent.

"Good. Time's running out for Evert and the woman. We need to get them in before it's too late. I want you to go down there. Talk to him. If anyone can convince him that I mean them no harm, it's you."

"Yes, sir. I'll leave immediately. By the time I hit the border, my men should have them in custody. Should I tell them to transport Tarik and the woman to the hospital in White Moose?"

"No. They're going to need very specialized care. We're better off if we can get them back here. As quickly as possible. Dispatch the helo. I'm coming too. I want to be down there before they're taken into custody. We have one shot at this. No one can afford for something to go wrong. We're cutting it too close time-wise."

"Very well, sir."

"Go. I'll be there in twenty minutes."

As soon as Zant left his office, Torborg picked up the phone to call The Director. Finally, some semi-good news to share. He hoped it wasn't too little too late.

* * * * *

Since arriving in Alaska, Abby had witnessed some ah-*maze*-ing sights but the one that took second only to seeing Tarik naked was finally seeing Katie.

Because Tarik was afraid of being spotted by the Omega goons or Canadian police, Abby had to play it real cool when she finally spotted her friend. Although her insides were hopping around like grasshoppers on crack, she had to swoop around the corner and snag her friend before she made it to the hotel's check-in counter.

Since Katie was clueless, Abby made sure Katie saw her face right away. She had to know things were serious and she had to be quiet.

Because they'd known each other forever, all it took was a second for Katie to register what Abby was trying to tell her. She acknowledged with a nod then followed Abby toward the back door. Tarik was waiting in the woods at the rear of the parking lot.

"What's going on? What's with the mime act?" Katie whispered as she hurried along beside Abby.

"This is what you get for sending me to Alaska alone. Oh my God, I'm glad to see you!"

Katie hesitated, pointing at the motel, visibly confused. "Where are we headed? Why aren't we going to your room?"

"Long story. Can't talk now. Where are you parked?"

"Around front." Katie pointed back in the direction of the road.

"Can you pull the car around back? Just stop right there, by the woods. I'll explain as soon as we're safely on the road."

"Sure, but—"

"Oh shit!"

A white van rolled around the side of the building. There were no cars to duck behind so Abby did the next best thing— she ducked behind her friend.

"What? What?" Katie stuttered.

Ducking down low in a futile attempt to keep out of the van's driver's view, Abby whispered, "Why, oh why couldn't you be at least three inches taller and about fifty pounds heavier? I'm no Amazon, but you're a midget. Just walk casually toward the building. Try not to call any attention to yourself."

"Like the girl who's not really hiding behind me won't call any attention to me?" Katie asked too loudly.

"Shush! They're after me."

"Did you become a paranoid schizophrenic overnight?"

"No. Take my word for it. This is no delusion. Fuck!" The van was stopped directly in front of them and a door swung open. "Go get your car." Abby turned around and sprinted toward the woods.

A man's voice followed her, "Stop!"

Sure the man was following her, she ran with all she had toward the forest and toward Tarik. It was probably not a good thing, leading that Omega jerk toward Tarik's hiding spot, but she was hoping Katie would see those guys meant business and they'd be getting a ride before they were in handcuffs. She didn't slow down when she broke through the bare brush at the forest's front but a pair of strong arms jerked her to a sudden, tooth-jarring stop a few yards into the woods.

She just about screamed, until she realized it was Tarik. "They're here. Omega," she whispered between huffing breaths. Oh man, she was going to puke. She hadn't run that hard since grade school.

"Yes, I see that. I know this guy, but I don't know if he'll help us. I tried to call him on the phone."

"He might help?"

"It's hard saying. Depends upon what kind of lies Torborg told him. I don't believe Raul would ever do anything intentionally to hurt me, but he might do something equally bad if he was misled into believing he was helping me."

"Got it. What do we do?"

"We wait for him to come to us. Which won't be long." He pointed over her shoulder and she spun around. "You go back there and hide behind that tree. If it's safe, I'll give you a signal. I'll wave like this." He lifted both arms over his head. "If I don't signal, I want you to sneak around to your friend's car."

She caught his hands in hers and squeezed. "What do I do if something happens to you?"

"You go with your friend and get far, far away. As fast as you can. Now, go. He's coming." He gave her a not-so-gentle push and swallowing a few choice words, she marched off into the woods. No man pushed her around! No man. Bad guys or not, she'd make sure he understood that.

And there was no way in hell she'd abandon him if things went bad. Hadn't he figured that out already?

* * * * *

It couldn't have been an accident that Raul Zant was the one to have found him. Tarik knew better than that. No, Torborg had planned this. Which meant Raul was probably being used as a pawn, lied to and manipulated, much like Tarik had been all these years.

He hoped he'd be able to convince his old friend of the truth. He had to try, if they'd have any hope of escaping. He wanted a chance to do some research, see exactly what Torborg had been up to, what kinds of experimentation Omega was conducting. He hadn't had time to do anything yet. The motel in Bear Creek didn't have the internet. How could he possibly blackmail his way to freedom without information?

Raul slowed as he reached the outer fringes of the woods. He peered between the trees, pushed aside some branches and stepped into the cool shadows. Being careful to stay hidden from the van and whoever else might be in it, Tarik approached his friend.

"Tarik," Raul said on a sigh. He looked and sounded relieved. "I wasn't sure what to expect when I found you. I'm glad to see you're okay still."

"Still?" Tarik asked, not ready to say much yet. Raul had been a true friend for several years now, but it was hard knowing what he knew, what he thought he knew, and what he intended to do about both. If there was one thing Tarik was sure of, it was that Raul was one very strong and very determined individual. If he was on your team, you had a guy who would move Mt. Everest to make things happen. If he was on the other guy's team, well, then you'd be damn lucky to finish the game at all, let alone win.

Whose team was Raul on?

"Yeah," Raul said, giving Tarik a thorough once-over. "Torborg told me you've been exposed to some kind of contaminant that's making you sick. If what he said is true, you need medical care. Now. Not two days from now. Or even two hours. He even sent the helo."

"Is that right? What kind of contaminant did he say I've been exposed to?"

"He didn't go into any details but with the kind of stuff you guys work with in the labs, it's not hard to figure it's possible."

"That's interesting." He eyed his friend. "Now that you see me, do you believe him?"

"Honestly? I don't know what to believe. You yourself said you looked at him as a mentor, a friend. The man claims you're like the son he never had. And you have to admit he's always treated you like you're special. So why would he lie? Why would he go to all this trouble and expense if it wasn't true?"

"Yes, why do you suppose he'd do that?"

Raul didn't speak for a long time. Looking like he was contemplating the future of all mankind, he regarded Tarik with narrowed eyes. "Do you know for a fact you haven't been exposed to anything dangerous?"

"Yes. I'm positive."

"Because if you were and I didn't haul your ass into the hospital, I won't be able to forgive myself."

"Believe me, I'm not dying from some kind of poisoning or exposure to a virus."

"Then tell me what this is all about."

"I can't. Not yet. Not until I know more. I need to get to a computer. I need a few hours at least. Will you help me?"

He heard the hum of an engine. It had to either be the van Raul had been driving or Abby's friend. He glanced in the direction of the sound but his view of the parking lot was cut off by the scrub at the front of the forest.

Raul glanced in the same direction.

"Who's with you?" Tarik asked.

"No one. At least not in the van. I left Torborg and Verga off at the front door to check in."

Tarik glanced back toward Abby's hiding spot. Had she walked around them? If she had, she'd been quieter than he'd given her credit for. "Then that must be my ride. I have my friend's cell. I'll give you the number. Abby's friend probably has a pen in her car. We can keep in touch. I won't call you. You call me. Okay?"

"Wellllll…"

"Torborg's feeding you lies. I'm not sure exactly what he's up to, but I know this must be important or he wouldn't be going to such trouble and expense to find me. I will face him. Soon. But not yet. Not until I get some answers."

"Okay. But don't wait too long. If there's any chance he's telling the truth, I don't want anything to happen to you."

Tarik nodded and pushed through the bushes, heading toward the parking lot. "What're you going to tell him if he asks what kept you so long?"

Following, Raul answered, "I don't know. I guess I'll say I saw something in the woods."

Tarik fought his way through the thick brush but halted midway between two lines of thorny bushes. "Fuck."

Standing about twenty feet away, facing Tarik, was Torborg. And worse, the man was holding Abby, hostage-style, her back snug against his front, his arm across her chest, and a pistol in his hand. The barrel was pressed to her temple and Torborg's finger was positioned on the trigger.

The blood pumping through Tarik's veins turned to acid. "Let. Her. Go." Even to his own ears, his voice had taken the pitch of a growl. He glared at Torborg while considering his options. He sensed an uncertain desperation about the man, like he felt as trapped as a rat in a jar.

Tarik knew the feeling all too well.

Torborg tipped his head, lifting his chin in a show of defiance. "I can't. You have to come with me. Now. Why would I let her go when I know she's my ticket? To you. She's your mate. You'd die for her."

"*You'll* die if you hurt her."

"It's your choice." The hand holding the gun trembled slightly and Torborg's face slowly took on a pale, ashy cast.

This only made Tarik more desperate to get Abby away from the man. What if Torborg jerked his hand and accidentally discharged the weapon? He was obviously barely holding it together. The scent of his fear was thick in the air, pungent and acrid like burnt plastic.

What the fuck was going on? Why was Torborg doing this? Holding innocent women hostage? Clearly, there was more to this situation than he'd had shared with anyone.

Between Tarik's worry for Abby's safety and the smell of Torborg's fear, Tarik had to struggle to keep from shifting. His muscles burned. His skin tingled. He tried to ignore the scent carried to his nose on a chilly gust, but it stirred his instincts and made his nerves fire up like mini-explosions.

He felt himself losing control. He staggered backward, bumping into something behind him. A set of hands closed around his upper arms and he jerked, yanking himself free before turning to give the offender a warning snarl.

Raul. He stared at Tarik gape-mouthed as a goldfish cradled in a cat's tongue.

Tarik didn't have to look down to know he was about to lose the battle with his body. The thick white hair had begun sprouting from his pores and his bones ached as they began to stretch and reshape. No matter how hard he tried, he couldn't hold back.

"Tarik." Abby's whisper reached his ears just before he closed his eyes against the mounting agony.

Temporarily crippled while his body changed, he endured minutes of torture, coupled with the terrifying thought that something was happening around him that he couldn't stop. He heard shouting, men and women. A hollow pop that could've been a gunshot. A scream that chilled his burning blood.

By the time he opened his eyes, he figured a whole lot of something had happened.

What he saw knocked him breathless. In full bear form, he staggered backward and fell on his rump. It took a while to comprehend the sight before him—Torborg and Raul stood bent over a fallen Abby. She was positioned between sitting and lying down, holding her shoulder. Her face was the hue of a clouded fall sky. A pasty grayish-white.

Tarik lifted his nose, catching the scent of fresh blood. He saw the red patch staining her sleeve and slicking her fingers. A bizarre hunger gripped him, threatening to overtake him and lock away what little remained of his humanity. Saliva flooded his mouth. He stood on all fours.

The two men lifted their heads simultaneously, looking like twin puppets being controlled by one player. Or little dolls. Delicate and weak. When he took a step forward, toward Abby, they both stood and shuffled backward.

A chase! What fun!

Now able to push aside his hunger for blood, he took a second and third step toward the men. In response, they turned tail and scampered, like a couple of kicked-up rabbits. The thrill of the chase pushed him forward into a full run. He caught Torborg first, knocked him to the ground with a swipe of a paw.

The smell of his prey's terror spiked Tarik's hunger. He roared and lunged at the man, now rolling on the ground, trying to get back on his feet.

No sooner had he stood than Tarik hit him again, this time harder. Torborg sailed several feet through the air before landing heavily on the gravel. Tarik stood over him, lowered his head to draw in a nice long breath. The smell was intoxicating.

"Tarik!" someone yelled.

He ignored the voice, content to breathe in the delicious scent of his quarry. Barely capable of thought, he stared down at the man's face.

He knew that man. He recognized him, yet didn't know him either. Like fading dreams at daybreak, his memories of life as a human were dimming. Like he had woken and the images he'd seen as he slept were drifting away…gone…

All he saw now was a meal laid out at his feet, not a man. Not a person. Starving, he lowered his head to take a bite. His teeth broke the skin and his mouth filled with the sweet flavor of blood. His hunger increased a hundredfold and he bit again.

"Tarik!"

He lifted his head and turned toward the sound. He knew that voice from somewhere. But where?

That face. That scent. A woman…a woman he knew. She was staggering toward him, one hand stretched out in front of her, the other clasping her dampened clothing. Blood. He could smell it. Sweet, sweet blood.

He licked his mouth, and forgetting the man at his feet, walked toward her. His instincts told him she was easy prey. There'd be no chase. Just the satisfaction of an effortless meal. But something held him from charging her. Something he didn't understand.

"Abby!" someone shouted.

His head hurt. Strange sensations buzzed through his body. He felt something. A heaviness inside. And a lightness.

"Tarik, it's me. It's Abby. I'm hurt but I'll be okay. Stop this. Please. Come back. Fight."

Fight? Come back? The words barely made sense to him at first. Then the sensations increased, the pain in his gut, the chill that had nothing to do with the temperature in the air. Slowly his head cleared. It was like flying an airplane through a cloud. Suddenly, he could see again. He understood what was happening. The light filled him.

Abby.

She was shaking, wide-eyed and terrified. Pale. Weak. She needed him to protect her.

Torborg.

He turned and was sickened by the sight of his former boss and mentor lying on the ground, his abdomen torn open. A crimson puddle stained the gravel of the parking lot. Raul stood dazed, not far from Torborg, a gun raised and aimed at Tarik's chest.

Look at what he'd done! He'd killed a man. Not just any man. A man he'd admired for years. The one man who had the answers he needed to hear. Torborg lay dead, silenced forever.

He briefly considered moving toward his friend, knowing he'd shoot out of fear.

The beast had taken over, totally wiping out his ability to think, feel, comprehend the consequences of his actions.

"Tarik, it's okay."

He felt Abby's light touch on his back through the thick coat of fur.

Abby.

He raised his head and looked at Raul again. *Shoot me. End this now. Before I do something else. Something worse. Something to Abby.* He took a step toward Raul and he stiffened.

"No!" Abby screamed. "Don't shoot him. Don't. Oh God, no!"

Raul's gaze shot to a point behind Tarik. It didn't stay there long. Tarik drew in another breath and took another step toward his friend.

Shoot me. I can't stop this. I can't control it. I'm dangerous to everyone.

Raul flinched again, but he didn't shoot.

"Noooo!" Abby scrambled around him, stopping in the line of fire. She turned a tear-streaked face to Tarik and gently stroked his chest. "I won't let you do this, Tarik. There must be another way. There has to be. If anyone can find it, you can. Please, please don't give up." She shouted over her shoulder, "See what that man did to him? See now? Who's the beast? The one who was forced to suffer or the one who created the suffering?"

Raul lowered the gun and Tarik knew he'd lost his chance at freedom.

He felt the first twinges as his body started to change back. Within a few heavy heartbeats, he was once again swept up in agony. Muscles and skin stretched and burned. Bones cracked and popped. It felt like it took forever for the change to end. He was left limp, trembling and nude. The gravel bit at his exposed skin.

Abby knelt beside him and wrapping her arms around his weak form, fell into heartrending sobs.

Looking over her shoulder at his friend, he held Abby until she had stopped crying. Her hot tears chilled as they dripped down his arm.

Raul put a shaking hand over his mouth.

"This is what Torborg created," Tarik said. "This is what he's trying to hide. I didn't know until a few days ago. I had no idea. And I have no idea if I can stop it."

Another woman ran from a nearby car, Abby's friend, no doubt. She shouted, "Time to go!" The two struggled. Abby's friend yelled again. Abby yelled back.

He gently pushed Abby toward her friend. "Go."

She visibly swallowed several times. Her eyes were watery and bloodshot, the hue of the stain on her sleeve. "No. You need help. Where will you go?"

"You're shot. You need to get to the hospital," her friend said with a shaky voice. "We can find him later. Right?" She lifted begging eyes to him. "Right?"

"Yes. I have my cell…" He looked around, spotting his tattered clothes about twenty feet away. He doubted his phone was intact but he wasn't going to tell Abby that.

"But you're hurt too. Look!" Abby pointed at his left leg.

He hadn't felt anything before, but with the pain of the change fading, he became aware of the itchy burn. His leg was wet. A cool breeze chilled the dampness, giving him goose bumps on the left side of his body. He reached down. His fingers found the source of the blood, a hole just above his knee.

The scent of his own blood filled his nostrils and he groaned. A familiar tingle charged up his spine.

No. Not again. He didn't have the strength to endure another change. Would he lose himself again? Lose his mind? His heart? His soul? Forever?

"You need a doctor," Abby said.

"No!" His voice had deepened again, signaling the change.

Abby didn't move away but the others did. Raul lifted the gun again but didn't aim it.

"If I change again, Raul, shoot me," Tarik demanded.

"No!" Abby shrieked. She caught his face between her hands. "Listen to me, Tarik. You can't give up. I love you, dammit! Do you hear me? I love you and I need you and I won't let you give up. You're a strong man. A human being with a heart and soul and mind. Don't believe what that animal told you." She indicated Torborg. "You deserve to live. You deserve love. You deserve everything that bastard took from you. You deserve a future. Don't let him take even that away. Don't let him win!"

Abby's friend stepped closer, stood next to Abby in a show of support. "I don't understand what's going on here, but I know Abby. I've never seen her like this. She loves you. I mean really, really loves you. And this woman hasn't loved a man in a long time."

Raul lowered the gun. "I don't want to shoot you. Dammit, what the fuck did he do?"

Breathless from the effort it took to fight with his own body, Tarik shook his head. "I'm not sure if I'll ever know now. And I don't know how much longer I can hold on. Look what I did to him. I was gone. It was like I'd left my body. I didn't think. I only smelled and tasted. All that I knew was the hunger. The awful hunger." He pushed himself off the ground. The gravel bit into his feet but he didn't give a damn. He needed to get away from them. He didn't know himself anymore. He didn't trust himself.

"You need some clothes. Some money," Raul said, seeming to understand what Tarik was about to do. He picked up Tarik's shredded clothes and shook his head. The phone fell out of Tarik's pocket, revealing its less-than-intact status. It was a cell phone pancake. Raul blocked his path to the woods.

"You can't run around like this. You'll die of hypothermia, even if you don't bleed to death. At least let me get you some clothes from the hotel room."

"No." Tarik pushed past his friend. "I need to leave. It's better this way. No one else will get hurt. If you can't see that then fuck you."

"Bastard!" Abby screamed behind him. "You blind, selfish bastard."

What? Tarik briefly considered ignoring her but he couldn't do it. It was the tone in her voice. The anguish. "I'm doing this for you, for all of you, not me."

"Fuck that." She glared at him. Furious and defiant and beautiful. "Forget about me."

"I can't."

"Think about the others," she shot back, taking a step toward him.

"What others?"

"The others like you." She took a second step toward him, and a third. She didn't speak again until she was standing less than three feet from him. Her chin was lifted in hard determination but her eyes were soft, pleading. "Do you suppose Omega made more like you? Do you think those other people might be suffering too? That they might need your help? Children. Women. Men." Her voice softened. Her lower lip trembled. He ached to taste it. To kiss her until the trembling stopped. Until they both had forgotten about all their troubles. "Do you think those people might deserve your help? With Torborg gone, who's going to find them? You're the only one right now who knows about this. Maybe this is what you're meant to do."

He hadn't thought about the possibility of others, or of what he might be able to do for them. But who was to say he could do anything at all? There were so many things he didn't know, like precisely how his genetics had been altered. "The chances that I can help anyone else like me are slim to none. I have no answers."

"Not yet, perhaps." She moved closer, until her fiery eyes were mere inches from his and her breasts didn't quite brush against his bare chest. "I believe you can find the answers. I believe in you so much..." She turned toward her friend and smiled then turned back to him again.

Abby pulled in a deep breath, hardly able to believe what she was about to say. If someone had told her a couple of weeks ago that before she left Alaska she'd sleep with a man who turned into a bear, would fall in love with him and decide to make Alaska her permanent home—all in a span of less than a week—she would've peed her pants laughing so hard. But the past few days since she'd arrived in Alaska had been so intense. Intense sex. Intense danger. Intense connection. All that intensity had acted like a catalyst. She hadn't been able to stop it. The bond between them had taken on a life of its own and she was powerless to stop it. By the end, she hadn't wanted to stop it.

Now she could see her former life for what it truly had been—basic survival. She hadn't been living life. She'd been surviving. Tarik made her feel alive. He was strong and sexy but not so strong he wasn't able to admit he needed her.

He was looking at her now, his eyes full of so many emotions she couldn't sort them all out. Her own eyes were burning with the tears she'd been holding back all day. It was time. Time to lay everything on the table.

She was both scared and exhilarated.

Blinking, she said, "Tarik, I believe in you so much I want to stay here in this Godforsaken place with you. I want to help you. I want to love you."

"Oh God," Katie squeaked.

Abby felt like her face was going to split open she was smiling so wide. "I came to Alaska for the adventure of a lifetime. What I found is my life...and a very new and thrilling kind of adventure."

Tarik's shoulders dropped and for a moment, Abby feared he'd tell her no. Then he swept her into his arms and held her so tightly she could hardly breathe. Loosening his hold a smidge, he tipped his head down to kiss her. She gladly returned the kiss.

"Okay, okay," she heard Katie say behind her. "Enough already. He's naked. Get a room! God, now what am I going to do for the next week?"

Abby smiled at Tarik. "So, does that mean you aren't going to run off into the woods to die a slow and painful death?"

"Yes. I mean no."

"Thank God!" Tarik's friend said.

"Tell me about it," Katie said flatly. "Is he always so dramatic?"

"Yeah," the guy standing next to Katie said. Abby couldn't help noticing the way those two were looking at each other all of a sudden. She had a feeling Katie would have no problems keeping busy over the next week. "Tarik's a regular drama queen. He played Dolly in our senior year musical. You'd never know it, but he has a mean falsetto."

Tarik's laughter echoed off the trees and vibrated through Abby's body, leaving her feeling dizzy and happy beyond words. "You promised to never tell a soul about that."

"Oh. Yeah." His friend didn't sound regretful in the least.

Tarik looped his arm around Abby's neck and started walking toward the hotel. "That's okay. I'll get you." He poked his friend's chest. "If I were you, I'd grow eyes in the back of your head because you're going to need them."

"Tough talk coming from a guy who runs around naked," his friend challenged. "So, what's the plan, Tarik? And what do we do about Torborg?"

"Plan? Who knows? And as far as Torborg goes, I guess we call the police and tell them he was attacked by a bear. I'm going inside to get me some clothes, food and sleep." He winked at Abby and her cheeks heated. "Not necessarily in that order. Then I guess I'll tackle everything else. One thing at a time. How's your arm, kitten?"

"It stopped bleeding. I guess it wasn't as bad as I thought. I always get woozy at the sight of my own blood." She gave him a reassuring smile. "Honest. I think everything's going to be fine." Happy and eager to meet every new challenge with Tarik, Abby mooshed herself into his side. This was where she belonged, with this man and in this place. "What about your leg?"

"Like you said, I think everything's going to be fine. As soon as we get some answers. And as long as we search for them together." He raised her fingers to his lips and kissed each fingertip. "Before I met you, I didn't have room in my life for love. But now my love for you is my life. You are my life."

TOUCH OF THE BEAST

Trademarks Acknowledgement

೫೦

The author acknowledges the trademarked status and trademark owners of the following wordmarks mentioned in this work of fiction:

Catwoman: DC Comics E.C. Publications, Inc., a New York corporation and Warner Communications Inc.

Doritos: Frito-Lay North America, Inc.

Lifetime: Lifetime Entertainment Services Cable LT Holdings, Inc., Disney/ABC International Television, Inc., Hearst LT Inc., and Hearst Holdings, Inc., and Hearst/ABC Video Services

Lord of the Rings: Saul Zaentz Company, The DBA Tolkien Enterprises

Lycra: E. I. du Pont de Nemours and Company

Mapquest: MapQuest.com, Inc.

MP5: Heckler & Koch, Inc.

OnStar: General Motors Corporation

Slim-fast: Lipton Investments, Inc.

Chapter One

ഔ

Katie Spenser arrived in Anchorage after spending eight dreary hours staring at the walls in Chicago's O'Hare airport, another fifty-eight tedious minutes cooped up in a grounded airplane—what idiot made up the rule that an airplane with a broken toilet wasn't fit for flight?—and six miserable hours and thirty-three minutes trying to ignore the woman next to her vomiting nonstop. Only to discover her ride from the airport had pulled a no-show.

Exhausted. Smelly, woozy and abandoned. Wasn't this a nifty way to launch a girl's vacation? Where the heck was Abby?

"Girl, what's up? I'm sitting here at the airport. Waiting for you. You're going to owe me big time for this," Katie said into her cell phone before snapping it shut and stuffing it into her pocket. "I can't believe she isn't answering her phone," she said to no one in particular as she wearily dragged her luggage behind her, in search of a rental car counter. After signing her life away to rent a truck, and taking a half-dozen wrong turns, she found the remote cabin they'd leased for two weeks.

No Abby. The place was empty.

Now Katie wasn't just annoyed. She was *worried*. It didn't look like Abby had been there at all. No suitcases. No clothes. No food.

Because Abby had left Detroit almost a week ago, that made no sense. Had something happened to her? Or had she decided to stay in a hotel the whole week? It was most likely the latter, but since Katie knew her friend was operating on a tight budget, she couldn't deny the first was possible. Abby was definitely short on cash and out of her element.

Katie hadn't worried too much about the fact that she hadn't heard a peep from Abby in close to a week. She figured her friend had been too busy enjoying her vacation to bother calling. Truth be told, she'd been relieved Abby hadn't been calling her every five minutes, moaning about being stuck in the Alaskan wilderness alone and making her feel guilty. Alaska hadn't been Abby's first choice for vacation destinations. Unlike Katie, Abby was a city girl to the marrow. She'd wanted to go to New York, max out her credit cards, see a show, do some sightseeing, shopping.

Boringggggggg.

Fighting a weird, sick feeling, Katie flopped onto the couch and crammed her hand into her jacket pocket. Her cell phone started vibrating the instant her fingers curled around it. "Thank God!" She checked the phone number on the lit screen then lifted it to her ear. "Hey, stranger! Wh—"

"Oh. My. God!" Abby shouted, sounding close to hysterical. "Katie! Where are you? I have so much to tell you but I don't know if we'll get cut off."

"Where are you?" Katie started pacing the room to keep warm. The place was like an icebox. She needed to get a fire started.

"I'm not sure. Somewhere in Canada." Abby paused a beat before continuing, giving Katie a chance to digest that first bit of information. "We're next to a road—"

"Canada?" Katie picked up a piece of firewood and tossed it in the fireplace, kicking it into position with her boot. "What're you doing in Canada in the middle of the night? Why aren't you at the cabin?"

"Long story. Where are you?"

She stacked a second log on top of the first and turned to look for some newspaper. "At the cabin, which, by the way, is empty. Where's your stuff? And I'm not happy with you. You didn't come and get me at the airport like we'd planned. I had to rent a car. Didn't—"

"You're here? In Alaska? And you have a car? And your phone works? There is a God!"

Katie scrunched up her shoulder to wedge the phone under her chin. She needed both hands to ball up some paper. But when she bent over, the phone slipped free and landed on the braided rag rug with a dull thud. She scooped it up, catching Abby say to someone, "She's here! She can come and get us."

Us? Who was she with?

Katie stuffed the wadded-up paper under the unlit logs in the fireplace and reached for the box of matches.

"Listen," Abby said, before Katie had a chance to ask her any questions, "I'm going to give the phone to somebody else, and I want you to take down some directions. Okay? And make sure you bring all your stuff. And your driver's license. You're not going back. Got it?"

"What's going on?" Katie set down the matches and rubbed her eyes. They were blurry, like they'd been rolled around in Vaseline.

Not coming back? What was with all the drama? Not that drama was anything new to Abby. She was a regular Sarah Bernhardt. A broken heel on a new pair of shoes qualified as a major catastrophe. And the world nearly came to an end a month ago when her credit was cut off by her bank. The bank, of course, had been looking out for her best interest, since there'd been an unusual amount of internet purchases all of a sudden. But get Abby Clumm to understand that. It was like trying to explain the value of honesty...to a politician.

She'd hate to see how her melodramatic friend would react if she faced a real tragedy.

"Just get a pencil and listen," Abby said. "I'll tell you when you get here."

Katie sighed and turned to look for something to write with. She found an old Chinese carryout menu and dull pencil in the kitchen.

A man's voice came on the line, "Hello?"

Ah, now things were making sense. Abby'd found herself a vacation flame. Interesting.

He must really be something to look at.

If Abby was begging her to pick them up in BFE Canada, Mr. Studly either had unreliable wheels or no wheels at all. Generally speaking, in Abby's book no car meant zero interest. Unless he was a total babe.

Then again, Abby should've rented a car for herself. Strange...

Katie scribbled down the directions Mr. Vacation Flame gave her, down to the last detail. After he hung up, and she had a chance to read them over, a minor fact dawned on her.

She was in for a long effing drive.

"Aw, fuck."

She made herself a pot of coffee, filled a thermos she found under the kitchen sink and then reluctantly left the cabin.

Despite the fact that Katie knew Abby had to be exaggerating when she'd claimed her situation was dire, Katie had to do the good-friend thing and drive down there tonight.

She was so not in the mood to deal with this stuff, more Abby drama. Why hadn't she stayed home? Who cared if she'd spent the last eight months of her life in a haze? Not really living, just sort of there. She was fine.

To think she could have spent the week at home with an endless supply of ice cream and Lifetime movies. Now that was living.

* * * * *

After driving for friggin' hours down dark, abandoned roads to BFE Canada—the coffee gone hours ago, and crackly music playing on the stereo grating on her nerves just enough to keep her awake—Katie pulled into the hotel parking lot. She parked the truck, and feeling like she hadn't slept in days, headed inside the building.

Abby caught Katie in the hotel lobby, as she was walking up to the check-in counter.

Katie noticed right off the bat that Abby was giving her a strange look. A look that told her something was going on. Unfortunately, Katie was too exhausted to figure out what her friend was trying to communicate via pantomime.

Visibly frustrated, Abby frowned and jabbed an index finger at the door.

At least that was one signal Katie could comprehend. She nodded.

She blamed the fact that she didn't realize how truly odd Abby was behaving on her sleep-deprived, semi-catatonic state. It took her several minutes, until they were halfway across the lobby, before it all sunk in.

Abby was far from what anyone would call a quiet girl, yet there she was, silent, and creeping around on tiptoe, looking left and right and then left and right again, like she was expecting the boogey man to jump out from some hiding spot and scare the piss out of her.

Normally Abby'd screech and squawk like a rooster with its toe caught in a fence whenever she saw Katie. Weirder yet, Katie realized as she got closer, Abby's eyes were wide, and there was a wild look about her, like nothing Katie had ever seen before. Abby caught Katie's arm and yanked hard, pulling her toward the door.

"What's going on? What's with the mime act?" Katie whispered as she hurried outside.

"This is what you get for sending me to Alaska alone. Oh my God, I'm glad to see you!"

Katie hesitated, pointing back toward the hotel. "Where are we headed? Why aren't we going to your room?"

The whole vacation thing had been Abby's idea — meant to lift Katie's sagging spirits. Katie hadn't wanted to go, and Abby'd known it. Even so, Katie hadn't expected such an over-the-top, enthusiastic welcome. Her friend looked almost hysterical.

"Long story," Abby whispered, sobering. "Can't talk now. Where are you parked?"

"In front." Bewildered by her friend's wildly fluctuating emotional state, Katie motioned toward the road.

"Can you pull the car around back? Just stop right there, by the woods. I'll explain as soon as we're safely on the road."

"Sure, but —"

"Oh shit!" Abby ducked behind Katie as a white delivery van rolled around the side of the building.

"What? What?" Katie stuttered, trying to turn around to see what her friend was doing. Concern was quickly morphing to genuine fear. This crazy act was so unlike Abby in so many ways.

Hiding from delivery vans? What was up with that?

Still huddled behind Katie, Abby whispered, "Why, oh why couldn't you be at least three inches taller and about fifty pounds heavier? I'm no Amazon, but you're a midget. Just walk casually toward the building. Try not to call any attention to yourself."

"Like the girl who's not really hiding behind me won't call any attention to me?" Katie said, starting to feel a little frantic herself.

"Shush! They're after me."

Katie started shuffling toward the hotel. "Did you become a paranoid schizophrenic overnight?"

"No. Take my word for it. This is no delusion. Fuck!" Abby whispered. The van stopped directly in front of them and a door swung open. "Go get your car." Before Katie could say anything, Abby sprinted toward the woods.

What the hell?

A man jumped out of the van, shouting, "Stop!" Then he broke into a full run, chasing Abby into the woods.

What the fuck?

Obviously, it was safe to say that for once Abby was not creatively embellishing—or even slightly exaggerating—the truth.

Why would anyone be chasing Abby? She was honest as they came, to a fault. She never did anything bad to anyone, not even when they deserved it.

Wasting time standing in the parking lot, wondering about things she couldn't begin to understand, was not particularly helpful. She ran to get her rental, started it and drove around the building, parking as close to the woods as she could get. The engine idling, she waited.

Although she could hear the rustling of leaves and cracking of sticks in the woods, no one came out, no one spoke. Nothing happened for several agonizing minutes.

Then everything went quiet. Eerily silent. The snapping and rustling in the woods stopped. Even the insects and birds ceased making noise. Shivering, she flipped on the heat. It was dark. Really dark. And the forest was one big, scary, silent shadow.

An owl hooted somewhere far away. The creepy sound added to the tension winding up Katie's spine. Little shivers crawled up her back, tickling her insides like spiders.

Should she go in after Abby and try to help? Undecided, she opened the door and stood outside, staring at the woods, wishing Abby would come out. It was so friggin' dark. If she left the car, passing Abby somewhere in the woods, Abby could end up waiting for her instead.

What to do?

There. A shadow was moving. A smallish shadow, about Abby's size. Could it be? God, she hoped it was Abby.

Katie glanced back toward the white van, which was still idling in the middle of the mostly empty parking lot. She climbed back in the truck and watched, holding her breath as the shadow came closer.

"Abby," she whispered to herself as she recognized her friend's very noticeable jacket, bright pink and lined with faux lamb's wool. "Thank God." She put the truck in gear and waited for Abby to climb inside.

Abby didn't come.

Katie heard scuffling. Something big slammed up against the back end of the truck. She jerked and the vehicle lurched forward a few feet before she gathered her wits enough to put it in park. She hopped out and dashed around the side to see what had happened, all the while wondering what she'd do if she discovered Abby was in trouble. She had no weapon and she didn't want to take the time to go rooting through her luggage for something. She'd have to wing it.

She halted mid-stride as she rounded the side of the truck. Oh no, there'd be no winging that.

Abby was there, all right. But she wasn't alone. A man stood behind her, hostage-style, holding a gun to her head.

Fuck and double fuck!

"Oh, shit!" Katie said. "Abby, what's going on?"

"Long story." Abby looked like she was about to piss her pants, and Katie felt awful for not knowing what to do to help. It wasn't like she'd come armed for battle with gun-toting bad guys.

She'd driven all this way, exhausted and addle-brained, expecting to pick up her friend and attempt to get through a week's vacation with her sanity intact. She'd never dreamed her law-abiding, good-girl best friend would be running from psychos with guns.

Had they walked into an episode of *24*?

Abby was staring at a huge guy standing about twenty feet away. He was...niiiice. Big. Good looking in a tall, dark and studly kind of way. Definitely Abby's type. Katie guessed he was The Fling.

"Let. Her. Go." The Fling's voice was a low growl. He glared at the guy holding Abby hostage, shooting him death-daggers from his eyes.

A girl who could smell danger from a hundred paces, Katie took a few steps back. Things were going down. No use getting in the middle. She'd wait for the right time to help Abby.

The guy holding Abby tipped his head. "I can't. You have to come with me. Now. Why would I let her go when I know she's my ticket? To you. She's your mate. You'd die for her."

What was with the mate thing? Who called their girlfriend a mate?

"You'll die if you hurt her," The Fling grumbled.

"It's your choice." The shithead holding Abby jerked her tighter against his body.

Good God, was that asshole going to shoot her friend? What the fuck was going on? The Fling tipped his head and sniffed the air like an animal.

Weird. Then again, all she'd seen since arriving in BFE Canada had been fucking strange. Maybe they'd walked into an episode of *Smallville* instead.

No one did anything for several long minutes. No one spoke, threw a punch or pulled a trigger, yet The Fling's face pulled into a contorted mask of pain. He staggered backward like he'd been sucker-punched, bumping into a third guy who'd come out of nowhere. The guy grabbed The Fling's arms but he jerked, yanking himself free. His lips curled into a lopsided snarl.

Then, as Katie stood by, her eyeballs practically bugging from her head, something straight out of effing Van Helsing happened. No computer animation. No stunt doubles or makeup.

This was fucking real!

It started slowly. Thick white hair literally sprouted all over The Fling's arms, legs, face. Then the changing sped up. He dropped to his hands and knees. His body thickened. His legs shortened. His face elongated.

It was so freaking bizarre, Katie couldn't look away.

In the space of a few seconds, The Fling became a polar bear.

"Tarik," Abby whispered before launching into Catwoman mode.

Still dumbstruck by the Van Helsing act, Katie stood frozen in place, watching Abby swing an arm up, knock the gun away from her head, and spinning, wrestle the asshole for the weapon.

Wow. She hadn't seen that coming. Abby was as anti-violence as Gandhi.

In an effort to keep her friend from getting her ass beat, or worse, Katie shook away her shock and staggered into the fray. Unfortunately, Asshole kicked her away before she was able to help. As she scrambled back to her feet, Asshole turned and aimed the gun at Abby's chest.

Time slowed to a crawl.

Katie heard herself scream.

He pulled the trigger.

Pop.

Abby did a three-sixty then landed on her butt. She lifted a trembling hand to her shoulder and looked up at Asshole, her face a mask of disbelief.

Katie screamed again. She tried to move but she couldn't. She couldn't breathe, couldn't speak.

Abby? Shot?

No. That's not what just happened. No, no, no! Katie's insides twisted into an excruciating knot.

Abby slumped, catching herself before she fell flat on her back. Her face went white.

The Asshole, still holding the gun, bent over Abby, inspecting her wound.

What the fuck? Did he want to finish her off? Not happy with the shot he got in?

Katie wanted to lunge forward, tackle him and beat him with her bare hands, but she was still numb from shock. Black patches and sparkling stars partially blocked her vision. Frantic to regain her composure, she dropped to her knees and put her head down.

The other guy, the one who'd grabbed The Fling before he'd morphed into a bear, ran to the man.

The bear sat back on its rump. It lifted its nose, rubbed a giant paw over its snout then stood on all fours again. When it took a step forward, both men jumped to their feet and shuffled backward, leaving Abby defenseless. She was sitting up now, but she still looked pale and disoriented.

"Abby." Katie scooted around the side of the truck, where she could keep an eye on her friend but would hopefully stay out of the way of the bear.

Think! Think! How do you distract a polar bear?

The animal lumbered toward the men. Like a couple of chickens — although she could hardly blame them — they turned tail and scampered for the woods. While Katie tiptoed around the truck, heading toward Abby, the bear ran after the men, easily outpacing them by double. Katie focused on the animal as she slowly and silently made her way to Abby.

The animal caught Asshole first and knocked him to the ground with a swipe of a paw. The gun flew from the man's hand.

That was the beginning of the end for that guy.

Until recently, Katie had believed people got their just desserts in the end, but this...this guy must've done some awful things to deserve what he got.

The guy looked like a boneless rag doll as the bear mauled him, biting, tearing, knocking him around with those huge paws. The attack went on for who knew how long. Could've been a few seconds. Could've been several minutes.

Continuing to keep a sharp eye on the bear, she inched closer to Abby. But before she'd gotten close enough to get a good look at her friend's injury, Abby waved her off.

"Tarik!" Abby yelled. She slowly stood.

Despite the red stain on Abby's jacket, seeing her stand up made Katie feel a little better. Abby had been known to howl in agony over a paper cut. The wound couldn't be too bad. Either that or her friend was in shock.

The bear stopped moving for a second then dropped its head and took one giant chomp out of the Asshole's gut.

Ew!

Disgusted, Katie spun around and covered her face. Her throat closed in on itself as she gagged.

It was too freaking awful.

"Tarik!" she heard Abby shout again.

Blinking away the tears gathering in her eyes from the retching, Katie turned around again.

The bear left the poor guy—who Katie hoped was dead by now—and started walking toward Abby.

Oh God, no!

"Abby!" she shouted, not sure if she should retreat or run out and drag her insane friend the hell away from there.

Abby didn't move. She didn't flinch or blink, even when the bear came closer. "Tarik, it's me," she said, sounding calm as could be, certainly not like she was standing nose to bellybutton with a thousand-pound bear who'd just had a taste of blood. "It's Abby. I'm hurt but I'll be okay. Stop this. Please. Come back. Fight."

Wow. That was just…wow. Insane but wow.

Katie had to admit, she admired her friend's newfound courage. The Abby she'd known a little more than a week ago would've never able to stand up to this kind of terror. She didn't even do haunted houses at Halloween. They scared her too much.

Some movement to the left caught Katie's attention. The other guy had the gun now, and he was aiming at the bear's chest.

Now that was an intelligent man.

"Tarik, it's okay," Abby said, stepping forward. She reached out and touched the animal's back.

Damn crazy, that was.

The bear noticed the guy holding the gun. It took a step toward him and the guy stiffened.

"No!" Abby screamed. "Don't shoot him. Don't. Oh God, no!"

The guy glanced at Abby then refocused on the bear. He flinched but didn't shoot when the bear took another step forward.

Why wasn't he pulling the trigger? It was like the animal was taunting him, trying to force him to shoot.

"Noooo!" Abby did something completely baffling — flung herself into the line of fire. Crying, she stroked the animal's chest like it was a big effing teddy bear. "I won't let you do this, Tarik. There must be another way. There has to be. If anyone can find it, you can. Please, please don't give up." She shouted over her shoulder at the guy holding the gun, "See what that man did to him? See now? Who's the beast? The one who was forced to suffer or the one who created the suffering?"

The man lowered the gun.

Seconds later, Tarik's body changed. Fur shed away, exposing the smooth skin of the man underneath. His face changed back. His legs lengthened. Finally, he lay on the gravel parking lot, nude. Abby knelt beside him and fell into hysterical sobs.

The guy with the gun put a shaking hand over his mouth.

Katie didn't know what to do. Abby was a wreck but Katie felt like she hadn't wanted her help when she'd offered it.

She had no idea what guy they were talking about or who'd done what to whom. She had no idea if Tarik would change back into a bear and start chewing someone else to bits…

She'd been a lot of places in the world with her father, to wild places where danger lurked all around her—in the trees, in the grasses, below the surface of a mirror-smooth lake, yet in all her life, she could remember only one other time when she'd felt so helpless.

"This is what Torborg created," Tarik said. "This is what he's trying to hide. I didn't know until a few days ago. I had no idea. And I have no idea if I can stop it."

Come on, girl. Snap out of it! You would've been 'gator lunch ages ago if you'd acted like this the first time you'd been to the Everglades. Things were semi-calm at the moment. It was time to get Abby and make a run for it, in case the shit started flying again. She dashed to Abby and tried to drag her wailing friend to her feet.

"Time to go!" she shouted.

Abby shoved her away. "No!"

"What's wrong with you? Let's get the fuck out of here!" She grabbed Abby's wrist but Abby wrenched it free.

"No! I'm not going anywhere."

Tarik gently pushed Abby away. "Go."

Abby visibly swallowed several times. Her bottom lip trembled. "No. You need help. Where will you go?"

"You're shot. You need to get to the hospital." Katie pointed at Abby's shoulder, desperate to reason with her friend. All of this was so unlike her. "We can find him later. Right?" She turned begging eyes to The Fling. "Right?"

"Yes. I have my cell…"

"But you're hurt too. Look!" Abby pointed at his left leg.

He reached down and closed his eyes, cringing.

"You need a doctor," Abby said.

"No!" His voice had deepened again.

Was he going to change back into the bear?

Oh shit! Katie shuffled backwards, trying to take Abby with her, but again Abby shoved her away. The man lifted the gun but didn't aim it.

"If I change again, Raul, shoot me," The Fling demanded.

Finally, the voice of reason.

"No!" Abby shrieked. "Listen to me, Tarik. You can't give up. I love you, dammit! Do you hear me? I love you and I need you and I won't let you give up."

Love? Aw, fuck! Why this guy, Tarik the Bear Man? Why?

"You're a strong man," Abby shouted in his face. "A human being with a heart and soul and mind. Don't believe what that animal told you." She pointed at the poor guy who'd been eaten alive.

That poor SOB had been an animal too?

"You deserve to live," Abby continued, "You deserve love. You deserve everything that bastard took from you. You deserve a future. Don't let him take even that away. Don't let him win!"

Dammit, Katie had no choice now. Stirred by the emotion in Abby's voice—she knew Abby meant every word she'd said, including the "L" word—she stopped trying to grab at Abby.

If her friend loved Tarik, then whether Katie thought it was insane or not, she had to put up a show of support. At least until later when things had settled down and they could have a heart-to-heart.

That was so coming. As soon as possible. Abby was not in love with this guy after only a week. It wasn't possible.

Katie stepped closer to Abby. "I don't understand what's going on here, but I know Abby. I've never seen her like this. She loves you. I mean really, really loves you. And this woman hasn't loved a man in a long time."

The guy Tarik had called Raul lowered the gun. "I don't want to shoot you. Dammit, what the fuck did he do?" He motioned to the dead guy.

Tarik shook his head. "I'm not sure if I'll ever know now. And I don't know how much longer I can hold on. Look what I did to him. I was gone. It was like I'd left my body. I didn't think. I only smelled and tasted. All that I knew was the hunger. The awful hunger." He pushed himself off the ground.

"You need some clothes. Some money," Raul said. He picked up Tarik's shredded clothes and shook his head. "You can't run around like this. You'll die of hypothermia, even if you don't bleed to death. At least let me get you some clothes from the hotel room."

"No." Tarik shoved by him. "I need to leave. It's better this way. No one else will get hurt. If you can't see that then fuck you."

"Bastard!" Abby screamed. "You blind, selfish bastard."

Tarik looked shocked. Katie figured he hadn't yet seen the more vocal side of Abby.

"I'm doing this for you, for all of you, not me," he reasoned.

"Fuck that." Abby's voice shook as she shouted, "Forget about me."

Man, Abby had it bad.

"I can't," Tarik said.

So did he. This was so not going to end well.

This was the weirdest, most depressing scene she'd witnessed in months. When would it end? Abby? In love with some guy from Alaska? Who changed into a large carnivore? She needed a stiff drink and a soft bed…and about twenty hours of sleep…unless it was all a terrible nightmare. She could only hope.

"Think about the others," Abby shouted.

"What others?" Tarik countered.

"The others like you." Abby stomped toward him, defiant and courageous. "Do you suppose Omega made more like you? Do you think those other people might be suffering too? That they might need your help? Children. Women. Men. Do you think those people might deserve your help? With Torborg gone, who's going to find them? You're the only one right now who knows about this. Maybe this is what you're meant to do."

Children? Someone was hurting kids? That did sound bad.

Tarik slowly shook his head. "The chances that I can help anyone else like me are slim to none. I have no answers."

"Not yet, perhaps," Abby said. "I believe you can find the answers. I believe in you so much…" She turned to Katie, smiled then turned back to him again.

Katie knew that look. It was the same one Abby'd given her right before she'd quit her sucky-but-well-paying accounting job a few years back. Up until today, that was the most impulsive, shocking thing she'd ever done.

What was the crazy girl going to do next?

"Tarik, I believe in you so much I want to stay here in this Godforsaken place with you. I want to help you. I want to love you."

"Oh God," Katie squeaked. Abby move? To Alaska? Forever? No!

"I came to Alaska for the adventure of a lifetime. What I found is my life...and a very new and thrilling kind of adventure."

Tarik's shoulders slumped.

Katie held her breath, not sure what she hoped for. Would he tell Abby to leave? Or would he tell her he loved her too? Either way, she figured Abby was toast.

He swept Abby into his arms and kissed her.

Yeah, she was toast.

"Okay, okay," Katie said, figuring she had no choice but to hide her true feelings until she had time to talk to her friend in private. "Enough already. He's naked. Get a room! God, now what am I going to do for the next week?"

Abby giggled. Giggled! Katie couldn't remember the last time she'd heard her friend do that. Seventh grade?

"So," Abby said, grinning from ear-to-ear, "does that mean you aren't going to run off into the woods to die a slow and painful death?"

"Yes. I mean no."

"Thank God!" Raul said.

"Tell me about it," Katie said flatly. "Is he always so dramatic?" If those two weren't friggin' made for each other she didn't know who was.

She took another look at the guy who'd been about to shoot Abby's bear-man. Hmmm...Raul. Interesting name. An unexpected tingle zipped through her body.

"Yeah," the guy standing next to her said, giving her an assessing look back. "Tarik's a regular drama queen. He played Dolly in our senior year musical. You'd never know it, but he has a mean falsetto."

Tarik busted into a throaty guffaw. "You promised to never tell a soul about that."

"Oh. Yeah." Raul didn't sound regretful. Didn't look regretful either. He winked at Katie. He was flirting? With her?

Tarik looped his arm around Abby's neck and started walking toward the hotel. "That's okay. I'll get you." He poked his friend's chest. "If I were you, I'd grow eyes in the back of your head because you're going to need them."

"Tough talk coming from a guy who runs around naked," his friend challenged. "So, what's the plan, Tarik? And what do we do about Torborg?"

"Plan? Who knows? And as far as Torborg goes..." His expression turned troubled, guilty for the briefest of moments. Then it became hard, resolved. "I guess we call the police and tell them he was attacked by a bear. I'm going inside to get me some clothes, food and sleep." He looked at Abby, giving her a man-on-the-hunt look. "Not necessarily in that order."

Obviously, their girl talk would have to be later.

He continued, "Then I guess I'll tackle everything else. One thing at a time. How's your arm, kitten?"

Kitten? He called Abby *Kitten*? Actually, the nickname did fit her friend pretty well.

"It stopped bleeding. I guess it wasn't as bad as I thought. I always get woozy at the sight of my own blood." After a beat, Abby added, "Honest. I think everything's going to be fine."

Katie shook her head and watched her friend walk into the hotel with Tarik the Bear Man.

She had quite the opposite feeling. Everything was not going to be fine.

Chapter Two

ฬ

So, that was the first day of Katie's vacation. In a nutshell, it sucked. People died. Her friend was in love and wanted to move to Alaska...

She knew she should've stayed home.

The only part of the last twenty-four hours that didn't stink worse than the skunk she'd hit on the way down to Bear Creek—or Running Bear or whatever the little Podunk town was called—was Raul.

For some unknown reason when he was nearby, her worries faded. Her mood lifted. Her body warmed.

Raulllll...His name made her think of all things beastly. A roaring lion, lazing under a tree.

While she had to admit, the morphing bear-man and pistol-flaying bad guy had distracted her from noticing Raul for a while, once things had settled, and the police, fire department and EMTs had arrived and left, she couldn't help but notice him. No matter how hard she tried not to look his way, her gaze ended up there anyway. On his face, which was really breathtaking. His shoulders. His broad chest.

Before she realized what she was doing, she had lobbed a few eyelash flutters and shy smiles his way. He tossed a few naughty grins back.

Wow, she couldn't remember the last time she'd flirted with a guy. She'd forgotten how much of a stress-reliever it was.

"How about grabbing some breakfast in the hotel restaurant?" Raul offered, making full eye contact with her for the first time since Tarik and Abby had scooted off.

His smile widened.

Her gaze followed the motion of his hand as he stuffed it into his pants pocket. It strayed slightly to the left.

Hmmm. More than her drooping mood was lifting, if that bulge was any indication. "Sure. Sounds great. With all the commotion, I'd forgotten I was hungry."

He gave her a look that promised a lot more than a ham and cheese omelet. "Me too."

Whew, these Alaskan men move fast. Her cheeks warmed. A few other parts did too.

Was she game for this? For what Raul clearly had on his mind? Something told her he wasn't just after some small talk over processed pork and burnt toast.

She was tired and still a little in shock. Considering her current state, was it smart to jump into bed with the first hunk she laid eyes on? With any hunk?

Probably not the best idea.

Besides, there was still the matter of a much-needed conversation with her temporarily insane best friend. The sooner things were dealt with, the better.

"I should check in with Abby. We have some things to talk about."

"I doubt you'll be able to drag her away from Tarik just yet. It looked like he was going to keep her...busy...for a while."

Raul did have a point there.

"Yeah. Sure looked that way," she admitted. She thought about it for a few seconds then decided she should still try to talk to Abby. Even though there were probably few things in life that would be more pleasant that getting cozy with Raul in a restaurant booth, she had other priorities that had to come first.

Like saving her best friend from making the mistake of a lifetime.

She rubbed her neck. It was stiff and she was getting a headache. "You know, I'd better go find her anyway. We have a lot of…catching up to do."

"Okay."

"It was a sweet thought though." She got in the truck and slammed the door.

He walked up to the open window. "How about I meet you in the lobby in an hour? Do you think that'll give you enough time?"

Wow. He really wanted to take her to breakfast. She wasn't sure if she should be flattered or creeped out by his persistence. She put her foot on the brake. "Well, I don't know…"

"I'd like to buy you a meal. Just. One. Meal."

She put the truck into gear then gave him another long look. He was so gorgeous. He had the world's perfect face. Dark hair cut short on the sides, but with longer, sexy waves on top. Tanned skin. Dark-chocolate eyes that glittered when he smiled. A mouth that made her heart hop around in her chest like a caged rabbit. He had a shallow cleft in his chin. She'd always had a thing for cleft chins. Diamond studs graced each earlobe.

She'd never been big on guys with pierced ears, but those bits of bling looked fine on him. Better than fine.

Gosh, he was…beautiful. Her eyes didn't know where they wanted to stay. There was so much amazing terrain to cover on his face alone. "I…well…"

"From the looks of it, your trip to Alaska didn't start out too great. I'd like to change that." He blinked and smiled again, flashing brilliantly white teeth and adorable dimples on either side of his mouth.

She practically melted.

There was absolutely no way she could shoot him down. It just wasn't possible.

Besides, it was only breakfast. He'd promised. She was hungry. She needed food.

"Okay. An hour sounds like enough time." *To talk some sense into my crazy best friend.* "I'll meet you in the lobby."

The wattage of his grin cranked up to near blinding.

The vision of his face lingered in her mind as she parked the truck and headed into the hotel. She'd dated some gorgeous men but Raul was beyond compare. He had a face that could be in movies. And in magazines. And…everywhere if she had any say.

While she asked the desk clerk to call up to Abby's room, she sensed Raul coming up behind her. The skin on her back did that little tingly thing again.

She glanced to see if her instincts were right.

Yep.

"I can take the next person in line," a second clerk said.

"Excuse me." Raul touched the small of her back as he stepped around her.

The innocent contact just about brought her to her knees.

While she waited for the clerk helping her to return from wherever he'd run off to, she watched Raul register for his room. He had a nice profile. Hell, the guy looked great no matter which angle you inspected him from. He caught her staring and she nearly died from embarrassment.

He leaned over and whispered, "See you in a bit."

Tempted to either fling herself at him like a wanton hussy or climb over the counter and hide, she nodded. "Okay."

"I'm sorry, miss," the clerk said, returning to the counter. "I've tried three times. There's no answer."

After watching Raul walk to the elevator—it was tough deciding which side was his best, but the rear view was a contender—she turned her attention back to the clerk. "No answer? That brat. I'll have to go up and knock. What's her room number?"

"I'm sorry, but I can't give you that information."

"But you don't understand. I have to make sure she's okay. She had…er, a little accident outside. You saw the police, right?"

"I'm aware of the activities that occurred in our parking lot, yes. But she left no messages. I can't give out room numbers to just anyone."

"I'm not 'just anyone'. I'm her best friend."

"For all I know, you're her worst enemy."

Obviously this was going nowhere.

She heaved a sigh meant to let the clerk know precisely how difficult he was being. "Fine. Fine! You win. Will you deliver a message at least?"

"Yes. That I can do." He picked up a pen and pad of paper.

"Good. Tell her she'd better get back to me on my cell phone within the hour, or I'm going to leave."

The clerk scribbled down the message. "Your name?"

"Katie."

"Very well." He set the paper aside.

She sighed again. Didn't he know the rules? He was supposed to turn around and put her message in a mailbox, so she could read the room number, like the guy in *Digital Fortress*. "Can I help you with anything else?"

"Sure. I guess I'm going to need a room, since she's not answering her phone." *And you're not giving this Stephanie Plum wannabe a break.*

"Now *that* is something I can help you with. I'll need a credit card and your ID."

Grumbling to herself about uncooperative clerks and best friends who were too busy boinking man-bears to take care of more pressing matters, she forked over the required items, signed the paperwork, and went out to her truck to get her luggage. She decided to take only the small bag in. Barring a major catastrophe, it had everything she needed for one day — makeup, pajamas, and a single change of clothes. The goliath suitcase, which weighed more than a full-grown man, could sit in the truck until they went back to the cabin. She doubted anyone was going to steal it. For one thing, they'd need a forklift to get it out.

Feeling more tired with every step she took, she headed to her room and made a halfhearted attempt at prettying herself up. A part of her — the dead-dog-tired part — wanted to forget about breakfast and just go to bed. But another part refused to listen to reason. Thus, she continued with her preparation, with the expectation that she'd have a pleasant meal and then crash.

After a long, scalding shower, fussing with her hair and makeup, and putting on some fresh clothes, she almost felt human again. Normally, when she prepared for a date, she tried to look her best. Today, she'd settle for presentable.

Among her friends, getting ready for a first date normally involved hours of exfoliating, plucking, shaving, waxing, drying and curling, not to mention the shopping trip for the perfect outfit.

Nine-tenths of that wasn't happening this morning. Oh well.

It wasn't like Raul was going to get more than a distant view of at least half of the body parts requiring such thorough grooming.

Unlike Abby, Katie wasn't looking for a vacation fling. The last thing she needed right now was a roll in the hay with a stranger.

Long distance romances never worked. Living in Alaska — of all places — meant that Raul could at most qualify for the revered title of "guy friend".

141

Yes, fit, athletic, friendly, Raul was definitely a candidate for Vacation Guy Pal. Things being what they were, it wasn't looking like she'd be spending a whole lot of time with Abby over the next few days anyway. She could use the company, especially if she did any hiking.

She hoped Raul would understand.

Her footsteps light, her heart hammering the backside of her breastbone for some reason beyond her comprehension, she hurried to the lobby. Raul was waiting by the front desk. She held her breath as she walked up behind him and tried to think of something clever to say.

Then he turned around and words failed her.

"Hi," he said in a low voice, dripping with promise and male satisfaction. His gaze caressed her skin as it swept up and down her body.

Battling a tremor that had started at the base of her spine, she drew her hands behind her back and clasped them together. Her eyes did a little wandering of their own.

He looked amazing, better than he had an hour earlier. How was that possible? How did a guy's skin get tanner? Okay, she could see that happening if the hotel had tanning beds. But how could his brown eyes gain a hint of shadowy danger? And how could his shoulders get broader?

The obvious answer was they hadn't. She was simply more attentive to those fine details now.

Wow.

Made a girl wonder what he'd look like after she'd rested and was no longer gathering and interpreting sensations through a haze of exhaustion.

She wasn't sure it was safe to find out.

Raul knew he shouldn't be there with this woman. His baby brother Bryson was in deep shit.

He'd received the anonymous call hours ago. If Tarik and Abby weren't returned to Omega by tomorrow night, Bryson would die. That call had been followed by a second, less than an hour ago, a message from Bryson.

As if the first one hadn't been bad enough, the second had left Raul's blood running cold. There was no chance the caller had been bluffing.

The irony was, a helo waited for him a couple miles away. A helo that was worthless at the moment, thanks to strong northerly winds.

Yes, there were other ways to travel, car being the most obvious. Which was why he couldn't really justify his procrastination.

He was sitting in a restaurant, having breakfast with a woman, instead of driving back to Anchorage to save his brother's life?

Did not compute.

Yet, he was there because he had to be.

No one was holding a gun to his head. No one had threatened him. It wasn't anything like that. No, it was something much more primal, more urgent and beyond his full comprehension.

He simply had to be there. He had to be near Katie. He had to see her. To touch her. He wasn't sure why he was reacting this way to her.

Yes, she was beautiful. She was slim, with soft curves, long blonde hair and eyes that reminded him of cat's eyes. They were green with flecks of gold and their corners slanted up. Her lips were full, like Angelina Jolie full. He knew they'd taste amazing.

The entire time they sat in the restaurant, he stared at her, trying to figure out why he was going so nuts. There was no logic to his reaction.

After a while, he decided it didn't matter. Why question the inexplicable? All he cared about was how he'd get closer. How he'd convince her to let him touch her stomach. Her breast. Her thigh.

He purposefully left his leg resting against hers under the table. That small bit of contact eased the burn at first, but later he wanted more. Much, much more.

She shoved her half-full plate away and dabbed at her mouth with a napkin. Her lips curved into a smile.

Damn.

His cock strained against his underwear.

"So you came here to catch Tarik?" she asked, referring to a statement he'd made earlier. "I'm still trying to sort out what happened in the parking lot. It was weird. Like scary weird. It was real, right? I wasn't seeing things?"

"Oh no, you weren't seeing things. It was real all right. But I don't know much more than you," he said, focusing on her eyes. Damn if they weren't the most amazing color... "Torborg, the guy Tarik...er, attacked...was our boss and the CEO of Omega Corporation. Somehow, Torborg did something to Tarik—I have no clue what—to make him turn into a polar bear. At least, that's what Tarik's telling me."

"Do you believe him? I mean, we both saw him change. Can't hardly deny that." She gave a nervous giggle and raised a hand to her chest. Her index finger traced the neckline of her top.

His mouth went dry.

She licked her lips. Her index finger moved a little lower, sliding into the cleft between her breasts. "But do you believe what he said about your boss?"

He coughed and pried his gaze from her chest. What was with him? He'd never stared at a woman like that, practically drooling like a dog. And damn if his cock wasn't about to bust out of his pants. His testicles felt like they were heavier than bowling balls. "I don't know what to believe." In more ways than one. "I'd never heard of such a thing. People turning into animals. But considering the work Omega does, I guess if it's possible, Omega might be the company to make it happen."

She glanced down at her hand, as if she hadn't realized what it had been doing.

It fell to her lap.

A sexy pink hue washed over her neck and face. "What's Omega do?" she asked.

Some kind of sweet scent tickled his nose. He inhaled once, twice, drawing it in. *Mmmmm.* His balls got another ten pounds heavier.

Uncomfortable, he shifted in his seat. "Conducts medical research for drug companies. They specialize in genetic research."

The color in her face deepened. "Ah. I see now." She fanned her face with her napkin.

He scooted down a bit and let his knee rub up against the inside of her thigh. Her eyes widened but she didn't move away.

Promising.

It wasn't easy, considering he was so hot he could hardly think of anything but snatching Katie up in his arms and hauling her to his room, but he struggled to continue their awkward conversation. "I'm not into the science end of things, so I have extremely limited understanding of Omega's work." He moved his leg back and forth, caressing the length of her thigh. "I guess we've helped develop some treatments for some pretty serious diseases." When he felt her hand brush over his knee, he just about jumped her. Right there.

Her fingers returned to the neckline of her top.

The corners of her lips curled up into a nervous smile that sent more of his blood to parts south of his bellybutton. "What do you think'll happen to Omega, with Torborg being dead? And what about Tarik?" she asked, her voice wavering.

Unable to stop himself, he slid both his knees between hers and pressed them out, forcing her legs apart.

Those pretty green eyes nearly bugged out of her head. Her mouth formed an adorable O of surprise and she sucked in an audible breath. Her jaw dropped when his hand found one of her legs and started exploring...

"The Board of Directors will probably have someone in Torborg's office before we get back to Anchorage," he said, sliding down in his seat so that he could reach further up her thigh. "And Tarik...I'm not sure. He's got to come back and see if he can get a hold of Torborg's files. I hope he finds what he needs. Can't be easy living the way he is. I can see it's killing him, not being able to control himself."

"Yeah," she said on a shaky sigh.

He moved to the other leg, sliding his hand up as far as he could reach and then drawing little circles over the silky material of her pants. He wished she was wearing a skirt.

He smiled when she inched down a bit, allowing him to reach the warm juncture of her thighs. Her eyelids fluttered, long lashes fanning out over her flushed cheeks as they dropped closed. "If you're worried about your friend catching whatever Tarik has, we can have her checked out. I mean, I don't know if it's contagious. Torborg kind of hinted that it might be. That's why he sent me. To get them both back to Anchorage and have them checked by a doctor. Maybe he has a cure? Hadn't thought of that, but I suppose it's possible."

"That might be a good idea then." Her eyes suddenly wide, she reached under the table and knocked his hand away, looking over his head.

The waiter set the check on the table and asked if they'd like anything else.

Nothing you're going to be able to give us.

"No thanks," she said, giving the server a jittery smile. "I think I should get back to my room—" She shifted back in her seat.

"How about dessert?" Raul offered, not ready to let the "date" end yet. Just a few more minutes. That would be enough.

He hoped.

She pursed her lips.

He'd be satisfied with having those for dessert.

She fiddled with her napkin. "Dessert sounds...good, but I'm really tired."

He lifted a hand to the waiter, to let him know he shouldn't go anywhere yet. "To go, then. You can take it back to your room."

"You're doing my diet no favors."

"You don't need to diet. You're perfect the way you are."

"Nice line. Someone's taught you well."

"I have an older sister." *And a younger brother who's been kidnapped.*

What the fuck am I doing?

* * * * *

Minutes later, Katie found herself sitting in a dumpy hotel room in Bear Creek or Crippled Bear or whatever, having dessert with the most gorgeous man she'd ever laid eyes upon.

Later, after giving her friend some shit for even considering moving to Alaska—and for a man! Insanity!—she'd have to thank her for giving her some time alone with Raul. She was having a great time, even if she was so tired her eyes felt like they'd been sandblasted.

She was dizzy and hot. And a little confused. And hot. And ready to jump his bones. And feeling really, really good for the first time in many months.

She smiled.

His eyebrows smooshed down and made an attempt at meeting dead center in his forehead. Didn't quite make it. "Good cake?"

"Yes. The best I've ever had. Want a taste?" She cut a piece and lifted the fork. She licked her lips while waiting with clichéd bated breath.

How she loved to watch his lips close around the tines of a fork. She'd stared at his mouth the entire time he'd been eating. Luckily, he didn't seem to be overly self-conscious about women sitting dumbstruck, staring at him like he was a god incarnate while he was gulping down toast and bacon. Made her wonder if it happened a lot.

Of course it does. Look at him!

And wonder of all wonders, although he didn't seem fazed by her gaping, he didn't appear to realize how absolutely gorgeous he was. He wasn't strutting around like a proud peacock, tail shaking. He was sitting there, being real. Polite. Funny.

And extremely naughty.

"...and that's how I met Tarik. We've been friends ever since."

God, she hadn't realized he'd been talking all that time. "What a great story," she said, trying to sound amused instead of guilty.

"What about you and Abby?" He licked a bit of frosting off the tip of his thumb and she stifled a whimper.

"Us? Me? Abby?" she squeaked. Damn voice. A shrill impersonation of a chipmunk couldn't be very attractive. She cleared her throat and then tried talking again, "Well, that's a funny story. You see, as it turns out, we were in love with the same asshole, not that either one of us knew he was an asshole. We both were convinced he loved us and we'd get married someday and live happily ever after."

"And you became friends after that?" His tongue darted out to capture a speck of frosting that had been perched on his upper lip.

She swallowed a happy sigh. "Hey, we were ten. We both got over it after a while."

His chuckle rumbled through her body like thunder. It was a very pleasant vibration. She sighed again.

She couldn't remember the last time she'd connected with a guy like this, so quickly. Yes, she was all but hurling herself at the man she was so in lust with him. A current of energy was zinging through her body and zapping in the air.

But there was something else between them as well—the kind of connection that should have sent her running for the proverbial hills.

She didn't need this now. Complications. An infatuation that could never lead to anything long-lasting. The temptation to throw away caution and do something crazy.

So why wasn't she running?

Chapter Three

Katie's earlier thoughts of heading for safer parts were quickly banished from her head the moment Raul leaned over to kiss her. She hadn't anticipated the kiss, although she'd thought about it enough. Oh hell, if she were honest with herself, she'd admit she'd begun to wonder what was taking him so long.

The kiss was lead-melting hot but not in a pushy or rushed way. His mouth brushed softly over hers at first, teasing and tickling. He had amazing lips. Soft and scrumptious. Then hard and demanding. They made her want to do things she'd never thought to try.

When his tongue got into the action she wondered what it would take to convince her to attempt every single one of those things. Today.

While his tongue stroked and tormented, his hands wandered. They started their journey on either side of her face. They smoothed down her neck, brushed over her shoulders then drifted down her arms.

She broke the kiss to drag in a much-needed breath. Oxygen deprivation had most definitely set in.

Their gazes locked. She saw something strange in his eyes, a shadow shifting across irises the shade of the earth, like someone walking by a window in a darkened room.

His fingers tightened around her upper arms. His mouth pulled into a narrow line. He looked like a guy who was about to lose it.

Her breathing quickened.

"I don't know what it is about you." He lifted one of his hands to her face again. His index finger traced her lower lip, leaving a trail of pleasant tingles behind. "No touch is enough. No kiss…"

She knew the feeling. Insanity or not, she couldn't deny it any longer. She wanted him to take her. Now.

She laid her hand over his and closed her eyes. The scent of man and crisp outdoor air drifted to her nose. Her pussy burned. The sound of his heavy breathing echoed in her head. Together, the sensations intensified her desire to new and urgent heights.

"Raul," she whispered. "What's happening?"

She opened her eyes as he eased her onto her back on the bed. He gazed down at her for a least a bazillion stuttering heartbeats, maybe more.

"I'm going to take you," he answered, his eyes telling her he'd accept nothing but acquiescence.

"Yes."

He kissed her again. This time his mouth was hard and demanding, punishing. His hands closed over her breasts and kneaded them through the material of her knit top and bra. She reached up and dug her fingernails into the crisp cotton covering his shoulders.

More!

Seeming to read her mind, he shifted positions until his body was pressed against her length and his erection ground against her pubis. The weight felt wonderful, the friction amazing.

Still not enough.

He sat back, caught her wrists in his fists and pinned them up over her head to the mattress.

Now he was getting somewhere!

"Yes," she whispered, writhing under him. She needed his cock between her legs. She needed it now. She'd suffered long enough.

She'd been stupid to think she could be friends with this man, that she'd be able to resist the sensual promise in his wicked grin and deep voice, or that she'd be able to stand firm against the desire he'd so masterfully stirred within her. The tormenting had started hours ago. The sly glances and teasing touches. The definitive moment, when her will had been thoroughly defeated, had been in the restaurant. When he'd forced her legs apart with his knees and traced soft, winding lines up her thighs. If his intention had been to seduce her today, he'd succeeded. In a big way.

She willingly submitted. Her body was his. She couldn't take another second of agony.

"Oh God," she repeated over and over as he nibbled her neck. Goose bumps coated the right side of her body.

"What is it, baby?" he asked against her throat.

"Dying."

"Good. Let me send you to Heaven."

She started to laugh at his cheesy line but her chuckle became lodged in her throat when he rose up on his knees, straddling her hips, and gathered both wrists into one hand.

Flush-faced and heavy-lidded, he dragged the index finger of his free hand down the center of her throat and chest. It stopped at the neckline of her shirt. "Hmmm. This is in the way." He hooked his finger under the fabric and yanked. The material stretched but didn't tear. "Damn."

For the first time ever she wished the material of her top wasn't fifty percent Lycra.

He tried a second option, grabbed the lower hem and pushed it up until her shirt was gathered in a lump under her chin. She gave a secret smile, knowing what he was seeing now—a black lace demi bra that pushed her tits up high and barely covered her nipples. It was the sexiest piece of lingerie she owned.

"Fuck!" he said.

"You like?" Of course, she knew the answer to that question.

"Hell yes. A fucking eunuch would love this." He lowered his head and licked the swell of her right breast. Then he bit it, and she yipped with both surprise and glee.

He used his nose to push the cup down and expose her nipple. It was erect already, almost painfully sensitive. When he flicked his tongue over it, white-hot blades of desire licked her body.

Her back tightened, lifting off the bed and pushing her breasts into the air.

More!

He ran his tongue round and round her nipple then pulled it into his mouth. She moaned as he suckled.

Dying.

He released her hands and set about yanking and tearing away every stitch of her clothing from her body. Most of the garments, she suspected from the sounds she heard, would be headed for the rag bin. She didn't give a damn.

Once she was completely unclothed, he stripped.

She sat up to watch him. Her gaze took in the sight of smooth, tanned skin stretched over toned muscles. His shoulders were wide and developed, his chest broad enough to make her sigh with appreciation, his stomach a delightful plane cut into six by deep grooves. A sprinkling of brown hair ran from his bellybutton to the base of his cock.

What a cock. Long and thick and perfect.

Her pussy clenched around aching emptiness. A gush of warm wetness slicked the insides of her thighs. She reached for him but he caught her hands in his and pinned them behind her back.

She loved how he took control. She'd never had a lover do that before. It was thrilling.

Way beyond the point of being able to speak, she whimpered.

He nibbled the sweet spot where her neck met her shoulder. He was standing. She was sitting, her legs hanging over the edge of the mattress. The position left her feeling helpless and small. He forced her legs apart with his knee and a blast of sensual heat flashed through her body. He reached down and traced an invisible line from her bellybutton to her pussy. Her thighs quivered, pulling further apart. Dizzy, she dropped her head back. A moan pushed up her throat and slipped between her lips.

His finger skirted her slick folds to tickle her inner thigh. She wanted to scream. She lifted her head and glared at him.

"I have to taste you." His hands on her knees, he slowly knelt before her. He tipped his head back to look into her eyes and audibly inhaled. "Your scent is driving me crazy. I've never smelled anything sexier."

Everything about him was driving her crazy. The feel of his skin, warm and smooth, under her fingertips. How his voice vibrated inside her body like earthquake aftershocks and his muscles bulged and rippled as he moved. The way his eyes seemed to see clear through to her soul.

Did he know her every secret? Did he see the pain of her loss? Her fears? Her needs?

He lowered his head. She watched as he moved closer, until his mouth was there, on her pussy, precisely where she wanted it. His tongue ran up and down her slit, teasing her labia through the nest of tightly trimmed curls between her legs.

The air in the room thinned, or at least it felt that way. She compensated by gulping air into her lungs in shallow, panting breaths. Her cheeks warmed.

She ached for his touch to become more intimate. Much more.

As if reading her thoughts, he used his fingers to part her outer lips, exposing her clit to his wonderfully skillful tongue. It danced over her nub, stopping a fraction of a second before she climaxed.

She whimpered and gave him a pleading look.

Seeming to enjoy her suffering far too much, he answered her silent plea with another round of torture, driving her to the crest once more.

And again he stopped microseconds before she had her release.

"Bastard," she muttered, digging her fingernails into the only part of him she could reach — his forearms.

He chuckled and resumed tormenting her. Using lips and teeth as well as tongue, he sent her soaring toward completion for a third time.

Every muscle in her body pulled tight, until she felt like they were all tangled into one big knot. Heat rushed through her body in wild, violent waves. She ached for the release he continued to deny her. Ached everywhere, from her scalp down to her heels. She lifted a trembling hand to her face and wiped away a droplet of perspiration dribbling down her temple.

No more!

She opened her mouth to literally beg him for mercy, but he stopped before she'd spoken a single word.

No tongue. No lips. No teeth.

Again? This was so wrong!

She opened her eyes — when had she closed them? — and sent him death daggers.

He smiled, clearly pleased with himself, stood and pushed on her chest until she was lying flat on her back. "I don't like to rush," he murmured, giving her a look feral enough to send the average girl into cardiac arrest. He lowered his head, his lips poised over hers, teasing, tempting.

The passing seconds measured by the rapid pounding of her heart, she closed her eyes, held her breath and waited to taste his kiss again.

He whispered, "Shoot me."

She would if she could! Perhaps not with a real gun, but with something that would cause adequate pain and suffering, while avoiding any long-lasting damage. She was a sane woman, at least for the moment. If he dared to drive her to the verge of orgasm again, she couldn't say that wouldn't change.

"You have no idea how much I want you right now. Or how difficult it has been to wait. No more." He caught the undersides of her knees and pulled, until her ass rested on the edge of the mattress. Lifting and hooking his elbows under her knees, he forced her legs wide apart. The tip of his cock prodded at her pussy before oh-so slowly gliding into her wet depths.

"Ahhhhh," she heard herself say as his cock moved within her. It must have taken an eternity and a second for him to complete the first inward thrust. Those were the most glorious moments of her existence, or so she figured. Though she suspected the ones following could very well be even better.

He withdrew from her in an equally deliberate fashion, his cock stroking every one of those extra-special places deep inside on its way out.

About the time he poised himself to thrust back inside again, she remembered to inhale.

And then he was filling her again. His hands smoothed down her thighs until they reached their junction. His fingertips probed her folds.

She heard herself speak as he stroked her way to the outer edges of the universe. Her words were disjointed, her voice breathy. "Yes...oh...God...there...more...no." She ached to touch him, to create another connection with him, besides the one between her legs. She reached down and tried to close her fingers around his wrists but he grabbed her hands and forced them out to her sides.

"Don't move," he murmured in a deep, guttural voice as he slowly withdrew his cock from her. She bit back a moan at the loss of his intimate strokes. He ran his hands up her arms, two flattened palms, gliding along her skin, barely touching it, and driving her insane. "I know what you need. What you crave." His hands skimmed over her nipples as they changed direction, now descending down her torso. "Don't move a finger. An eyelid. Don't do anything I don't tell you to do and I will reward you, over and over again."

Ooooh. She loved the sound of that! "Ohhh…kay."

His fingers tickled her lower stomach before parting her labia and teasing her clit again. He drew one, two, three circles over her nub, sending three blasts of heat raging through her body. Then he entered her with a hard, swift stroke.

"Yesssss," she whispered on a sigh.

He settled into a faster rhythm than before, one that had her trembling within moments and teetering on the brink of orgasm.

She held her breath, arched her back and clawed at the bedding. She didn't want it to end and yet she couldn't hold back.

He simultaneously pushed her thighs further apart and quickened the pace of both his thrusts and strokes to her clit. He drove into her with rapid, rough urgency. "Come for me, baby," he demanded. "Come for me now."

She felt his cock swell within her. The added sensation sent her hurling over the edge. Her orgasm charged through her system like a jagged bolt of lightning. It burned its way out from her center, to her limbs, her face, her toes.

Raul hesitated on an outward stroke before drilling her hard, over and over, while muttering words she didn't understand under his breath.

His frenzied movements within her drew out her orgasm. It seemed to last for ages. Heat pulsing through her body in liquid waves. Colors exploding behind her closed eyelids. Sounds and smells and sensations battering her system so relentlessly she couldn't sort them all out until slowly they faded and her mind became hers again.

Before the tingles and twitches had ceased completely, she was swallowed up in a moment of regret.

She was normally so much more responsible than this. She didn't do casual sex.

But it had happened so quickly...kind of. Yes, Raul had driven her absolutely crazy at breakfast and she'd sort of encouraged him. But she'd still returned to her room assuming they'd share dessert and then say goodbye. Sometime after the last nibble of cake smothered in chocolate sauce and now, she'd lost her ability to think.

This guy was dangerous.

What have I done?

But damn, that was amazing!

He seemed to sense her conflicting emotions. Deep worry lines cut across his forehead as he drew his eyebrows together. He pulled out of her, climbed up onto the mattress, and helped her scoot up toward the head of the bed with gentle hands. "What's wrong? Did I hurt you?"

Man...

How did a girl tell a guy this sweet—not to mention spectacular in bed—that she was sorry she'd slept with him? Sorry in some ways.

Only because it was a bad decision, not because it sucked.

She'd be going home in a week. Right now, she needed her life to be simple. She didn't have the strength to handle anything but simple.

He wouldn't understand.

She tugged on the coverlet until it was down low enough for her to slip underneath. It was only after she'd covered herself up to her armpits that she had the courage to try to explain. Her cheeks were so hot she thought they might blister. "My friends all say I'm a little old-fashioned."

God, that sounded lame. She forgot what she was about to say next.

He lifted a hand to her chin and gazed deeply into her eyes. "Old-fashioned is good. I like old-fashioned."

Heh. Yeah. Right. She indicated her disbelief with a lift of one eyebrow.

"Sometimes," he amended. "When it comes to certain things."

"Like sleeping on the first date?" she joked, trying to hide her unease.

"Usually, yes," he answered, his expression as serious as a blister on your big toe during a ten-mile hike. Then he soberly added, "Believe it or not, I've never slept with a woman on the first date."

How was he doing this? Being so serious and yet putting her at ease somehow? The regret that had been almost painful, like a big, heavy lump of concrete sitting in her gut, was fading.

She rolled her eyes. "Puh-leez."

"What?"

She nearly giggled at his wide-eyed expression. "You don't have to lie. Everyone knows it's okay for a man to sleep with anyone he wants, anytime, anywhere. It's the old double standard." She smoothed the covers over her chest, trying hard not to notice how absolutely scrumptious he looked sitting there naked.

Raul Zant was perfect. In every way. Even his hands and feet were nice to look at. His fingers were long and tapered. His feet not your typical ugly man-feet.

If he hadn't been so sexy—not to mention sweet, and sensitive...and apparently able to read her mind?—she'd never have lost her self-control.

Dangerous.

He settled in beside her and pulled her toward him, sliding one arm under her head. "Would you believe me if I told you I was a virgin until the age of twenty-eight?"

She didn't laugh, though a giggle bubbled up her throat. What was he trying to do here? Make her feel better about what they'd done by telling her silly stories? What a terrible liar. "No."

He kissed the top of her head. "It's true."

"Sorry, not buying it," she said, even as she snuggled in closer. He was so cuddly.

"I swear, it's the truth. Before I went into the military, I didn't do a whole lot of dating. And then once I joined the Army, I was too busy. Because of my job I didn't stay in one place long enough to form any friendships, let alone romances that lasted more than a few months."

"Okay, the Army bit I can buy. But why wouldn't you date when you were in school?" She tipped her head up to look at his face.

He shrugged his shoulders. Thick, black eyelashes that were too long to belong on a man swept up and down as he blinked, drawing her gaze to his eyes. "I was shy."

She made no comment to that one, mostly because she could believe it.

"Anyway, that was ages ago and none of it matters now. I don't sleep around. I'm healthy. Thanks to the good ole U.S.

government, I've been tested or inoculated for everything from the plague to hepatitis, so you have nothing to worry about. And there's no need for guilt. We were both...we got caught by surprise. It doesn't have to happen again. Unless we both want it to." He ran his palm over her face. "Now, sleep. You need to rest before we head back to Alaska. It's a long trip."

Cradled in his arms, she slipped easily into sleep.

When she woke an hour later, she was a little disappointed—though not surprised—to find he hadn't stayed with her.

Chapter Four

ဆာ

Five minutes. That's all she'd have in the next several hours. Katie watched the two guys amble toward the gas station, silently rehearsing her get-your-head-out-of-your-ass speech for her best friend. Since she'd slept while Raul'd been driving, leaving only a couple hours before they arrived in Anchorage, there was no time for niceties. Abby would have to receive the blunt version.

Wasn't the first time.

"Girl," Katie started, pivoting in the driver's seat to give her friend a glare, "have you lost your fucking mind?"

Abby frowned, crossed her arms over her chest, and flung one leg over the other. "Nice."

"I don't have time to be nice. They're men. Men don't take twenty minutes to pee like women do."

"Great. So you're just going to tell me I'm an idiot? What happened to 'My friend really loves you, blah, blah, blah'?" Abby mimicked, in a singsong voice.

Katie smacked the steering wheel with her palm. "Did you really expect me to tell you I thought you were being an idiot with all those people around, bullets flying and whatnot? I'm a better friend than that."

Abby turned to stare out the window. "Yeah, you wait until we're alone to insult me."

"I'm trying to save you from making one of the biggest mistakes of your life."

Abby shrugged her shoulder, sending an I-don't-want-to-talk-about-this vibe. "It's not the biggest mistake of my life. I know what I'm doing."

"You're going to walk away from everything and it's not the biggest mistake you've ever made?" Katie asked the side of her head. "From a great job? Friends?" *From me?*

"No."

"Argh!" If she could have, she would've reached back and throttled her best friend. Problem was that wouldn't do a damn thing. The only thing that would bring her friend back to her senses was logic. "You've worked how long to get that promotion? And now you're going to just quit?"

Still staring out the window and sending non-comunicado vibes, Abby murmured, "Promotion? Big whoop. It's not like I'm Vice President of Sales and Marketing. I'm Marketing Assistant, also known as Official Pee-on."

"Better than still being sales secretary."

"I can get a job out here. I'm sure it won't be hard finding a new position." She finally looked at Katie. The fire of cold determination glittered in her eyes. "I'll look under Pee-ons in the classifieds. There's probably a whole section of jobs to choose from."

"Shut up." Didn't she know there wouldn't be a whole section of best friends in the classifieds?

"Seriously." Abby blinked once, twice, three times. The whites of her eyes grew pinker each time. "I didn't expect you to jump for joy when you heard the news. I know you better than that. But I thought you'd trust me to make the right decision. We've been friends for a long time."

Yes, a long time. How would she go on without Abby? Especially now. Abby had always been there when she needed her.

"You should know by now that I'm no idiot." Abby sniffled and blinked a few more times. "And being my very best friend, I didn't expect you to put yourself before my happiness."

Oh man, Abby was going to cry.

Was she being selfish? Putting her own needs before Abby's happiness? Maybe. No… Or was she? "Maybe I am thinking about myself a little, but I'm thinking about you too," Katie said, softening her voice. "I've seen what happens to you when you get all starry-eyed over a man—"

"This is different," Abby said, dropping her gaze to her clasped hands, sitting in her lap. "Tarik's different."

"Yeah. You've got that right. He turns into a wild animal and eats people," she blurted. Why would Abby choose a guy who turned into an animal over her best friend? A friend who needed her? A friend who cared for her, had been there to hold her hand through every crisis, big and small?

Okay, she was thinking of herself. But this wasn't good for Abby either.

"I knew you were going to be this way," Abby grumbled. "All negative."

"Why wouldn't I? The whole bear thing. It's a problem. A huge, fanged, clawed problem."

"That's you, always looking for the bad in a situation."

"Duh!" Katie dropped her head, knocking it against the steering wheel. "Are you trying to say a guy changing into a huge bear is a good thing? Are you looking to get rid of a few enemies?"

The sound of scuffling shoes outside alerted her to the return of the guys.

"We'll continue this conversation later," she said, starting her rental truck. They'd turned Abby's into a local branch of the rental company, since they figured they wouldn't need both. Raul said his van wasn't running right, so it had been towed to a mechanic somewhere.

"No, I don't think there's anything more to be said. We're going to have to agree to disagree on this one. At least if you'd like to remain friends," Abby added, putting weight into her words.

Katie heard her message, loud and clear.

Damn it all, she was going to have to suck it up, let her friend make her own decisions. It would be hard. Lonely. Painful. But sooner or later, Abby's heart would be broken. Then, being the true friend she was, Katie would help scrape the pieces off the ground and glue them back together.

She heaved a sigh and gave Raul a weak smile as he slid into the passenger seat.

"Is something wrong?" he asked.

Two points for Raul. He wasn't as oblivious as most men were, outside the bedroom as well as inside.

"No, nothing," she said. "All set?"

"Yeah."

She shifted the truck into gear and turned the steering wheel. "Let's get going then. I'd like to get to Anchorage before sunrise, if that's possible."

He leaned over and whispered, "Me too."

A little shudder zipped down her spine.

So much for her renewed vow to keep their friendship strictly platonic.

Abby barked, "Hah! Might want to practice what you preach."

She stiffened, even as a second wave of wanting blasted through her system. This was going to be a long drive.

* * * * *

It had been hell, but Raul somehow resisted the urge to drag Katie to the nearest Anchorage hotel and fuck her until dawn. Between the urges coursing through his body the entire time they'd been driving, and the uncomfortable sense of time slipping away, he'd been ready to jump out of his skin.

It made no sense when he thought about it—the overwhelming wanting he felt for Katie.

Now.

The timing was all wrong.

He had a brother in danger. It was clear Omega would stop at nothing to contain whatever virus or germ responsible for Tarik's bizarre condition. He'd be a fool to doubt they'd kill his brother if he didn't deliver both Tarik and Abby to them by sundown.

The fucking clock wasn't just ticking, it was racing.

So why the hell was he thinking about how amazing Katie smelled, how smooth and warm her skin had felt and how sweet she tasted? His hard-on still hadn't gone down. If he didn't know better, he'd swear he'd overdosed on the little blue pill.

He shifted in his seat and cracked the window, welcoming the chilly early-morning air. It was crisp and fresh smelling, the scent slightly diluting the intoxicating aroma coming from Katie's general direction.

She was aroused.

"Turn right here," he said, directing her to Omega.

"Okay." She gave him a curious look. "Is this the way to our cabin? It doesn't look familiar."

"No, it's not," Tarik said from the backseat. "I wanted to run into work and see if I can get some stuff from my office. I also want to check my email. See what's going on."

"It can't wait until later?" Abby asked, echoing Katie's unspoken question, and sounding as exhausted as Katie felt, despite the hours she'd slept while he'd driven the bulk of their journey.

"Security's pretty light during second shift, and with Raul here, I don't expect to have any problems," Tarik reasoned. "As it stands now, I think I'm still working here but I didn't want to take any chances. It'll just take a few minutes. Promise. Then you and I will head back to my place and you can take a long bath."

"I'm not sure I have the energy to take a bath," Abby muttered. "I may just go to sleep."

Katie pulled the truck into a large, paved parking lot that stretched around the corner of a pale gray concrete building. The word Omega was spelled out on a small brass sign next to the single glass door.

"Well, here we are." Katie cut off the engine. The two guys opened their doors.

"Do either of you ladies need to use the bathroom?" Raul asked.

What a sweetie. So thoughtful.

"I don't. But I wouldn't mind stretching my legs," Katie said.

"Me too," Abby agreed.

They climbed out of the truck, gave each other a look, and headed toward their respective guys. It was no use hiding her attraction to Raul. Abby had already come to some accurate assumptions about how she'd spent her free time back at the hotel. She'd also made a point of lobbing a few cheap shots her way.

Katie slid an arm around Raul's waist and fell into step beside him. He was moving pretty quickly and flinched when she pressed her side up against his.

"In a hurry?" she asked, dropping her arm. She was catching a clear don't-touch vibe. Was he the kind who didn't like to bring his personal business into his work? Or were Abby's little barbs getting to him?

"Yeah. I'd like to get this over with and get home." He punched in a few numbers on the security pad under the sign and a click sounded as the lock disengaged. He pushed open the door and held it for her.

"I hope you're not always in a hurry." She gave him a nervous smile as she passed by him into the semi-dark lobby.

He answered with a lick of his lips and a crooked grin.

Oh, mama.

She prayed Tarik was telling the truth, and this would be a very quick thing. After yesterday's brief bout of after-sex regret, and a foolishly misguided attempt at convincing herself she'd keep Raul at arm's distance for the remainder of her vacation, she'd spent the past several hours trying to concentrate on driving while fighting the urge to pull over and molest him on the spot. Even with Abby hurling poorly disguised insults her way.

Her friend and Tarik be damned. Responsibility be damned. Sanity be damned.

There was something about him, something that was driving her absolutely fucking insane. She wanted him. Bad. Her determination to resist him was only making things ten times worse.

He held the door for Abby and Tarik, then pushed it closed and locked it after they were inside.

A little charge of apprehension skipped up her spine for some reason. Her palms grew instantly slick.

They were locked inside this building. What if something happened and they needed to get out quickly?

Duh.

She shook her head and eyed her surroundings again. It was perfectly safe. Dark and empty and kind of eerie. But safe.

She'd been reading too many Dan Brown novels lately. She was starting to imagine bad guys lurking around every corner.

"How about waiting here in the lobby?" Raul asked, giving her shoulder a quick rub. "The bathroom's down this hallway. The door next to it leads to the breakroom. We have a couple of vending machines in there. Snacks. Soft drinks. We'll be back in a few."

"Sure. Okay." She glanced at Abby. "You sticking with me, or going with them?"

"I'm not sure," she answered, turning to Tarik. "Mind if I go with you?"

Tarik shook his head. "Better stay down here."

Raul looked at Tarik then Abby. "It would probably be okay if she came up." He sounded unsure.

"I'd rather she wait down here."

"Okay." Abby looked disappointed as stood on tiptoe and kissed his chin. "See you in a few. Don't stay away too long." Turning to display a full frown, she motioned to Katie. "Come on. Let's see what kind of processed food we can find." She pointed toward the breakroom.

"I'm with you," Katie said.

"We'll be right down." Tarik caught Abby's hand and squeezed it before walking in the opposite direction.

Raul tossed Katie a half-smile then followed Tarik.

* * * * *

Raul was grateful for the fact that he didn't have to act like he wasn't nervous anymore. Considering everything that had happened lately, it was believable that he'd be a little anxious bringing Tarik into the building. Although he was far from a *little* anxious. He was freaking-the-fuck-out.

What if his brother was already dead?

What if the bastard who'd called him was lying?

What if this was a trap and they'd all end up dead?

Fuck and triple fuck.

The security office was empty. He checked it first, before going any further. The fact that there wasn't anyone monitoring the cameras did bother him on a professional level. His job was to make sure the building was secure at all times. Those monitors should never be unsupervised. Where the hell was Tom?

Then again, maybe Tom's absence was intentional?

No witnesses.

He'd managed to call back the fucking no-faced bastard who'd kidnapped his brother earlier, when he'd gone to the bathroom. Of course, he'd waited until Tarik had left so he wouldn't overhear anything.

At this point, he had no idea who the fucker was, but he had to assume it was someone at Omega, someone at the very top of the corporate ladder. Someone who had a lot to lose if news of Tarik's medical condition got out.

Evidently whoever it was had decided it was better to risk Omega being broken into than having Tom witness what was going down.

It made him wonder where that left him...and his brother, for that matter.

Exiting the security office, he gave Tarik a nod. "Security's empty. Must be...taking a toilet break."

"That's unusual, isn't it?" Tarik asked, falling into step beside him as they headed toward the elevator. "I mean, I don't usually pay attention to the comings and goings of your team, but I guess I assumed there was someone here around the clock."

"There should be. Two men, one in the office at all times. Those monitors are never supposed to be unmanned. But I can't say it doesn't happen. People have to pee." He hit the button for the third floor and it lit up. Conscious of the security cameras overhead, he lowered his voice. "I guess we'll just keep our eyes open for them, and give whoever we run into first our cover story if they wonder what you're doing here. I doubt that Mike, the other guy on second shift, would bother asking. He's new and doesn't know a damn thing."

"Got it."

The elevator doors slid open and they stepped inside. Despite the fact that he'd handled more than a few stressful situations—having served eight years in the US Army, two of them in Iraq—his heart was racing, and he was jumpier than a cat on a tightrope stretched over the Niagara Falls. Sweat beaded on his forehead. His palms were slick. Watching the numbers light up on the panel—two, three, he closed his fists and hid them behind his back.

The car stopped. The door slid open. Half expecting someone to jump at them, every muscle in Raul's body tensed.

Nothing happened.

He glanced both ways as he exited the elevator. His senses on high alert, he followed Tarik down the hall toward his office.

One of the fluorescent lights overhead blacked out a few feet from Tarik's door and Raul spun around, sure someone would be attacking them from behind.

No one. The hallway was empty.

"Jumpy a little?" Tarik teased, sliding his key into the door's lock and twisting it to the right. "Shouldn't I be the nervous one, not you?"

Considering the highly secretive nature of the work conducted at Omega, the security systems were extremely slack. A simple numeric security code kept any potential intruders out of the building, and highly fallible key locks protected individual offices, with the exception of the basement.

Of all places—where there were no offices, no computers, nothing worth a damn thing—the lower level was secured by multiple systems.

At least the janitorial supplies would never come up missing. Evidently, toilet paper rated a multi-million dollar security system. He'd never understand fucking corporate types.

Tarik closed the door before he reached for the light switch, leaving them standing in a dark-as-death room for several seconds. Raul stood with his back to the wall, his eyelids raised as high as they could go, his whole body wound tight.

Would someone jump them now? When they were closed in a dark room and vulnerable?

He heard the snap of a switch but the overhead fixtures didn't light up.

"Damn. No lights? What's up with that?" Tarik said from the general direction of the doorway. We can map the entire human genome but can't keep our lights working?"

Raul had a feeling he knew what was up. They'd walked into an ambush. His back firmly pressed against the wall, he squatted down, hoping whoever was about to jump them wasn't wearing night vision goggles. If they were, he was dead. He couldn't see his hand in front of his face.

The light switch snapped several more times.

And then a puff of cool air hit his right cheek.

Out of instinct, he dived to the left and slammed into a hard, large piece of furniture with sharp fucking corners, just as something big and heavy hit the wall he'd been leaning against.

Good. Served the fucker right.

He curled up into a ball and rolled onto his side. His head slammed into something else and he saw stars. As he struggled to find his way around the side of the obstacle, a heavy body landed on him, knocking him flat on his back. Completely blind, he swung, making contact with some part of his attacker. Encouraged by the grunt that followed, he fought for all he was worth. Hands. Feet. Elbows.

Suddenly, the office door banged open and a slant of light cut through the center of the room.

A man dressed head to toe in black—helmet and mask, coverall and boots—stood framed by the glaring light from the hallway. In front of him stood Raul's brother, Bryson, held at gunpoint. "Up. Now," the gunman said in a computer-altered voice.

Digital voice-changing system, strange goggles that looked more like diving equipment than night vision, body armor that was nothing like military issue, and a weapon that vaguely resembled an MP5 with a silencer but with a few notable differences.

Fancy toys, these guys had. At the moment, he'd give his left nut to get his hands on any of it, especially that weapon.

His gaze fixed to his brother's face, Raul stood and raised his hands.

Bryson's expression remained cool as he returned Raul's stare.

Someone grabbed Raul's wrists from behind.

Tarik, held by a third man in black, cursed. His skin rippled and the start of a thick white coat sprouted on his arms, but the guy holding him plunged a hypodermic into his shoulder.

A split second later Tarik dropped to the floor. He didn't complete the change.

These guys were well prepared—for everything.

What did they intend for Tarik, now that he was out cold?

What about Bryson?

* * * * *

The minute they were inside the breakroom, door closed and lights on, Katie said, "I know what you're thinking but—"

Abby stepped up to the snack machine. "What I'm thinking is you're a fucking hypocrite, yeah."

"It might look that way but it's not. I'm not planning doing anything crazy, like giving up my life for a guy." Her nerves on edge, Katie unzipped her purse and started rooting around in the bottom for change.

"You gave up your life a long time ago," Abby snapped.

Her friend did not just say that. No. "What are you talking about? Gave up my life? How?" She tipped her purse to the side and shook it. Hard. She wasn't talking about how she'd moved out of her apartment to help her father. How she'd refused invitations to go out because he'd been sick and needed her. "Was I supposed to go on like nothing was happening? Leave him home alone while I lived it up?"

Abby sighed. "I'm sorry. I shouldn't have said that. No. You shouldn't have. But—"

"I don't want to talk about this right now." Katie dug to the deepest corner of her purse and grabbed as many coins as she could. She checked. Three quarters, a dime, a few nickels and a couple of pennies. Not bad. Switching the hoard to the other hand, she went in for more. "What're you getting?" she asked, not giving a rat's ass what her friend's answer would be.

Abby slid a handful of coins into the machine's slot. *Plunk, plunk, plunk...* "A bag of Doritos. I shouldn't be eating these, but what the hell? I'll have a Slimfast for lunch later. What about you?"

"Not sure yet." Katie stared blindly at the machine in front of her.

"There's something between Tarik and me," Abby said, cutting through what was becoming an awkward silence. "I can't explain it."

She could almost relate to what Abby was saying. "Yeah." She shoved a quarter into the pop machine. It seemed Alaskan men were in a class of their own when it came to sex appeal. She had no idea what it was about Raul, but there was something there too. Something that made her ache to be near him, to talk to him, touch him, to submit to him in all ways.

She wasn't sure if she was more eager to find out what that special something was, or to get the hell away from him. This...connection...scared her.

Almost as much as it intrigued her.

"You ask me, I think we're both in for trouble," she admitted.

Abby ripped open her bag of chips. "I hope you're wrong."

Chapter Five

❧

"Take that one down to the truck," the gunman holding Bryson said, indicating the still-unconscious Tarik.

"Yes, sir." The hostile hefted Tarik over his shoulder with ease, as if the solid two-hundred-pounds-plus Tarik weighed no more than a bag of cotton balls. The man left the room.

With him gone, there were only two remaining. Two enemy personnel. Two guns.

And two unarmed brothers.

The chances they'd get out of this with their asses intact had risen from maybe one in a trillion to one in a million. Still sucked. And Raul could see no way to improve those odds.

"You delivered," the gunman said to Raul.

"Yeah," Raul said, testing the restraints circling his wrists. Felt like Nylon. The edges burned his skin as he twisted his hands. "So how about letting my brother go as promised?" he added, keeping what he wanted to say to himself.

The guy they'd just hauled out of the room was one of his best friends. If it hadn't been for the fact that these bastards had been holding his brother hostage, he would never have done this. Fuckers had given him no choice.

He had to wonder why Omega had employed a group like this — paramilitary, with high-tech equipment not even the US military offered its elite forces — to apprehend one unarmed man and woman. Supposedly to get them medical care?

There was a time when he'd believed Omega had Tarik's wellbeing in mind. He wasn't one hundred percent convinced anymore.

Tarik might be in danger. And if they apprehended Abby. She could be too.

He needed answers. Problem was, he knew the more information the enemy volunteered, the less likely they'd be to let him walk. Better to not ask questions if he was going to have any hope of perhaps helping Tarik later.

He didn't want to think about what they could be doing to his friend if his instincts were right.

There were several minutes of tense silence. While his insides churned, he fought to keep his mien cool.

"The women downstairs. How much do they know?" the gunman asked a hundred heartbeats later.

He fought to disguise the shock racing through his system. Was it possible they didn't realize one of the women downstairs was Abby? Was there still some chance he could protect them both? "Nothing."

The gunman shook his head. "I guess I shouldn't expect you to tell me the truth." He addressed the hostile standing behind Raul. "Go find the women. Take them to the truck."

Raul's gut twisted into a knot. Katie! What would they want with her?

"Yes, sir." The man left the room.

One hostile. One gun. Two brothers. Better odds.

Seething inside and desperate to get to Katie before the enemy did, Raul jerked against the restraints, as hard as he could.

Much to his surprise, the Nylon snapped.

Defective? Or perhaps not secured properly? Intentional or accidental?

Careful to keep his hands behind his back, as if he was still restrained, he moved closer to the only remaining gunman. "We need to talk about this," he said, enunciating every word. He glanced at Bryson.

As kids, he and his brother had played war with their neighbors, a boy named Thomas and a girl, Tina, who'd been a lot tougher than most boys they'd known. Tina was always the one to hold the war prisoners, and tall for her age and strong for a girl, she wasn't easy to escape from. Raul and Bryson had come up with a secret code, a system to alert each other to their intentions. It was the only way to take her by surprise and escape.

He hoped Bryson remembered their code after all these years.

He'd just told him to get ready to duck out of the way.

He took another couple of steps closer, bringing himself within striking distance, as well as point blank range of the weapon—not that a shot from ten feet would've done any less damage to his skull.

The man pressed the gun to Bryson's temple instead. "Back up."

"I just want to talk..." He pulled in a deep breath and shouted, "Now!"

Bryson dove.

Raul kicked the weapon out of the gunman's hand. It sailed across the room, hit the wall and landed with a metallic clunk about fifteen feet away.

"Run!" Raul shouted to his brother as he ducked a punch. A second one hit its mark, his left eye. Raul's head snapped back on impact but he kept fighting. When one of his punches left the gunman staggering and dazed for a split second, he glanced at Bryson.

Bryson hadn't moved.

No, no, no! His stubborn brother better not pull that shit now. "Go, dammit!" Raul shouted, taking another blow to the face before lunging forward to strike their assailant in the one place he was vulnerable, his throat.

"Fuck!" Bryson dashed from the room.

Raul felt the guy's airway collapse. The struck man staggered backward, audibly struggling to pull air into his lungs.

Raul had his chance.

Deciding it wasn't worth the effort to find the gun, he ran from the room.

* * * * *

The breakroom door crashed open, slamming into the wall.

Katie jumped, dropping her soda can on the floor. It clattered on the linoleum before rolling under the snack machine. She spun around.

Raul rushed into the room looking like he'd been on the losing side of a boxing match. His face was bloody, one eye nearly swollen shut and his lower lip at least double its normal size.

Worried he might collapse, she rushed to him and wrapped an arm around his waist. "What happened?"

He dabbed at the blood on his mouth with his sleeve. "I need to get you two out of here. Now."

"Where's Tarik?" Abby said.

"Can't. Talk. Now." Raul doubled over for a moment. Blood dripped from his face, leaving little crimson droplets on the white floor. Once vertical again, he reached out and yanked Katie toward the door. He was strong, despite his injuries. Damn strong. Caught off guard, she had to scramble to keep her feet under her.

"Why can't you talk?" Abby just about shrieked, stomping after them. "What happened? Where's Tarik?"

Raul spun around and grabbed Abby by the arms, hissing, "For God's sake, shut up! They'll hear you. I'll tell you everything as soon as we get the fuck out of here."

"Who? They?" Abby shouted.

"Not now."

"Fuck you!"

Raul pressed his back to the door, hauling Katie up against him.

She felt something...firm...against her lower back. Raul was hard? Now? With the whole running-from-danger thing going on? And the blood, fat lip and black eye? How was that possible?

"Fine. Stay here." Raul poked his head out, checking the hallway for someone or something. Once he must've determined the coast was clear, he grabbed Katie's wrist and ran.

Katie looked over her shoulder at Abby. "Come on," she whispered, stumbling along behind him.

Abby, being the stubborn twerp she sometimes was, crossed her arms over her chest and stood defiant. "I'm not leaving without Tarik."

"Abby! Damn you!" Katie shouted, when Raul continued to pull her down the hallway. She tried to break free from his grip, but he was holding her too tightly. So firmly, her hand was going numb. "Stop, Raul. Abby. We have to make her—"

"I don't think anyone's going to make her do anything she doesn't want to do. And if I try to explain all this to your friend now, I'm afraid none of us'll get out of here." He halted mid-stride, turned and led her back the way they'd come. She slammed into his back and then half tripped, half ran after him. "I'll come back for her if I have to." He led her around a corner and down a narrow corridor. A sign, lit red and suspended from the ceiling, indicated an emergency exit at the end.

Scared and confused and worried about Abby and Tarik, she kept quiet as she followed him outside and around the back of the building. When he reached the truck, he threw open the passenger side door, indicated she should get in with a stabbing index finger, then ran around to the driver's side. Once inside, he looked down at the ignition, thrust a hand her way. "Keys?"

She shoved her hand into her coat pocket but didn't pull out the keys. "What about Abby? I thought you were going back in for her. We can't leave her here."

Motioning with his hand to hurry up, he explained, "I have to get you somewhere safe first. They have a vehicle. Tarik's already been taken into custody. I need to hide you and the truck. I'll come back for her. If she's smart, she'll stay quiet and they won't find her. I don't think they know where you two were or they would've beat me to you."

This felt so wrong. But she had to admit this stuff was way beyond her. The only people she ran from were bill collectors and the occasional Jehovah's Witness, and they didn't punch people in the face. "You promise?" She reluctantly held the keys over his open hand.

"Yes." He snatched them from her and started the vehicle. Seconds later, they were driving down the road. Miles passed. Too many miles. And several gas stations. A restaurant. A market. He could have left her at any one of those places.

"Where are we going?" Suddenly sick to her stomach, she twisted at the waist to look back. The road was too twisty-turny to see Omega anymore. "Abby."

"My friend's place is only a couple more miles up the road. I'll leave you there and then head back. Okay?"

Even though he was concentrating on the road up ahead and probably couldn't see her, she nodded. The huge lump of worry in her throat wouldn't let her speak.

"I'm sure she'll be okay," he said, clearly sensing her concern.

She nodded again.

Her mood didn't lift until he pulled into the driveway of a tidy little ranch. She scrambled out of the truck, hoping he'd open up the front door, let her inside and then leave right away.

Much to her relief, he moved like a guy on a mission. Opened the door with a key he found under a nearby bush. Flipped on some lights. Escorted her through the house, pointing out a few key rooms — kitchen, bathroom, bedroom.

There was only one bedroom.

He rushed to the front door, leaving her to trail behind him. The man moved fast. "I'll be back as soon as I can." He pulled her roughly against him and kissed her like there'd be no tomorrow. Then, leaving her barely standing, on legs that felt as sturdy as molten cheese, he ran out to her rental truck and drove off.

Abby.

She was too nervous to do anything more than use the bathroom or pace back and forth in front of the wide living room window.

Dawn had started to tint the sky to the east a purple-pink and a few early rising birds were tweeting. She could hear them through the three panes of glass. The sound did not calm her shredded nerves. Not at all.

Would she die from anxiety? She felt like she could jump right out of her skin. Her heart pounded against her breastbone in a quick staccato beat. Her legs still hadn't firmed up. They were soft and unsteady. She was sweating all over, despite the fact that the room was cool.

"Hurry, dammit!"

She glanced at the clock on the mantel. It was one of those old-fashioned reproductions. The kind that actually ticktocked. She had a similar clock in her house. Most of the time she found that sound soothing. Not this morning. Each tick marked another second she'd been in agony.

What a weird twist this trip had taken! When she'd left Chicago, she'd expected to come up here, veg out in front of a fire for a night, maybe drag Abby outside to do some hiking.

Lose herself in the beauty of her surroundings. Certainly not dash between the Yukon and back, it seemed one step ahead of disaster the whole time.

Gosh, what would she do if Raul didn't come back?

She'd been on many a camping trip. Before he'd died, her father had been an avid outdoorsman, and had insisted on hauling her around whenever he did anything outdoorsy. She'd known how to field dress a dear before she'd turned ten.

But this, this insanity was way beyond her comfort zone.

People turning into animals. Bad guys. Guns not sighted at clay targets or animals, but at people.

Her best friend alone in that building, in who knew how much trouble.

Ack!

She widened the range of her pacing, hoping some new terrain would distract her. Down the narrow hallway, into the bedroom, back down the hallway, into the kitchen. The living room. Then to the bedroom again.

Finally, the crunch and pop of gravel under tires signaled the approach of a vehicle. She ran to the front door and threw it open. It was fully daylight outside now, although the sun squatted low in the eastern sky.

He climbed out of the truck.

She waited.

No other doors opened.

She dashed outside. "Where's Abby?"

Raul's shoulders dropped several inches. He blinked slowly, like it was hard to find the strength to lift his eyelids.

"What?" she urged.

"I'm sorry." He shook his head. "They got her too."

"Who? Who got her?" Her wobbly knees turned to molten marshmallow. Afraid she was going to collapse this time, not him, she grabbed his arms and held on. "What happened?"

"I don't know what the hell is going on. I didn't know who the guys were that attacked us when we were in Tarik's office. No one's telling me anything. All I know is what I read, that a woman was escorted from the building at 0400 by an outside security team. It was on the security log."

"Security team?" Her racing heart rate slowed. "That could be good, right? Maybe they took her to jail or something. For breaking and entering or something." She'd take a felony over the alternative right now.

"Not likely. I think someone's covering up something big. The guys who attacked Tarik and me weren't security guards. They were paramilitary, dressed in body armor and carrying high-powered weapons."

"Oh my God. I knew we shouldn't have left her." Her knees buckled. She made her way on quaking legs to the front porch and sat. She cupped her hands over her face. Tears gathered in her burning eyes. "Why'd I let you leave her there?" she shouted. "I didn't want to! I knew it wasn't safe."

Raul stooped down and pulled her hands from her face. His expression softened. "We did what we had to. It was that or have all of us caught. And then we'd have no way of helping anybody. Would that be better? Remember, Tarik had already been taken into custody—"

"No, but..." Katie's hand trembled as she rubbed the tip of her nose. One fat tear dribbled down her cheek.

Raul wiped it away tenderly, and she inexplicably started aching for more of his touches. A kiss. She needed a kiss.

Now? Not now!

Raul palmed her cheek, his gaze fixed on her eyes, his brows heavy with concern. "They caught Abby within minutes of our leaving. If we'd stuck around, we would've been captured too." He licked his lips. "I've been looking for her, but just driving around any longer made no sense..."

She stared at his mouth. A sudden charge of yearning blazed through her body, literally knocking the air from her lungs.

Why was she getting turned on now? What was wrong with her? She shook her head in a feeble attempt to throw off the lust blasting through her body. "H-How will we find her?"

"I don't know."

"We have to." Desperate to put some distance between them, possibly the only cure for her raging hormones, she pushed to her feet and spun around to head back into the house. Her foot landed on a stone and her ankle twisted. Off kilter, she let out a little shriek, stumbled and nearly fell to the ground. "Dammit!"

Raul caught her and held her until she'd steadied herself. She was uncomfortably aware of the precise positions of both his hands, as well as all points of contact between his body and hers.

Tempted for some insane reason to sink into his embrace, she pushed away from him.

Releasing her, he said, "I'm sorry, baby. I did what I thought was best. There was no perfect way to handle that situation."

"Yeah, I know." Angry and confused and flushed with the heat of a yearning she didn't understand or want, she hurried inside.

She was not horny! Not while her friend was sitting somewhere, being held captive by assholes who would do who-knew-what.

Raul took one of her hands in his and, stepping around her, pulled her toward the bedroom. "Come on. You need some rest. While you're sleeping, I'll make a few phone calls, see what I can find out."

She swiped at her forehead as she followed him into the room. "Are you crazy? I can't go to sleep now. Abby needs—"

"We'll see about that." He pushed open the door.

Chapter Six

ೋ

Katie blinked open her eyes. For several seconds she had absolutely no clue where she was.

Then *he* shifted beside her and she remembered.

Raul.

She slowly rolled onto her side, moving carefully to avoid waking him. She glanced up. The shades were drawn. Was it daytime? Nighttime? How had she fallen asleep? Had Raul drugged her? How long had she been sleeping? Where was the clock?

Abby!

She jumped out of bed. Bathroom. She needed a bathroom. And she needed Raul to wake his ass up. "Raul! Raul!" she shook his shoulder.

He didn't budge.

Effing men. They slept like the dead.

She glanced at the clock. She was so out of whack, having been up for twenty-five hours straight the first day of her so-called vacation, then conking out in the car on the way back to Alaska. And then crashing again after coming to the cabin. She hadn't slept so much in years.

Was it five in the evening? Or five in the morning? Did it matter?

She needed to find Abby. Who cared what time it was?

A girl on a mission, and gratefully free of the distracting and bizarre horniness of earlier, she headed into the bathroom, took care of some personal business and freshened up a bit. No sense scaring everyone she came into contract with.

Once she was reasonably satisfied with the image in the mirror, she returned to the bedroom.

Raul was lying on his side, facing away from her. He was undressed, at least from the waist up. In his sleep, he'd pushed the covers down, giving her a clear view of his back and shoulders.

Clear lines defined his muscles and his skin was smooth, tan. A mini-wave of heat whooshed through her body.

Oh no.

Not wanting to risk getting turned on again and becoming distracted, she spun around and clamped her eyelids closed.

What the fuck was wrong with her?

"Raul!" she shouted, refusing to look at him. "Wake up!"

"Huh?" he said, sounding sleepy. His voice was a low, sexy rumble. "What're you doing? Come back to bed."

Suddenly there wasn't anything else she'd rather do.

"I can't," she said, even though she was slowly backing toward the bed. A soft touch on her shoulder made her stop moving. Made her stop breathing too.

"I made some headway while you were sleeping," he murmured into her right ear.

Goose bumps coated the right side of her body. "What'd you find out?" she asked, standing stock-still on the outside while quaking like a blade of grass in a hurricane on the inside.

A puff of warm breath caressed the side of her neck, just below her ear. "I have a lead on where they might be holding Abby and Tarik. But we need to wait until nightfall to go check it out."

"It's daytime?"

"Just after five in the evening. It'll be getting dark around seven, which means we have almost two hours...to rest." He reached around her back, placed his hands over her clothed breasts, and kneaded them.

"Are you sure…we shouldn't…be doingggggg…" A sigh slipped between her lips. Her neck became spineless, allowing her head to fall back against Raul's chest. Little tremors of pleasure rippled through her body.

Raul's hands strayed from her breasts. One skimmed over her shoulders until it reached her neck. The other ran down her side to her hip. His fingers combed through her hair before catching it. He pulled, semi-sharply, forcing her to drop her head to one side.

Soft kisses and nips, tongue and teeth on her neck raised goose bumps all over her upper body. Hot and cold. Chill and fire. She flexed the muscles of her back, arching it. Her bottom rubbed against his erection. He groaned softly into her ear, bit the tickly spot where her shoulder met her neck, and released her hair.

She reached around her back to fondle his cock but he grabbed her wrists and pinned them against her clothed backside. This did not make her happy. Now there was a barrier between her bottom and his cock. Plus she couldn't play with him.

She whimpered to communicate her frustration.

"Not yet, baby. I want to touch you first. Give you pleasure. Taste every inch of you." He wrapped an arm around her chest, just above her breasts, and pulled, dragging her backward. She shuffled with him until the back of her knees hit something and she dropped onto her butt. Raul released her hands a split second before she landed on his lap, her back against his chest.

He reached around with both hands now, caught the hem of her knit top and pulled it over her head. "I don't know what's happening. I want you. All the time. When I'm asleep. When I'm getting my ass beat. When I'm running for my life or fighting for my friend's life. It makes no fucking sense." He tossed her shirt aside before reaching for the center clasp of her bra. He licked a tickly path down one shoulder while unfastening her bra and pushing the straps down her arms.

She disposed of that garment the same way he had her shirt.

"But I'm tired of trying to figure it out." His hands closed over her breasts, kneading, pinching, pulling. Simmering heat pooled between her legs. She used her toes to push against the floor, leverage, allowing her to ground her bottom against his lap. "And I'm tired of fighting it."

Her body craved more. She reached down to unfasten her jeans.

Hot. Too hot.

Her eyelids shuttered out the room, enclosing her in a world of swirling colors and building need. The button holding her pants fastened sprang free of the hole. Burning up from the inside out, she fumbled with the fly. Raul's hands came to her aid. They pushed, pulled, until her jeans were down around her thighs. She had to tip her hips up to free them. Once they dropped below her knees, she kicked them off.

Only a pair of satin panties remained. They had to come off. Now.

She lifted her bottom, prepared to pull them down. But Raul stopped her. He held her hips, his fingers digging into her flesh, lifting her off his lap. She felt him slide out from underneath her. She opened her eyes to see where he was going.

He stood directly in front of her, completely nude, and sporting both a raging erection and a strained, desperate expression, like a starving man looking at a juicy steak he wouldn't be allowed to eat.

She smiled. "Are you okay?"

"I'm not sure. I've never felt this way before. I...hurt...I want you so bad. I ache to take you. To have you submit to me.

To make you mine. Yet at the same time I know I have no right." He closed the distance between them. Despite the fact that she was standing, he towered over her. It was one of those moments when she truly felt small, even a little powerless. For once, it wasn't a bad feeling. Not at all.

"I know what you mean." She stared at his chest because it was oh-so worthy of several minutes — make that hours — of her undivided attention. Normally, she didn't go for the smooth-as-a-baby's-butt look, but on Raul it was beyond perfect. His skin was deeply tanned, just the way she liked it.

She reached out to touch him but he caught her hand in his fist and jerked it behind her back. She made a little yip of surprise. He'd moved so quickly, she hadn't anticipated it.

The chest she'd been admiring was now much closer, licking proximity. Her nose at nipple level. Her tongue darted out, moistening lips that felt like they'd been exposed to at least eighteen straight hours of desert sun.

Raul shifted, pressing his bulk even more firmly against her. She felt his chest inflate with every inhalation. He rocked his hips, grinding his rigid cock against her abdomen.

Little wakes of pleasure rippled up and down inside her. She stood very still, not sure what to expect. Her nerves were jittery and raw. Uncertainty and arousal blended, producing a bizarre reaction inside her body. Heat and cold. Tremors. A racing heart, beating too fast to deliver adequate oxygen to her brain.

There was a strange sense of danger in the air. She could almost smell it, slightly tangy like citrus.

He grabbed her free hand and pulled it behind her back too, gathering it with the other into one of his fists. One hand free now, he ran light, teasing touches over her buttocks, up to the small of her back and then back down. He trembled against her.

Or was that her quaking against him?

"I'm trying…holding back," he murmured.

Was he speaking to her?

Did she want him to hold back?

He tightened his hold on her wrists, until the bones ground into each other.

The mild pain only amplified the sensual tension thick in the air, the heat buzzing through her body like zaps of electricity. Her nipples hardened, the tips skimming against his warm skin, the slight touch adding yet another sensation to the already overwhelming mixture pummeling her body.

She closed her eyes again and inhaled deeply.

There it was again, the spicy scent. The smell of danger.

She liked it.

"Have you ever had a man take complete control? In every way?" he asked, his breath warming her left shoulder.

Every way? More than he already had? What did he mean? She shivered as goose bumps popped out of her skin, coating the entire left side of her body. "No."

"I will be the first." He bit her neck, not so hard he'd break skin, but hard enough to get her attention.

She stiffened against him again. A breathy moan slipped between her lips. The muscles along her left side tightened, her shoulder lifted and her head tipped slightly to the side.

He released her neck and swirled his tongue over the stinging skin, licking away the pain. Pleasure. Pain. The line between them blurred. Her body was swept up in a swelling need. What had started as a mild burning was quickly growing into an uncontrollable blaze.

She let her head drop back, welcoming him to bite her again, to take her, to do whatever he wanted.

He pushed her backward, until the backs of her legs struck the bed, and she landed on her butt on the mattress. She lifted her eyelids as she lowered herself to her back.

He stood over her, seeming to be part man, part beast. Not in a literal sense, like Tarik, but in a purely sexual sense.

His expression was fierce. Focused. His eyes narrowed as he stared down at her, as he reached down to lift her into his arms. He held her against him for a moment, and she closed her eyes and soaked up the heat radiating from his skin. It was a tender, sweet moment where neither spoke and their breathing slowed, falling into a synchronized pace and rhythm, as if they were one, breathing together.

After at least twenty heartbeats of quiet bliss, he positioned her on the bed, spread-eagled. There were no ties to bind her. There was no need for them. His dark gaze held her in place.

She physically felt the weight of his gaze upon her body, felt its heat as it drifted from her face, over her chest, stomach. It rested at the apex of her thighs, where it kindled the blaze that had been burning since she'd woken.

She ached to open her legs wider, but she resisted the urge to move. Somehow she knew he wanted her to stay still. Stone still. And she wanted to please him. So much that her heart felt heavier than concrete.

He ran a finger up the sole of her foot, tickling it.

It was difficult, but she kept still.

He bent over and licked a winding path up the side of her leg, beginning at her ankle and ending at her hip. Again, she remained motionless.

He smiled at her with raw male satisfaction. "You're naturally submissive. It's in your blood."

If it was, this was the first she knew of it. Her mother, in particular, probably wouldn't have agreed with that statement. But at the moment, she reveled in the affirming glimmer in his eye.

"You've remembered my promise. You'll get your reward. When this is all over and we can return to my house, I have some things I'd like to show you. Some things I'm sure you'll enjoy."

She wished they could go there right now!

"Spread your legs for me. Show me how wet you are. How much you want me."

She dragged her ankles further apart, leaving her legs lying flat on the bed. The muscles lining her inner thighs burned from the stretch. A lot of other parts burned too, from the flares blasting from his eyes as he watched her.

His tongue slipped between his lips, moistening them before he spoke again, "Wider."

Another wave of wanting surged through her body at the single word, at the way he was looking at her, at the swell of his biceps when he lifted his arm to comb his fingers through his hair.

There was only one way she could open her legs wider. She bent her knees and pulled them back.

So open. Exposed.

Would he touch her? Please?

"At home, I have a dildo. If I had it right now, I'd fuck your pussy with it while I fucked your ass with my cock."

How she longed for that!

"Have you ever been fucked in the ass?" He ran an index finger along her slick folds, dragging some of her juices back, to her anus.

"No."

"You'll like it. I know you will."

She wasn't one hundred percent sure, but a part of her was curious to see if he was right.

His finger pushed at her hole, begging entry. It burned a little as he increased the pressure. She sucked in a little gulp of air. Her pussy contracted.

He pulled his finger away, replacing it with his tongue.

"Ohhhhh," she heard herself say as he teased her anus. Saliva and juices from her pussy ran down between her ass cheeks. His finger returned, this time aided by the cool slickness. It slipped inside.

She trembled.

His finger slowly pistoning in and out of her ass, he turned his attention to her clit. His tongue danced over it, assaulting it with quick, teasing swipes that made her breathless and panting and on the verge of orgasm.

When the agony was beyond her ability to take, he pulled his finger from her ass, kneeled before her, gripped her hips in his hands and entered her pussy.

He drove in and out of her, pelvis slapping against her bottom with each inward thrust. The air blasting from her lungs with each withdrawal. She closed her fingers around the scratchy covers, a desperate attempt at anchoring herself.

Unlike the last time, this time he fucked her hard and fast, not a bad thing at all. Her body reacted swiftly, the proof of its appreciation blasting out from her center. Hot surges of wanting, like rolling waves on the shore. Crashing over her.

They were coming closer, harder, faster.

And then he stopped, pulled out and pushed her over on her belly. "I'm going to fuck your ass now."

She nodded. "Yes. Do it now." She raised her hips up and scooted her knees underneath. She left her chest flat on the bed.

Tingles and twitches erupted all over her skin, like mini fireworks, as he spread her juices between her cheeks and gently prodded her hole with his cock. He was huge. What was she thinking?

He pushed harder. Her anus burned, but the pain only increased her pleasure. When he slipped inside, thrusting a finger into her pussy at the same time, the first spasm of a powerful climax rippled through her body. The second, third and fourth were intensified by the added sensation of Raul's cock and finger stroking her intimately. At the fifth one, he growled, dug his fingers into her hips and seated himself deep inside her anus.

"Ohhhhh yesssss," he said in a voice that suddenly sounded much deeper than it had a few moments before.

Was she imagining things?

A bizarre sensation charged through Raul's body as he climaxed, a weird buzzing that started in his center and spread out. Pleasant at first, it swiftly changed, becoming painful then excruciating. He withdrew from Katie, rolled to his side and cried out in agony, but the voice he heard blast from his throat wasn't his own.

What was happening to him?

His muscles were stretching and tearing. His bones popping and cracking. It felt as if he was being torn apart from the inside out.

He prayed for unconsciousness, but it didn't come. Just one second after another of agonizing torture.

His mind was slowing, his thoughts growing muddied, like he'd had too much whiskey. Sensations took over where thoughts had faded, growing stronger until they were almost painful. Scents invaded his nostrils, some pleasant, like the lingering aroma of an aroused woman, some bitter.

The pain inside his body was easing, allowing him to focus on the sounds he heard. Breathing. Was that his own or Katie's?

He opened his eyes, discovering he'd fallen to the floor. Katie was clear over on the other side of the room, visibly shaking and pale. He felt strange, wild and predatory. The way she looked at him intensified that feeling. She was terrified. Her gaze dropped and he looked down, curious to see what she was staring at.

What he saw made him stop breathing mid-inhalation.

Two thick legs had taken the place of his arms. Shaggy dark brown fur, thicker than a dog's hair, coated them. He raised a hand and stared at the huge paw that had replaced one of his hands. His fingernails had lengthened into hooked black claws.

What?

"R-Raul?" Katie whispered through chattering teeth.

He lifted his head and tried to nod. Would she understand him? Would she stop fearing him? He could smell it, her terror. The scent was doing things to him, stirring desires and urges.

Chase. Take. Possess.

His thoughts were getting cloudier, images taking the place of words in his head. Images of Katie's body, lying under his.

He closed his eyes and inhaled. The scent of her, his woman, was everywhere. Sweet.

Still inhaling deeply, drinking in her aroma, he moved closer. He sniffed the bed, the sheets. Hunger raged through him. Not a hunger for food but a hunger for Katie. He felt a growl vibrate in his chest. It rumbled up his throat and out his mouth, taking the form of a deep roar when it escaped.

Katie screamed, the smell and sound of her fear driving him to her. He jumped over the bed, clearing it easily, and raced across the room. He stood on his hind legs and pinned her between the wall and his body. He bent his head down and sniffed her hair.

The sound of her crying was muffled at first, but it grew louder. She was saying something but he couldn't understand. What language was she speaking?

Her neck. He had a strange urge to take her neck in his mouth, to taste her skin. He towered over her, had to bend slightly and shift positions to reach.

Slowly he closed his mouth around the slender column. He felt her stiffen against him, heard the sound of her shallow breaths in his ears.

Oh yes! Yes. She was submitting to him. He tightened his hold.

Chapter Seven

ℰↃ

Jonathan Westlake had dreamed of this day for many years, when he'd sit in this office, at this desk, and see the words "Chairman and Chief Executive Officer" after his name. But he'd never expected that dream to actually come true.

It was too fucking good to believe!

To think just last week he'd been V.P. of Corporate Communications, and now he was The Guy, The One On Top, in charge of everything. He'd spent the better part of his first day on the job in a daze, too overwhelmed by it all to absorb much of anything. Huo Kwan, President and COO, had done his best to help. But there was so much to learn, and for being The Guy On Top, he had a lot of people to answer to.

Now, hours after most of Omega's staff and management had left for the day, he was sitting at his desk, waiting for a virtual conference with a key scientific advisor in Europe, Albert Manassa, Ph.D.

The flat panel computer screen in front of him showed a room but no man. It had displayed this scene for over an hour. Omega's new CEO was getting impatient. He'd made reservations at his wife's favorite restaurant for tonight, to celebrate his promotion. And after that...he had big plans for the evening.

"Perhaps we should reschedule for another time," he said yet again into the computer cam.

"Dr. Manassa will be with you in just a moment," a female voice repeated, the speaker's face out of range of the camera. "He was unexpectedly delayed, but he'll be here shortly."

"Very well." Evidently the doctor had a thing for keeping his appointments, no matter who he inconvenienced.

Knowing there was no chance he'd make the reservation for six-thirty, he muted the web cam's microphone and called the restaurant back to change his reservation. He'd damn well better be able to make a nine o'clock. It was almost six now. Taking drive time into consideration, that gave Manassa a couple of hours. He hoped the delay meant the doctor would be in a hurry to take care of whatever business they had and move on.

He called his wife's cell and left an apology and peace offering then reactivated the microphone again.

Moments later, he heard shuffling from his computer speakers. And voices, a man and the woman who'd spoken to him — without having ever shown her face, which he found a little odd.

Finally, a gentleman he guessed to be in his mid-sixties took a seat in front of the computer. His hair was neatly trimmed, white and silver, as was his beard. He was wearing a white lab coat, his name embroidered on the pocket in black thread. "My apologies, Mr. Westlake," he said, with a slight Spanish accent, "for making you wait."

"No problem," he lied. "How may I help you?"

"Before Dr. Torborg…had his unfortunate accident, he had promised to deliver to me a list of names, the participants in a clinical trial of an experimental drug labeled, 'Trofim'. I am hoping you are able to locate the information. I need it if I am going to review the findings of this trial in time."

Being the former head of Corporate Communications, he was a little surprised to learn the former CEO had sidestepped him in dealing with the doctor. He quickly made the assumption the project had to have been top priority. "Let me see what I can come up with." He swiveled in his chair, facing a second computer screen. "How do you spell the drug?"

"T-R-O-F-I-M"

Jonathan called up a "find" screen and typed in the drug name as it was spelled. He located several files, all password protected.

He hoped Torborg had stored the passwords in his computer, to allow him to open the documents, or he was screwed. He double-clicked on the first.

A password screen popped up but the password was not automatically inserted like he'd hoped.

He turned toward the video-conference monitor. "Sorry, it's going to take some time. I don't have the password."

The doctor shook his head. "Do you want your client to take this drug to the FDA without my reviewing this material?"

"I don't know if I have a choice." He stared at the screen for a second then searched through the desk drawers, Torborg's planner, his calendar, assorted office supplies. No list of passwords. Finally, at a loss where to check next, he looked up Kwan's cell number and gave him a call. Less than a minute later, he had the one password that opened all of Torborg's files. Torborg had thankfully been lax in the security department.

The document opened.

He read the first dozen or so names on the list, surprised to find he recognized one. Tarik Evert.

He skimmed the rest of the document before saving an unprotected copy. Turning again to Manassa, he asked, "What's your email address?" He typed in the address and fired off a quick email before printing off a copy for later perusal. His curiosity was piqued.

The doctor verified he'd received the message and thanked Westlake, promising to make quick work of reviewing the study, before their team turned in the results to the FDA. Then he signed off.

Eager to meet his wife for dinner, and knowing an evening out meant hours of fucking, he shut down his computer, locked up his office and headed out. He left the document sitting in the printer. He'd look at it tomorrow.

This CEO had had enough work for one day. Time to play.

* * * * *

Alberto Guzman made sure the video conference was disconnected before speaking. "You have your orders and the first payment," he said in Spanish as he queued the document to print. "They all must die. You have forty-eight hours."

The assassin took the list off the printer and left without speaking a word.

* * * * *

Standing there, a prisoner of the largest animal she'd ever come into contact with, a million thoughts raced through Katie's head.

Oh my God!

I'm going to die! I don't want to die.

I'm going to be eaten alive by a bear!

Please, just let it end quickly!

Ohmygod, ohmygod, ohmygod!

Once the flurry of panic had subsided, eased somewhat by the fact that the bear pinning her to the wall hadn't broken skin yet, despite the fact that she'd been standing there at least an eternity and a minute, her brain set about constructing more rational thoughts.

Raul was like Tarik. They changed into animals somehow.

How exactly had Abby reacted to Tarik in his bear form?

Naturally, Katie had been a little overwhelmed by everything going on in the hotel's parking lot to notice nuances, but she had noted one thing because it had been so obvious—Abby had shown no fear.

Damn if that wasn't nearly impossible with an animal nibbling on a girl's neck! How had Abby managed?

Must have been that yoga-or-whatever Abby did religiously, every night, come hell or Midnight Madness at the mall. Katie teased her about it all the time. Now, she was wondering who the moron was.

Figuring she had no other choices, besides flipping out and becoming a snack to a bear, she closed her eyes and made a halfhearted attempt at turning her mind to more pleasant thoughts. Initially, the images that came to mind were far from delightful—her poor little self being torn apart by the beast holding her. But slowly, her fear faded. More peaceful images took their place in her head—a stream in the woods. Sunlight glittering off the water. Little critters skittering about. A naked Raul—human—standing waist-deep in the water, crooking a finger at her. An invitation she had no interest in ignoring.

The bear's hold on her neck loosened. Its hot breath slowed. Despite her eyes still being closed, she knew the instant the bear had backed away.

She just about collapsed from relief. It was working! She continued to think happy thoughts, of a naked Raul. Her body warmed. Her cheeks. Her stomach. Her pussy.

A soft touch ran up her leg.

God help her, she shouldn't feel this way about an animal, but that touch felt soooooo good.

"Katie," he whispered.

The bear could talk? She opened one eye.

Whoo hooo! Raul wasn't a bear anymore. He was a man…an extremely *happy* man.

She was quickly becoming one very relieved—not to mention happy—girl, too. Mild ripples of arousal blended with the huge waves of relief at not being eaten alive, until she was warm and giddy. "Wow," was all she said as she stared at the evidence of his emotional state — all ten inches or so. "Glad to have you back."

"Are you talking to him...or me?" Raul teased.

Her checks about burst into flame. "You." She intentionally dragged her gaze away from his erection, up over lean, tight abdominal muscles, a chest that made her drool, to his face.

He was smiling. God, what a smile. She liked him a whole lot better as a man.

"Hi," he said.

"Hi," she echoed.

His tongue darted out and swept over his lower lip, leaving a sheen that made it look more scrumptious than ever. "I don't know what happened a few minutes ago, but I can tell you this — I want you. Now." He lunged forward, swept her into his arms and tossed her onto the bed. He crawled toward her, giving her the kind of look she'd dreamed about on many a lonely night.

She held her breath as she fell onto her back. His chest pressed down on hers, his widespread legs pinning her hips to the bed. She hadn't fully recovered from her earlier scare, but the smidge of fear that lingered only made the desire simmering within her veins all the more potent. She closed her eyes and succumbed to the sensations sweeping through her body. The chills elicited by his tickling touches to her neck. The heat stirred by the scent of man and sex carried to her nose on a cool draft. The sound of her own soft moans and sighs.

"Shit." Raul abruptly stopped what he was doing and lifted his head.

Bewildered and a little disappointed, she blinked open one eye. "What's wrong?"

His head was turned, his gaze focused on the bedroom door. "I thought I heard something."

"Something? Like what kind of something?" She tried to sit up but his weight held her pinned flat.

He grumbled a few words under his breath and rolled off her. "I'll go check. Stay here." He scooped up his pants and stepped into them.

She hadn't heard anything. What did he think was out there?

"Okay." Curious but also worried, she scooted to the edge of the bed, halting only long enough to watch the muscles of his back and shoulders ripple when he pulled a T-shirt over his head.

Raul's mind and mood came crashing back to earth, his sudden change having nothing to do with Bryson's untimely interruption. If anything, he'd done Raul a favor by forcing him drag his sorry ass out of bed and his mind back to reality.

Everything had changed. He might not have wanted to accept that fact earlier, when he'd been too distracted, by desire, to think. Now that his hunger for Katie had eased—for the time being—he was thinking much more clearly now.

It had been painful, turning his friend Tarik over to the goons Omega had hired. He'd done it only because of his brother.

Granted, earlier this morning he'd done what he could to help Tarik. Once he'd made certain Katie was safe and he'd tracked down his brother, hiding deep in the woods about a quarter mile from Omega, he'd tried to go back to Omega and find Tarik and Katie's friend. He'd intended to make sure they received the medical care he'd been assured they'd needed.

Despite his source's constant assurances, something didn't feel right about all of this.

Not sure what kind of reception he'd face, he'd been tense as he punched in the security code. He'd been met at the door by a security team he didn't recognize. No one could tell him where Tarik had been taken, even though he was still officially the head of Omega's security department. They all claimed to know nothing about the evening's activities. There was nothing on the log about Tarik. The attack. Katie's friend.

It was as if nothing had happened.

He checked the security tapes.

The footage from cameras one, three and four had been tampered with. Three and four should have shown them entering the building and going to Tarik's office. Three was positioned in the lobby, near the entry to the breakroom. Four was up in the hallway, outside Tarik's office. One was outside, positioned at the front door.

The footage supposedly taped by all three cameras showed absolutely no activity. The time and date running along the top of the recordings were accurate.

Someone had gone to some length to hide the evening's events.

One of the new security officers, a young guy with a military hair cut and crooked nose, probably from having been broken more than once, stuck pretty close to him as he reviewed the tapes. He watched every move Raul made but didn't say anything to stop him.

Regardless, Raul bristled.

He hated it when people watched over his shoulder. Figuring he'd wait until night shift to do any more investigating at Omega, when the security team would be smaller and hopefully less nosy, he'd headed out.

Hopefully he had plenty of time to find Tarik and Abby. He couldn't see a reason why a company like Omega, respected in the industry, would want anyone's blood sullying its reputation. Come to think of it, if those guys last night had meant business, they could have killed Bryson days ago, instead of keeping him alive, a captive, a potential witness.

Right?

Damn, he hoped so!

He'd planned to continue the search after picking up Bryson and swinging by the cabin to drop him off and check on Katie. He wasn't exactly crazy about bringing Bryson to the cabin, knowing the kinds of questions his presence could raise, but there was no other choice. Bryson was in danger. He had to protect him.

He hadn't expected to lose so much time though, thanks to a new but major weakness—his urgent need for Katie.

When he was around her, he could barely think about anything else. He'd never taken drugs, never had a physical dependency on any substance. But he had a sudden appreciation for how quickly an addiction could take over a person's life. He felt crippled, like he was losing control. Of his mind. His body. His life. How would he hold on?

Worse yet, how long would he be able to fight the temptation to just give up?

Now that he too was infected with the virus, or whatever it was that caused him to turn into an animal, the clock was racing. He needed Tarik, sooner rather than later, and alive.

He needed help, a cure. He could see already he didn't like what it was turning him into—a guy held slave to his baser urges.

Damn it! He cursed himself and the position he'd been put in. He kissed Katie's eyelids. "Be right back," he whispered. "Stay here until I tell you it's safe."

She hiked herself up on one elbow when he bent over and pressed a kiss to her forehead. "Should I get dressed? Will we be leaving in a hurry?"

"I doubt it. The sound I heard is probably only an animal that's found its way into the attic. I just want to be sure. And as far as Tarik and Abby are concerned, I need to talk to a few people before we go anywhere. We need answers."

She gave him a worried look.

"Get dressed. Put on something comfortable. I'll be back in a few." He closed the door behind him as he left, hoping she wouldn't follow him out. No doubt she'd be surprised to find Bryson on the couch.

He hadn't told her about his brother for a reason, because he hadn't wanted to explain what his brother was doing here. Or more specifically, how he'd traded his brother for his best friend...and hers.

Made him look like a first-class shit.

Which he was, of course. But he didn't want her thinking that.

"Hey." He nudged his sleeping brother. "Get up. What are you making all that noise about?"

"What?" his brother said, sounding exasperated as he tended to do when roused from a deep sleep. "I didn't make any noise."

"You're pounding on the wall like jackrabbit trying to kick its way out of a trash can. We have a problem."

"What's that? Did the bastards find us already?" Bryson did a lot of blinking as he sat up. He stretched, rolled his head from side to side. His vertebrae snapped.

"No. But I caught it."

"Caught what?"

"I caught the virus or whatever it is. I just turned into a fucking bear. Just like Tarik."

"You did what?" Bryson froze mid-roll and snapped his head up so fast Raul thought he might get whiplash. "Did you say you turned into a bear?"

"Yeah. Tarik did too. Evidently that's why those bastards kidnapped you—to make me chase after him and drag his ass back here. They said they wanted to get him medical care."

"Ohhhhh. Shit." Bryson dropped his gaze, looking very much like the little boy who'd once been caught stealing money out of their mother's purse.

"What?"

"I had no idea why they'd taken me."

"Yeah. Sooooo?" He encouraged his brother to elaborate with a wave of one hand. Bryson was hiding something. Something important. Raul could feel it in his gut.

"I didn't want to tell anyone, not even you. I-I thought I was going nuts..." Bryson looked up and swallowed and Raul knew instantly what he was about to say. "It's happening to me too. The changing. I thought at first I was hallucinating or something. But then it happened again and again. I-I finally learned to control it. Kind of. It still takes over sometimes and I can't stop it."

Raul's heart halted, mid-beat, or at least he could swear it had. His brother too? What the hell was this? "We have to find Tarik...if it isn't...God, I hope they were telling me the truth. For his sake as well as ours. We have to find out what's causing this. How to stop it. Obviously, Omega has something to do with it. The research they're conducting—"

"Raul? Are you out there?" Katie shouted from the general direction of the hallway.

"Shoot!" Raul spat as he yanked on his brother's arm, half dragging him toward the door. "Get up and pretend like you've just come in."

"Yeah, yeah. Got it." Bryson caught his coat in his fist as he stumbled by the coat tree toward the front door. "You didn't tell her I was out here all night?"

"No, and I'm not going to explain it now."

"Raul?" Katie repeated. She was in the room now. He turned to face her. Her head was tipped, her brow furrowed. She was dressed, although her feet were still bare. She crossed her arms over her chest. "We have a visitor? Where'd he come from?"

"It's okay. This is my little brother, Bryson. He...uh...I called him last night and told him what's up. He lives down the road. Not far. That's the sound I heard, Bryson knocking. He's going to help us find Tarik and your friend, Allie."

"Abby. Her name is Abby." Katie's gaze dropped to Bryson's unshod feet.

"I left my boots outside. They were muddy," Bryson explained.

Quick thinking.

"How...thoughtful," Katie said flatly.

Diversion. Time for a distraction. Before Katie started asking the kinds of questions that would get him into trouble. "So, my brother here is a world-class hacker. Can get into any computer system on the planet. He's going to hack into Omega's system and see what he can find out."

"I...? Yes, I'd better get right on that." Bryson shuffled past Katie. "Computer?"

"In there. Everyone has a computer these days." Pointing toward a pine electronics armoire, Raul gave Katie a reassuring smile. "We'll find them."

"You said you had a lead. Right? You found out something last night while I was sleeping."

"I did say that..." *Shit!* "And I did...have a lead. A good lead. But I...checked it out this morning and it looks like..."

Katie frowned.

"Okay, I wasn't exactly honest with you when I said I had a lead."

"Then you don't know where they are? And you delayed looking for them, telling me we had time to..." she glanced Bryson's way, "'rest'? When we should have been looking for them? My best friend! They have my best friend!" Her voice was rising with each word she said. Her face was growing redder too. Morphing from a soft pink to a deep magenta.

Oh boy. That was one angry woman. "There's no reason to assume—"

210

"Bastard!" She swung at him, slugging him in the chest. He didn't bother to block it. "You fucking...jerk!" she screamed, pelting him with her fists. One, two, three blows landed on his chest, stomach, face. He didn't care. They weren't particularly painful. Not to mention he really did deserve every single belt. And some.

He had no excuse. His brother had been safe, and although he'd hoped to search for Tarik during the daylight hours, he'd been too overcome by his need for Katie to leave the cabin. He'd tried. At least a dozen times but he simply couldn't walk out of the room.

He was fucking weak!

While his friend was being poked and prodded by doctors of unknown repute, he had been prodding Katie.

He was a fucking lowlife shit. Worst than that. Lowlife snail-scum shit.

Clearly running out of gas, Katie stopped swinging and just glared at him. "Aren't you going to say anything?"

Was it time to come clean and tell her everything? For some reason her looking at him like that, with something damn near hatred in her slitted eyes, made his insides feel like they'd been put through a meat grinder.

He needed everything to be okay between them. Now.

He drew in a much-needed deep breath and prepared to tell her everything, even the part about him leaving Abby behind on purpose, hoping she'd buy all of them some time. "I—"

"It was my fault," Bryson said before Raul had gotten more than that one word out."

"Really." Katie's response wasn't a question. It was a statement. A very clear statement. She didn't trust either one of them to tell the truth.

"Yes," Bryson said, from the other side of the room. He was perched on a wooden chair, the computer booting up in front of him. "He was waiting for me to get back."

"Back from where?"

Bryson turned around, punched a few buttons and then answered, "From Omega. I was supposed to be sneaking in to find out where Tarik had been taken. But I'm a better hacker than spy. Didn't find out a goddamn thing."

His baby brother was bailing him out. That was a change, a change he wasn't sure he liked. It was always the other way around. The older brother was the responsible one, the one who was supposed to take care of everyone else, younger siblings, mother. That's why he'd left the military—hadn't been there for his family when they'd needed him.

"Yeah," Raul agreed, reluctantly going along with Bryson's slight alteration of the facts, while adding a touch of the truth to make their excuse slightly more convincing. If Katie truly knew him, she'd never believe he'd send his baby brother on an errand as potentially dangerous as this. But she didn't. Not yet. At least he hoped not. "I was waiting for Bryson because no one at Omega is going to tell me a goddamn thing. I learned that last night when I went back. Whoever has Tarik is hiding things from me, from the head of security. Someone from Omega is tied to this somehow but I'm not sure who or how. Tarik and Abby are supposed to be receiving medical care, but I'm not sure where. Until we know exactly what's going on and who is involved, we need to be invisible."

"Oh."

"Take it from me," Bryson added, "these guys mean business. I don't know who they are, or what they want, but they aren't your average everyday ambulance drivers."

"We need to plan carefully or…"

The look on Katie's face kept Raul from finishing that sentence.

He pulled her to him and held her tightly. Her sweet scent filled his nostrils and the hunger he had hoped had been sated for a while stirred inside him again.

Not now, he silently chastised his erect cock.

He struggled to push his mounting lust aside. Control. That was the key. His mind had to control his body. He closed his eyes. His hand ran up and down her back in a slow, soothing motion. Little surges of raw desire rippled through his body and battered at his defenses but he dug in his mental heels and refused to give up. He concentrated on thoughts of Tarik. "We're going to find them. I don't believe whoever is behind all this wants Tarik and Abby dead. At least not right away. They want to do medical tests of some kind or treat them for some bizarre infection before it spreads. Or they're trying to get to the bottom of what's happening to Tarik. To me." He kissed the top of her head. The scent of her skin filled his nostrils, deflecting his thoughts for a brief instant. But he fought for control again. "That doesn't mean we should go rushing in like a bunch of half-assed fools playing hero. The men who attacked us at Omega had equipment I've never seen before. Weapons. Body armor. I haven't seen anything like it in the military. Not in private security either. It's right out of the movies. And for what? To take two unarmed civilians into custody to get them medical care?"

Katie nodded. "I see what you mean."

"Whoever is behind this has money. Power. And they're operating outside the law for a reason we don't understand yet. It's a very dangerous situation. We're operating in the dark. No intel. Outmanned. Outgunned…"

"I understand now," Katie said to his chest.

"I'm in," Bryson exclaimed, facing the computer. "Where to now?"

Katie stepped out of his embrace. It physically hurt to have her be so near but not touch her. Determined to win yet another battle, he bit his lip and curled his fingers into tight fists. He would not pull her back to him.

"See what you can find in Torborg's files. T-O-R-B-O-R-G. I don't know a lot about computers but I think most of those guys keep their files on the servers." His voice sounded strained, even to his own ears.

Katie looked over her shoulder at him, worry etching shallow lines across her forehead and at the outer corners of her eyes.

"Got it," Bryson said, calling her attention back to him. His fingers flew over the keyboard, typing in letters, numbers. "He has his files in a password-protected folder."

Raul stared at Katie's back, at the slender column of her neck and asked, "Will you be able to break the password?"

"Yeah. No problem. Omega's security sucks. A five-year-old could hack into this system. What a pathetic excuse for a firewall."

Strange, that Omega would hire a group of men with the latest technology in body armor and weaponry to muscle a couple of unarmed civilians into protective custody for supposed medical care while being so lax in day-to-day security. It made no sense.

A guy who'd been trained to expect the worst, regardless of the facts presented to him, it made him nervous as hell.

All around, virtually as well as physically, Omega's security systems sucked. He'd suggested upgrades several times and they'd been quickly refused. Why?

"Come here and tell me which ones you'd like to see," Bryson said.

Raul stood next to Katie, behind Bryson's chair. Struggling to concentrate on the conversation, instead of the point of contact between her arm and his, he read the file names in the directory. My Documents. Letters and Faxes. Cost Analyses. Trofim? What was that? "That one." He pointed at the screen.

Bryson clicked on it, opening up a file with several documents in it. "Now where to?"

"I guess start at the top."

Bryson pointed the mouse at the first document and clicked. A window popped up, asking for a password. "Let's see if this guy's as lazy as I think he is." Bryson typed in a password. The document opened. "Oh yes, he is. Probably used the same password for everything. Not the smartest thing to do from a security standpoint."

Raul skimmed the document, a written report of some kind, detailing the procedure and results of some study. It was clinical, written in medical jargon he didn't understand. But from what he was able to interpret, nothing stood out. "Try the next one."

"Okay."

The second file was a spreadsheet, with names, addresses and phone numbers.

"Looks like a list of the people in the trial," Bryson reasoned, echoing Raul's thoughts.

"Yeah." His eyes ran down the first part of the list, until he hit the bottom of the page. "Page down. I want to see if I recognize any of the names."

"Okay." Bryson scrolled down.

Raul skimmed to the center of the second page and then halted. "Tarik Evert," he read aloud. "Go to the last page."

"Okay." Bryson scrolled to the last few entries.

Bryson Zant.

Raul Zant.

"What the hell?" Raul said, knowing in his gut that this was it, the connection they were looking for. "Print it out."

"What? The spreadsheet?"

"All of it, every single document in this file. None of it may make sense to us, but maybe it will to Tarik, and we don't want to take any chances that someone could delete these files before he has a chance to look at them." He reached down to pull the first page of names off the printer. "I think we should take a drive, see if any of these other people have been 'contacted' yet. Maybe if they have, they can tell us something."

"Or maybe they're all gone too," Katie said softly.

He hadn't wanted to think about that possibility, although it had been lurking in the back of his mind.

Then again, if Omega had wanted all the people on that list to disappear, why hadn't he been taken into custody when he'd gone back to Omega last night?

"They're not. At least not yet. Because if Omega had wanted everyone on that list, they would've captured me. I don't know what's going on. The pieces still aren't fitting."

"Oh boy, look at this," Bryson said, his voice low. He pointed at the computer screen.

There, in black and white, typed into a saved email were five words that turned Raul's blood to ice, "Abort. Eliminate all subjects."

Chapter Eight

❧

"Oh. My. God!" A jolt of fear shot through Katie's body exactly three seconds after she read the email on the computer screen. "What is this? What's going on?"

"Looks like we're subjects of some kind of experiment," Raul reasoned as he grabbed her arms and pulled her away from the computer. "You don't need to read any more."

"Like hell I don't!" She jerked, trying to shake herself free. Why was he holding her so tightly? Not letting her read more? He needed to help her. Help her find Abby, not manhandle her and hide information. "My best friend is tied up in this somehow, not to mention…" She stopped struggling when he flattened her against him. She looked up, into his face.

What did she see in his eyes? Could it be…genuine concern?

Her heart stopped beating for a fraction of a second.

Impossible. He couldn't…not really…it was too soon. Men didn't develop those kinds of feelings so quickly. They simply weren't capable of it.

But she was.

"In case you haven't noticed," she said, "I kind of like you, despite the fur and fangs."

He turned her around, placing his bulk between her and the computer. "And I like you too." He used his fingers to make quotation marks in the air as he said the word like. "A lot more than I ever thought possible. Which is why I think you need to leave. Tonight."

She shook her head, and continued to do so for the next several minutes, despite his drawn mouth and slitted eyes. "No. No, no, no!"

"Go. Home!" He tightened his grip on her upper arms and gave her two gentle shakes, one to punctuate each word. "Go back to Michigan and forget about all of this. I don't want you to get hurt. I can't say what I'll do if… You have to listen to me."

She heard the desperation in his voice. It couldn't be clearer if it was written on his forehead in glaring magenta ink. But she still couldn't even think about leaving now. This was no longer a semi-scary situation, with armed bad guys whose actions were being dictated by a company run by semi-moral individuals. No sirree. This was about bad guys with guns being told to kill people to cover something up.

Tarik. Raul. Abby.

The only way she'd leave was at gunpoint. And since no one was currently aiming a gun at her head, she was going nowhere.

Although Raul was clearly desperate to keep her out of harm's way, he wasn't going to do something that crazy to make her leave. She knew that much, just like she'd come to realize he hadn't wanted to eat her when he'd been a bear. He'd wanted to hold her. To control her, maybe. But never to harm her.

She had to admit she'd never been with a man who possessed such power. Physical. Mental. Emotional. Raul had it all. He was the total package. The kind of man she'd never expected to find.

Now that she'd found him, she wasn't ready to give him up. Not yet. Perhaps not ever.

It was suddenly easy to understand Abby's seemingly hasty decision to relocate to Alaska. If Abby felt even half as strongly about Tarik as she did about Raul, how could her friend not want to make such a move?

Oh God. She'd just kissed any thought of convincing her friend to rethink her move to Alaska goodbye. And possibly bought herself a shitload of heartbreak.

Raul released her and stormed toward the bedroom. She stood, dumbfounded, confused by her own thoughts, and watched him leave. He returned a few moments later with her overnight bag, gaping open, her clothes balled up and stuffed inside. One sock dangled half out. He set the bag beside the front door and picked up her hiking boots.

"I'm not leaving, Raul. I'm going to help you find Abby and Tarik."

"We need to get moving," Raul said, directing his words to Bryson. He dropped her boots at her feet then turned to his brother. "You're heading to the first name on the list. I'm taking this stubborn woman to the airport—"

"Like hell you are." Her actions carefully measured to communicate her determination, she calmly walked to the door, picked up her bag and headed toward the bedroom with it.

Raul started to reach for her as she swept past but he stopped short of grabbing her.

She lifted her chin in triumph as she continued into the bedroom, dropped the bag on the bed, sat and slipped on some clean socks.

When she returned to the living room to put on her boots, she found both men were gone.

He wouldn't!

She ran to the front door and yanked it open.

Raul was in her rental truck, in the driver's seat. His brother was sitting in the passenger seat beside him. He gave her a little smile then jerked the steering wheel and hit the gas, pulling a tight U-turn on the gravel drive. Pebbles tossed up by the tires struck the huge boulders lined up in front of the house's wooden foundation.

Bastard!

She slammed the door and headed for the computer, hoping Bryson hadn't shut it down.

Raul had underestimated this girl! She had brains and knew her way around a computer...and a forest. She was no sissy city girl who got lost without her *OnStar*.

She poked the power button on the computer monitor with an index finger and dragged the mouse over the Lord of the Rings mouse pad. The computer hadn't been shut down completely, but he'd closed the spreadsheet and disconnected from Omega's network.

"Shit!" she pounded a fist on the workstation's tiny desktop then dropped her gaze to the printer.

It was one of those nice laser models. Big. Powerful. Multifunctional.

With lots of memory.

Was there any chance...?

She scrolled through the printed documents on the printer's display panel, selected the first one on the list and hit the print button on the machine. The motor inside came to life with a whir. A piece of paper was swept up from the tray. The rollers turned and spit it out into a slot under the flat bed scanner.

She picked it up and smiled.

"Thank God for printers with memory chips."

The page in her left fist, she opened the internet browser and typed a single word, *Mapquest*.

* * * * *

Raul parked the truck about a quarter mile from the first address on the list. It had only taken them about ten minutes to reach their destination. Wasn't far from the house where he'd left Katie.

He felt no guilt over that one. She'd forced him to leave her, by being pigheaded.

He only wished he'd have the opportunity to teach her a lesson. A heaviness settled in his gut at the thought of eventually watching her leave. God help him. He knew he'd never be the same without her. Somehow, she made him whole, completed him. But there wasn't another choice. She had to go back home, forget about him.

Even if he found Tarik, things weren't going to be *normal* for a while. Their troubles weren't going away overnight. Would Tarik find a cure before it was too late? Before they both lost their tenuous grips on their humanity and hurt someone they loved? Could he trust himself with Katie? Would he spend the rest of his life running?

"You stay here," he said to Bryson as he cut the truck's engine. He left the key in the ignition and pulled on the door latch. "I'll give the signal if it's clear."

"I'm going with you." Bryson opened his own door.

What was with everyone refusing to listen to him? He glared his disapproval and laced his voice with heavy warning. "I don't have time to set you straight right now, baby brother."

"Fuck that. We're both men now. I don't need your protection anymore."

"Ha! Do I need to remind you who saved whose ass last night?"

Bryson gave Raul a smug grin. "And who, do you suppose, rigged the restraints?"

What?

His surprise must have been plain on his face because Bryson nodded. "Yeah. That was me. I knew they were using me as bait. And I knew they'd probably try to take you down, along with Tarik. It just happened to work to my benefit that the dumbasses left all their restraints in my room. And they underestimated how resourceful a guy with a lot of time and nowhere to go can get."

"Those things can't be cut with a butter knife. They wouldn't be stupid enough to leave you locked up with something sharper."

"No, but it's amazing what a little battery acid will do to them. My room was also a storeroom. I found a box of D batteries on a shelf."

His brother was a genius!

"So, let's go see if John Whatever has been hauled away yet." Bryson shuffled down the steep embankment, heading away from Smitty's Bait, Tackle and Taxidermy on Beaver Creek Road. Their destination was a home in the affluent housing development on the other side of a shallow stream.

Raul shook his head and followed. He wasn't exactly convinced he was making the right decision by letting his brother tag along, but he didn't want to waste time now convincing Bryson to change his mind. He'd just have to be extra cautious, not take the kinds of chances he would if he was alone.

Twilight had lengthened the shadows of the ancient oaks skirting the road, creating a decent cover for them as they ran. Once within the residential development itself, Raul felt a little better protected, not so out in the open and vulnerable. It was tough reading the addresses on the homes, large newer houses, built on single-acre lots and sold for a small fortune. Most of the porch lights were unlit, but after a fair amount of walking, they finally found their target, a contemporary, stone Cape Cod with an attached four-car garage.

He signaled to Bryson to drop back behind him as they approached the house.

There was no activity on the street, and the house looked empty, but he took no chances. He approached the house from the side, where a line of oaks, maples and pines cut a jagged line between the house's side yard and its neighbor.

Raul hurried to a back window. A weak light seeped outside, indicating the shades or curtains were open. He peered inside. The kitchen. A single incandescent light above the sink illuminated a room that was otherwise dark and empty.

He checked a bay window on the side of the house. The living room was empty too, a floor lamp the sole source of light.

"No one's home," Bryson whispered. "Maybe I should go around, check the mailbox to see if they've been gone more than a day."

"No. The mailbox is down by the road. It isn't safe."

Bryson sighed heavily. "No one's here. And this is the last house on a dead-end street. No one's coming this way. It's perfectly safe. Quit being so fucking paranoid or you'll never find Tarik."

Silence.

"I'm going to go ring the doorbell," Bryson announced.

"No you're not." Raul grabbed at his brother's arm but he missed. Bryson ran around the front of the house, leaving Raul to chase after him, whispering, "Stop! It's too fucking risky."

He dashed up to the front door and poked the doorbell with his fingertip. "Quit being such a fucking control freak. I know what I'm doing. It's perfectly safe. See?"

A soft cough sounded from the other side of the door. Raul grabbed his brother and yanked, pulling him off the front porch just before the front door blasted open and a spray of bullets whirred through the air, striking trees a couple hundred yards away.

They'd been waiting for them? Had it been a trap?

Raul dragged his stunned brother around the side of the house, zigging and zagging in an effort to avoid being struck by a bullet. He headed for the trees, which were thankfully less than twenty yards away. He flattened his back against the biggest oak he found and stopped running long enough to make sure Bryson hadn't been hit. "Okay?" he asked in between gasps.

"Yeah. They knew we were coming?"

"Maybe." Trying to catch his breath, he doubled over, resting his hands on his knees. "Then again, they might've just been there waiting for Stinson to come home from work." A bullet struck the tree, much too close to his right ear. A piece of bark cut loose from the impact struck him in the face, just under his eye. "We have to get out of here." He straightened up. "Ready?"

"Yeah. Which way?"

"Stay in the woods. We'll follow it as far as it goes."

"Okay."

Another bullet hit the tree, this one from a different angle. It came within inches of striking his shoulder. "Damn. They're coming fast. Go!" He broke into a hard run, his feet flying over crispy leaves and crackling twigs. He dodged saplings and pushed his way between shrubs. He leapt over fallen logs and stumbled over a tree root. The bullets pattered against nearby trees, sending bits of splintered wood and tree bark flying at his face and body.

And then they were at the end of the woods and the wide field stretched before them, a death sentence. A thin pine the only thing between him and death, he frantically searched the nearby landscape for an escape route.

"We're screwed," Bryson, also standing behind a pine, whispered. "Sorry."

Raul shook his head. "Not now." Time was running out. There was nowhere to go.

Fuck!

A bullet whirred through the air, less than an inch from his ear. He flinched, reflexively lunging in the opposite direction. Before he'd realized what happened, something hot seared his right arm, just below the elbow.

He'd been hit. He knew it. His brother would be next if he didn't do something. Now.

"Split up!" His arm burning, he headed for the field, hoping his brother wouldn't follow him, but would circle back, hiding behind the trees and staying out of sight.

He took a second shot in his left calf. His lower leg went instantly numb. It gave out and down he went, into the tall grass.

Bryson's voice pierced the night air, sharp like a dagger.

The bizarre buzzing feeling started deep inside, in his gut. It intensified as he lay in the cool grass, breathless and desperate, helpless to move, to save his brother or himself.

The sensation intensified until he was in the grip of agony, his muscles tearing, bones cracking, skin stretching. His mouth opened. Air found its way out of his lungs, but the sound coming from his chest was inhuman. A fierce growl.

The pain eased. His mind cleared somewhat. He felt strong. Big. Powerful. The world around him was visibly sharper, clearer, although everything was in shades of gray. The scent of blood, carried on a breeze, teased his nostrils. He inhaled. Sweet and tempting, like the smell of baking cookies.

He stood up on hind legs. His injured one was still a little numb but it supported his weight. He turned toward the woods. The bullets had stopped. Silence.

No insects. No birds. No movement. Something was wrong.

His skin tingled. On all fours again, he followed the scent of blood. It was getting stronger. Saliva dripped from his mouth. Hunger ripped through his gullet, twisting his insides into a knot so tight it was painful. He moved faster. Toward the smell. Toward the lights. The house.

Before he reached the building, something hit him from behind. Burning in his buttocks.

His strength drained away. Tired. He couldn't stand. He fell to the ground, looking toward the sound of footsteps.

Katie.

More footsteps coming from the other direction.

The enemy.

He tried to warn her, to shout, to move. No sounds came out. His paw was too heavy to lift. But to his relief she retreated before the men were upon him.

"Got him," one digitized voice said.

"Nice shot," a second one said. "But put the goddamn gun away."

Darkness. The world faded away.

Chapter Nine

∾

Katie choked on the sob she'd swallowed. Tears streamed down her cheeks.

That bear was Raul. She'd watched him change in the field and had followed him through the woods.

What to do? She had no gun, no weapons whatsoever. No vehicle, although she knew where her rental truck was parked. She'd passed it on her way into the subdivision. Would it do her any good, even if she had it?

No, not really, unless the guys dressed in black like ninjas were stupid enough to stand out in the open where she could plow them over.

She'd seen only two of them. At the moment, both were standing over an unconscious Raul, their rifles resting on their shoulders.

Why were they standing there chitchatting like workers around the water cooler?

She ached to go to him, to do whatever she could to save his life.

What if it was too late?

If there'd been any lingering doubt that he was more than a friend, it was completely gone now. It had been such a short time, but she adored this man. And more than anything, she wanted to have more time with him. A minute. An hour. A lifetime. Her insides hurt, like those bad guys had plunged a dagger into her stomach, sliced her open and dumped acid into the wounds.

She had to help. She had to know if he was dead or not. How?

They were moving him now, dragging him toward her hiding spot, behind a tree at the fringe of the woods. She tiptoed further back, taking up watch behind a pine tree deeper in the shadows. They stopped only twenty feet from her. She held her breath, sure they'd hear her if she didn't.

Raul was still in bear form. He looked limp, lifeless.

Her nose burned as tears gathered again in her eyes. She wouldn't cry. No, no, no. She pressed her hands over her mouth, stifling any sound that might try to slip between her lips.

The men stood erect and turned, heading back toward the house. She watched and waited, not daring to even blink her eyes until they were inside the building.

The second the front door swung closed, she ran to him, dropping beside him on her knees. Dried leaves crunched as she shifted her weight forward. Her hands wandered over his body. Warm. He was still warm. That had to be a good sign. She rested her head on his chest and again held her breath, listening, feeling, and praying she'd find some sign of life.

His chest rose almost imperceptibly then fell. Or had that been wishful thinking?

She waited. It moved again.

Thank God!

Alive. For now. But what could she do?

Wake him!

Her father had warned her to never, never, never, under any circumstances, wake a sleeping bear. What was she doing? Waking a sleeping bear?

Was she nuts?

Afraid to make any noise, she poked, shook and even kicked Raul—softly, of course.

He didn't wake but he did move a little. One huge paw swatted at her head, a testimony to precisely how stupid it probably was to be trying to wake him in the first place.

But she was undaunted. Sneaking frequent peeks at the house, she increased her efforts. She pushed. She smacked. She pulled his hair.

Her efforts got her nowhere.

Now what? From all she could see, he had no serious injuries. Had they drugged him? She stood up and tried to drag him but he was way too heavy. He didn't move an inch.

Should she take a chance and go get the truck? What if the men came back while she was gone? The vehicle was some distance away. It would take her more than a couple of minutes to run back to the store parking lot, start it and drive it down the winding road back into the subdivision.

The sound of gravel popping under tires called her attention back to the road. She slipped behind a tree and looked. A white Jeep was driving slowly down the road. It pulled into the driveway. The engine cut off.

Was this the guy they were after? Had he just returned home? And if so, were those men inside waiting to ambush him?

Should she warn him?

How?

Her mind grappled for an idea, like hands reaching for a lifeline that wasn't there. She was too far away to throw something at him. It was too dangerous to shout out. She had no light to flash.

The driver's side door opened. The man got out, walked around to the back of the vehicle and opened the rear door. He pulled out a box, shut the door and headed for the front porch. Something small and metallic caught the moonlight and flashed, his keys no doubt.

She couldn't sit there and watch the poor guy walk into a trap! She shuffled her feet in the leaves, making as much noise as she dared.

He glanced her way for a split second.

Desperate, she sent him danger vibes, knowing that only worked in the movies.

Didn't work. Of course. He let himself into the house. Minutes that felt more like hours later, the two bad guys ran from the rear of the house, something as long as a man held between them. They hauled their bundle to the woods on the opposite side of the backyard.

She guessed they had a vehicle parked over there. She also guessed that bundle had been John Whatever-his-name.

This was it, she knew time was about to run out. She pummeled Raul's chest with her fists as hard as she could. She pulled his hair and kicked him.

A low rumble emitted from his chest. She scuffled backward like a crab, on hands and heels when he opened his eyes and rolled over.

She could tell by the way he was moving, sloppy like a guy who'd been on a serious bender, that he'd been drugged. His head hung low, like it was too much work to hold it up. His paws clawed at the earth as he tried to push himself up onto all fours.

She stood. Her gaze pingponged back and forth between the beast struggling before her and the men heading back into the house. Because Raul was still under cover of the shadows, she hoped the men weren't prepared to find a conscious bear. The element of surprise was currently the only thing they had going for them. Granted, that would only work in their favor if Raul was able to fight them off.

He flopped onto his stomach. His fur rippled like something was brushing over it in waves.

He was changing back. Damn.

She tried to drag him behind a nearby tree but couldn't move him. His muscles were in a tight spasm, turning him into a tight, heavy mass of flesh and bone. Too heavy and immobile. She couldn't help him now. A sob of frustration blasted up her throat.

His gaze met hers. She witnessed such agony in his eyes she nearly reeled backward from the impact. A tear slid down her cheek and dropped on his chest.

His lips trembled. "Go," he whispered. "Go now."

She glanced up. The men hadn't come outside yet but she knew they didn't have long. "We need to go. Get up. Please. Please don't leave me alone out here. I can't bear to lose you too."

He shook his head. "Can't."

Furious, she smacked his chest. "Yes you can, dammit. You didn't drag me out of my cave and back into this world, of life and hope and love, just to leave me!" She lifted her head when she heard a sound, the snapping of a twig.

They were coming for him. Twenty seconds. She had maybe that long. She pressed a kiss to his mouth. "Please, don't give up. Fight."

"Trying, baby. Fucking shit. I'm numb. Can't feel. But here. Heart." He struggled for a handful of seconds before falling back to the ground. A gut-clenching longing filled his eyes. "I can't. Go. Help Bryson. Abby."

Her heart so heavy she could barely walk, she forced herself to leave him. "You might give up, but I'm not. I can't."

There was only one way she could help him now. She ran around the back of the house, hoping to find an unguarded vehicle parked on the other side.

She appeared to be in luck.

After spending several moments making sure no one was around to see her, she hopped up into the back of the white cargo van and hurried to the back, figuring she'd hide behind the bundle of blankets piled in the rear. The bundle, which was noticeably firm, most likely John Whoever, moved when she climbed over him. She wedged herself between him and the steel wall dividing the cargo area from the driver's seat.

Was the dead or unconscious John a man or a beast right now? She didn't want to think about it.

Voices. Shuffling feet. The bad guys were coming.

She closed her eyes and inhaled as slowly and shallowly as she could.

"This motherfucker weighs a ton, even in his human skin. No wonder it took two doses to knock him out."

"Still don't see why we couldn't just shoot the fucker and be done with it."

"You heard the boss. No evidence. No blood, you asshole. Now I've got to go spray down half the fucking yard. And you made a fucking mess in the house."

"Fucking stupid rule."

There was a loud thud. The van bounced. Then the doors slammed shut.

Was she an idiot or what? She was locked inside a van being driven who-knew-where by a couple of guys who had been hired to kill dozens of people. And she was trapped in there with one unknown occupant—of unknown species—and her unconscious…boyfriend? Lover? Love-of-her-life?

The van lurched forward, bounced up and down for a few minutes and then zoomed down the road.

No windows and nothing but a thin, three-foot tall steel divider between her and a pair of assassins, there was no chance she'd risk trying to get up to see where they were heading. The dividing wall wasn't solid all the way to the ceiling. It was more like security grating for the top foot and a half or so. She could try to peek out. But the risk wasn't worth it.

In foreign territory, how would she know where they were driving anyway? Unless she happened to peek at just the moment they passed a road sign. How likely was that?

She had her cell phone on her. Would it work in the van?

Being a huge fan of television police shows, she knew that at least in the world of TV detectives, a cell phone's call could be traced.

It was her only hope. She dialed 9-1-1 and whispered, "Help me. Being kidnapped in white van," into the phone when the dispatcher answered.

Despite the dispatcher's numerous questions, she said nothing more, simply turned down the volume and prayed the police would find them before it was too late.

* * * * *

Some hour or so later, the van pulled into a parking garage. The driver cut the engine, signaling to Katie that they had probably reached their destination. She checked her cell phone. The connection had not been dropped.

Thank God.

She flattened herself as best as she could when the back doors swung open. The two guys who'd lugged poor Raul to the van griped about some guy named Guzman as they dragged Raul's heavy frame from the van and carried him away. Katie didn't move, didn't blink, didn't breathe until she heard a door slam.

Taking the only chance she figured she had, she rolled over whoever—or whatever—was wrapped in the blankets and slid toward the gaping rear doors. She dropped to the concrete floor, and hurried around the side of the vehicle.

It was a warehouse of some kind. Mostly empty. A few skids scattered the area, stacked a good five feet high with shrink-wrapped cardboard boxes. A couple of fluorescent fixtures cast the interior in a flickering blueish light.

A door at the rear hung open, and she could see a bit of what was on the other side, a white-walled corridor. Her heart racing, she tiptoed closer.

Was it safe to look?

She pressed her back against the wall and peered through the doorway. Clear. She slipped inside.

She stood at the very end of a narrow hallway. There were no doors. A true dead end and a place she couldn't afford to be discovered in. No place to hide. She hurried up the corridor, stepping lightly so that her footsteps wouldn't be heard on the linoleum floor.

It led to a wide room lined on one wall by windows. The room was cut into workstations by temporary cubicle walls. It looked like they were all empty.

Thank God for small favors.

She stuck to a side passageway between the cubicles to try to avoid being discovered by the bad guys. They had to be heading back to the van for the other person, animal, whatever, soon. It had been several minutes now. How far could they have taken Raul?

She hoped they hadn't done anything terrible to him already, like killed him.

Surely they'd secure the second victim before taking the time to do something with the first, right? She definitely lacked the ability to read a criminal mind.

She rushed to the far end of the room and hid behind a mammoth supply cabinet next to the doorway.

Where would that door lead? Another open hallway with no place to hide?

Where'd the bad guys go with Raul?

Maybe she should wait there for them to return and then follow them—at a safe distance, of course?

Ack! She had no problems hiking through thick forests or climbing mountains. But this spy stuff was so not her thing!

She was so scared she felt sick. Her hands were shaking. Her knees quaking. Her heart zipping along at a rate that had to be at least ten times faster than normal.

The windows outside let in the slightest light, since it was now fully nighttime. And all but the first row of fluorescent overhead lights were off. Thus, she was pretty well hidden where she stood. But how would sitting behind a storage cabinet like a big chicken help Raul? Without Raul was there any hope of saving Abby?

"It's going to be a long fucking night," she heard a man say, from just outside the room.

Good thing she hadn't found the guts yet to leave her hiding spot! She crouched low and watched the two men walk by.

"How many more we got after this?"

"Not sure. I'd have to look at the list again. We got two this time. Probably won't be so lucky with the rest. At least twenty, I'm guessing."

"And we only have one more night? Fucking impossible. Unless they start letting us just shoot them."

"Can't."

"Fuck that."

The men disappeared through the warehouse door. Katie waited, silent, trembling, and wishing she had someone sitting next to her. Someone strong. With a big gun.

Was this a suicide mission? How could she possibly do any good here?

The men came back, visibly struggling with their load, carried between them. One guy was walking backward. Neither seemed to notice her.

She waited a full count of ten before following them. She trailed their voices down the hallway and through a door that led to a stairwell. They were below her, descending to the basement. She waited until the door underneath slammed shut with a bang before running down the stairs. She peered through the tiny window in the door to see if they were nearby.

Another hallway. Ack!

It had taken them a long time with Raul. She hoped that meant they wouldn't be coming back her way anytime soon. She pulled open the door and tiptoed down the passageway, peering in a small window cut into the first door on the right.

Looked like a hospital room inside. A man lay on a bed, IVs hung from a pole at the head. Monitors sat on a cart, counting out his heartbeats, respirations and blood pressure.

How bizarre.

She tried the door. Unlocked. Good to know. There was no reason to go inside so she moved to the next door.

The person lying on that bed she recognized immediately. Tarik! Did that mean Abby was somewhere nearby too? She opened the door and slipped into the room, pulling it shut behind her. She glanced at the bags hanging from the IV stand then looked at the monitors. "Tarik?" she whispered.

He didn't stir.

She tapped his shoulder. "Tarik, wake up," she hissed, growing desperate. If only he'd wake up! "Come on! I need your help!"

His eyelids slowly slid up, revealing a set of seriously bloodshot eyes. He didn't speak, just stared through her like she wasn't even there.

Had to be the drugs. She reached down to his wrist and unwrapped the tape. She wasn't a nurse, didn't even work in a hospital, but she'd seen enough IVs put in and taken out, thanks to her father's five-year battle with leukemia. She slid the needles out and applied pressure to Tarik's wrist to stop the bleeding.

She didn't expect his drugged, groggy state to change immediately, but she hoped he'd slowly come to.

The effect was somewhat quicker than she'd expected.

One second he was staring at the wall, the next, he was looking at her, seeming to actually comprehend what he was seeing.

"I know you," he murmured in a sleepy, slurred voice.

She nodded and pressed an index finger to her lips. "I'm here to help. Do you know where Abby is?"

He looked confused, glanced around the room like he was seeing it for the first time. "No."

"Don't know where you are, do you?"

"No."

She heard voices growing louder outside and crouched down. "Close your eyes and pretend like you're unconscious." When the voices faded, she stood up again. "I could use some help. Don't suppose you can stand up yet."

He blinked his eyes open again. "Uh...when I turn my head, the world spins."

She sighed. "Didn't think so." She patted his arm. "Okay. You stay here and play the unconscious good guy. I'll try to handle this by myself."

Was she nuts?

He grabbed her wrist before she stepped away and gave her a desperate look. "Find Abby."

"I'm doing my best."

"I love her," he added, still refusing to release her wrist.

"So do I." She gently pried his fingers off her wrist and crept toward the door.

No pressure here. She had at least a best friend to save, along with two men, one of whom she couldn't stop thinking about for more than a second. And she had to do this by herself. With no help. No gun. No plan.

Ack!

The police had evidently given up on her or weren't coming. She slid her hand in her pocket and pulled out her phone. The connection had been cut off who knew how long ago. Damn.

Chapter Ten

🆚

Katie dropped her phone back in her pocket and inched open the door, checking the corridor. No bad guys. Was it silly to hope she'd be fortunate enough to find Raul and Abby in one of the other rooms? She could only be so lucky!

She jogged, peering in one window after another. Empty, empty, empty, empty.

Damn. She knew it had been foolish to hope her friend and Raul would be close by. Of course they wouldn't. Because that would be too simple. Too easy. Too fucking convenient.

Ready to scream in frustration, she stopped at the last door and peered inside. Thank God!

Raul was lying on the bed, tied down with restraints. His eyes were open, his face was red and he appeared to be aware of his surroundings.

Miracle of all miracles!

She opened the door and slipped inside.

"No!" he shouted.

"Quiet! They'll hear you."

"They already know you're in the building."

Her stomach dropping to her toes, she turned around and prepared to run.

Too late.

The two bad guys stood framed in the doorway, smiling. "You made our job so much easier, doll. Maybe we should give you a show of appreciation, here, while your boyfriend watches."

One of them stalked toward her.

She backed away. Until the monitor cart stopped her from going any further. For a woman who'd once strived to be strong and independent, she was a big chicken.

She was an utter failure. She turned to Raul, prepared to apologize for letting him down, Abby. Tarik...

"Don't give up," Raul said, struggling with the straps binding his arms and legs to the bed.

Those were the exact words she'd spoken to Raul...and her father. Seconds before he'd died. She'd spent the last eight months angry at him for doing precisely that—giving up. For not loving her enough to keep going, keep fighting.

She looked at Raul again and caught the agony in his eyes. It was as if his eyes were a mirror to her soul, not his.

The bad guy sent her an I-know-you're-not-going-to-fight vibe as he slowly closed a fist around her upper arm. He smiled.

She drew in a slow, deep breath, reached down inside herself, gathered the bit of courage she possessed and lunged forward, aiming the heel of her hand at his throat like her father had taught her years ago.

The impact jarred her wrist, elbow and shoulder, but the results were worth the price of a few sore joints. There was a sickening crunch and then the man staggered backward, eyes wide, one hand at his throat. His mouth gaped open as he audibly struggled to inhale.

The second man charged forward, aiming for a full-body tackle. She had exactly one second to react. She dove to the side, slamming her shoulder into the wall. A blade of pain sawed up her arm. She scrambled to her feet, the world a blur, and dodged a second blow, this one clearly aimed at her head. The attacker's fist struck the wall behind her with a loud thud. His knuckles left a dent in the drywall.

He twisted around, his expression laced with menace. "Look what you made me do, bitch. You'll pay for that."

Horrified, Katie froze. But her mind whirred nonstop, thoughts flashing like bolts of lightning.

Why fight anymore? I'm going to be caught. And if I keep fighting, he'll just be more angry. More determined to hurt me. More dangerous.

Oh my God. What will they do to me? Will I be drugged? Killed? Used as a lab rat?

What about Abby? Tarik? If I'm captured, what will happen to them?

The man moved closer, his eyes slitted, his mien wary. "That's it, little girl. You just stay still."

"Katie? What are you doing?" Raul shouted. "Don't stop, dammit! I can't help you. You've got to do this on your own. Katie!"

She stepped backward. Her father's words playing through her head adding to the mental background noise.

I didn't give up. I'd never do that. There's a difference, you know. The choice was taken away from me. Don't ever let anyone take the choice from you. Don't ever give up on life.

When he'd said those words to her, she'd been too hysterical to truly comprehend them. But now, the meaning was crystal clear.

He hadn't quit on her. He hadn't wanted to leave her. He had wanted to live. And he'd wanted her to keep living, going on, no matter what.

Her attention snapped back to the present. God, what was she doing? She couldn't just stand there and let this man do what he wanted. Risk be damned, she had to keep fighting. To keep living.

She took another step backward, bumping into something low, something on wheels that rolled away from her. She heard the whirr of the wheels on the tile.

A stool.

Reacting out of pure instinct, she spun around, grabbed it and swung at him. It hit him smack dab in the gut, evidently knocking the air out of his lungs. He staggered backward, momentarily breathless.

She had a clear shot to the door. She could run. This was her chance to get away.

But what would that gain her? No. No running. She lifted her makeshift weapon over her head, closed her eyes and brought it down as hard and fast as she could. It struck the man with a sickening *thunk.*

She forced herself to open her eyes, fearing she'd missed her mark.

No, she didn't miss. Lots of blood on his head. His eyes were closed. He was half sitting, half lying, semi-propped by the monitor cart. She dropped the stool and went to work on the restraints. It felt like it took forever to get the first one. The second came easier. Raul unfastened the rest himself while she went to the doorway to see if there were any other bad guys headed their way.

So far, so good.

Too scared to have a well-deserved girly moment, fall into Raul's arms and let him hold her until she felt better, she grabbed Raul's hand and led him back down the hallway to Tarik's room.

Tarik was sitting up and looking shaky but stronger. He swung his legs over the edge of the bed and dropped to the floor. His steps were faltering, wobbly but he shook away Raul's offer of help. "Abby." He staggered out of the room, bouncing off the walls like a pinball. He headed toward the staircase. "Abby."

"She's not that way, unless they're keeping her upstairs somewhere." Katie motioned toward the rooms she hadn't checked yet. "I haven't gone all the way to the end. She could be this way but do we have time to look?"

"We have to." Pale, Tarik changed directions. He stretched his arms out to either side, using pressure against the walls to support him.

"Maybe you should wait here," Katie suggested, pitying the poor guy. He could barely stand yet there he was, dragging his body down the corridor, searching for Abby.

"No."

"I'll go." Raul ran ahead of them, zigging back and forth and peering in all the doors on alternating sides. He shook his head when he reached the end. "She's not here."

"Fuck." Tarik slumped against the wall and tipped his head back.

Raul jogged back to them, slid an arm around Katie's waist and pulled her tight against his side. "We'll find her. But we'd better get you out of here first. You're not in any condition to play the hero. You're going to have to trust us."

Tarik shook his head. "No way."

Raul released Katie and turned his full attention to Tarik. "I know I let you down once. But I promise I won't do it again. We aren't leaving without Abby."

Tarik didn't speak for a long beat. Stood and stared. The muscles along his jaw twitched. Finally he said, "Okay."

Raul and Katie helped Tarik up the stairs and outside the building. After making sure Tarik was safely hidden, Raul turned to Katie, gathered her hands in his and kissed every single one of her fingertips.

"Thank you for what you did," he said. "You were so brave. More courageous than I ever dreamed you could be."

"I had to. I couldn't just sit by and let you be hurt. Abby. Tarik."

"I've never seen a more daring woman, except for maybe that friend of yours, Abby. You two are amazing."

Her heart swelled at the compliment. "Thanks." She watched his Adam's apple bob up and down as he swallowed.

What was he thinking? And why wasn't he running back inside yet? "What's wrong?"

"Nothing. Just trying to get up the nerve to ask you something."

What kind of something was he thinking of asking her? Here? Now? "Oh?"

"Yeah. Will you..."

She held her breath. It was too soon to make promises of lifelong love and commitment!

"Help me?" he finished.

Huh?

"Will you come with me now? Help me find Abby?"

"Oh, God yes!" She flung herself into his arms, hugged him tightly for perhaps three seconds too long and then pulled away. "I thought you were going to ask me..." When he tipped his head in question, she shrugged, "Never mind. Let's go find Abby. Together. I think we'll make a kick ass team, you and me."

"Hey, what about me too?" someone said from the shadows.

Katie recognized that voice—Bryson, Raul's brother.

He stepped out from behind a garbage dumpster. "If it weren't for me hacking into Omega's computer network, you wouldn't have found John Whatever-his-name, who led you to this place. By the way, I did some work in here back when this building was a hospital, so I know this place inside and out..." He waved a hand behind his back, coaxing someone or something out from behind the dumpster. "Which came in handy when I ran into these two ladies while searching for you."

A woman Katie hadn't seen before stumbled out from her hiding spot, followed by a tousled and wobbly Abby.

"Abby?" Relief blasted through Katie as she lurched forward to steady her friend.

Abby rushed past Katie to Tarik, literally throwing herself into his outstretched arms. "Tarik!"

Tarik caught Abby mid-flight, the force making him take a shaky step backward. "Thank God!"

Katie blinked back hot tears of relief. Abby was okay. And she was happy. She'd found the man of her dreams.

"Thank you, little brother. Looks like you're the hero today." Raul tossed one arm over his brother's shoulder and looped the other around Katie's waist, hauling her flush to his side. "We're definitely keeping you around. From now on, it's all about teamwork." He turned to Katie and added, his voice thick with emotion, "I'm done being the lonely hero."

Her insides did a happy little trot. Too giddy to speak, she just blinked a zillion times and smiled.

He kissed her nose then gave her behind a sound smack. "Let's go. We still have a lot of work to do."

"Yes, work," Tarik said, his grin nearly as wide as Raul's as he gently unwrapped Abby's limbs from around his body and set her on her feet. "But after we take a little time to…recharge the batteries."

Katie and Abby gave each other knowing looks.

"Going to stick around the rest of the week?" Abby asked, obviously anticipating Katie's answer.

"I could be convinced."

Raul scooped her into his arms, and she yelped with surprise. "Just leave the convincing to me."

"With his skills of persuasion, I might be changing my permanent address too," Katie whispered to her best friend.

Abby nodded. "Exactly what I was hoping for."

Ready to face whatever lay ahead, Katie looped an arm around Raul's neck. Crazy thing, fate was. She'd had to travel thousands of miles to find the man who stirred her desires, challenged her to stand up to her fears, and embrace life again.

In the end he had helped her open her eyes and face the hurt and anger that she'd been struggling with for months.

Tarik and Raul still had things to sort out. There were bad guys still to be dealt with, but an odd kind of peace enveloped Katie. It was like a warm cocoon. She didn't know yet where things were headed with Raul. It was too soon to say. But it wasn't too soon to see he'd helped her find a strength within herself she'd never known she possessed. She'd never again cower away from life, afraid to live, for fear of losing.

He'd touched her heart, making her whole.

"Okay, Conan," she teased. "As much as I adore being carried around by your burly hunk of manliness, I'm ready to walk on my own two feet."

"You most definitely are."

The split second Raul lowered her to her feet, a blinding flash burned her eyes. A fraction of a second later, a bang slammed her eardrums. And a second after that, a blast of putrid, searing air threw her off her feet. She landed a distance away, in a daze, between Raul and a towering oak tree.

"Are you okay?" he asked, his gaze raking up and down her body, searching for injuries.

"Yes. I th-think so," she stuttered, shaken and confused. "What happened?" She could see the building, now engulfed in flames. "I thought we were safe...for now."

"Looks like the hospital blew up." Raul pushed himself to a stand. "Bryson? Tarik? Where are you guys?"

Bryson stumbled from behind an overturned car, Tarik, Abby and the strange woman trailing behind him. "I'm here. Damn, was that crazy or what?"

"Yeah." Raul's tone condemning, he scowled at his brother. "Did you blow up the place? That wasn't a good thing—"

"Hell no! Why would I do that? And how? It's not like I carry explosives in my pants pockets." Bryson shrugged. "But hey, I'm not going to complain. The bad guys are gone now, right? And we can head home and live the rest of our days in peace—assuming a life that includes the occasional transformation into a furry mammal 'peace'."

"I don't know…" Raul offered Katie a hand up. "I mean, don't you wonder? If we didn't blow it up, who did? And why?"

"That's simple." The woman stepped around Bryson, pulling a gun from her pocket and aiming it at Raul's forehead. "I did. But I'm afraid I can't share why—yet."

Why an electronic book?

We live in the Information Age — an exciting time in the history of human civilization, in which technology rules supreme and continues to progress in leaps and bounds every minute of every day. For a multitude of reasons, more and more avid literary fans are opting to purchase e-books instead of paper books. The question from those not yet initiated into the world of electronic reading is simply: *Why?*

1. *Price.* An electronic title at Ellora's Cave Publishing and Cerridwen Press runs anywhere from 40% to 75% less than the cover price of the exact same title in paperback format. Why? Basic mathematics and cost. It is less expensive to publish an e-book (no paper and printing, no warehousing and shipping) than it is to publish a paperback, so the savings are passed along to the consumer.

2. *Space.* Running out of room in your house for your books? That is one worry you will never have with electronic books. For a low one-time cost, you can purchase a handheld device specifically designed for e-reading. Many e-readers have large, convenient screens for viewing. Better yet, hundreds of titles can be stored within your new library — on a single microchip. There are a variety of e-readers from different manufacturers. You can also read e-books on your PC or laptop computer. (Please note that Ellora's Cave does not endorse any specific brands. You can check our websites at www.ellorascave.com

or www.cerridwenpress.com for information we make available to new consumers.)

3. *Mobility.* Because your new e-library consists of only a microchip within a small, easily transportable e-reader, your entire cache of books can be taken with you wherever you go.

4. ***Personal Viewing Preferences.*** Are the words you are currently reading too small? Too large? Too… ANNOYING? Paperback books cannot be modified according to personal preferences, but e-books can.

5. ***Instant Gratification.*** Is it the middle of the night and all the bookstores near you are closed? Are you tired of waiting days, sometimes weeks, for bookstores to ship the novels you bought? Ellora's Cave Publishing sells instantaneous downloads twenty-four hours a day, seven days a week, every day of the year. Our webstore is never closed. Our e-book delivery system is 100% automated, meaning your order is filled as soon as you pay for it.

Those are a few of the top reasons why electronic books are replacing paperbacks for many avid readers.

As always, Ellora's Cave and Cerridwen Press welcome your questions and comments. We invite you to email us at Comments@ellorascave.com or write to us directly at Ellora's Cave Publishing Inc., 1056 Home Avenue, Akron, OH 44310-3502.

Discover for yourself why readers can't get enough
of the multiple award-winning publisher

Ellora's Cave.

Whether you prefer e-books or paperbacks,

be sure to visit EC on the web at
www.ellorascave.com

for an erotic reading experience that will leave you
breathless.